sidelined

the draft

Bianca Williams

Bianca Williams Books

Bianca Williams Books, LLC.

Print ISBN: 978-0-9985146-0-4
eBook ISBN: 978-0-9985146-1-1

SIDELINED is a work of fiction inspired by true events.
Certain characters names, businesses, incidents, locations, and
events have been fictionalized for dramatic purposes.

For the untouchable and for those who have been sidelined

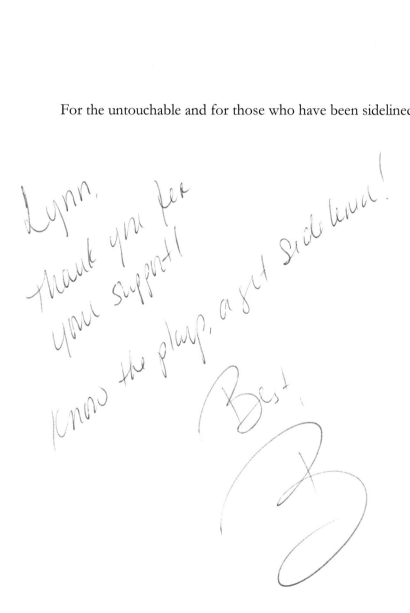

ACKNOWLEDGMENTS

GOD for HIS favor and giving me the vision. Jasmine, only Gayle and Oprah can understand our bond. Lisa, my dear friend, you gave me your shoulder to cry on and have witnessed the birth of SIDELINED. My circle of trust, Medeisa, Meneisa, Asia and Maurice, thank you for being honest and graciously telling me that my first draft was pretty much a piece of shit with promise! Gail, my editor, my writing coach, and my rock. You may be on the other side of the world but the universe brought us together for a reason. Keion, we started on this writing journey together and I'm finally taking that leap of faith. May you rest in eternal peace.

Briana, my ride or die, my reason for breathing. Without you, my life wouldn't have purpose. Thank you for being you and encouraging me to accomplish my goals. Mom, Dad, Cassie, Davonte, Kamari, Tony Jr, Carlos and Baby Cassie, you are an extension of me and I wouldn't be complete without you.

Last, but not least, I give thanks to heartbreak. Most nights, it was just us going at it for hours, bringing SIDELINED to life.

CONTENTS

sidelined

the draft

1

THE PLAY

As soon as he reaches for the pen, my stomach starts to churn. *Oh Lord.* I take a deep breath. Vomiting on the table would not only be a terrible first impression, but a long-lasting one. Still, my leg rocks, my heart races, and my eyes are wet with anticipation. And while countless scenarios of me losing consciousness play out in my mind, I fight to stay alert with a forced smile throughout the execution.

"There." He tosses the ballpoint onto the mahogany table, and when he stands, almost hits his head on the wrought-iron chandelier. I try not to laugh but he's clumsy *and* freakishly large. According to Wikipedia, the infamous Shane Smith is six-foot five and weighs two hundred sixty pounds. The day Jen, my best friend and event planner extraordinaire, bragged about pitching him, I Googled the NFL superstar. Initially, I shrugged it off as another one of her pipe dreams, yet here we are two weeks later in her dining room and he's signing her contract.

"I guess I owe you a deposit." He digs into the front pocket of his oversized jeans and whips out a wad of crisp $100 bills. After placing the stack of cash on the newly signed agreement, he reaches into his other pocket. "Three tickets to tonight's game."

"Really?" Jen, wide-eyed and flashing all thirty-two teeth, takes them from him.

"Bryn, there's one for you and your daughter."

"Wow!" I place my hand on my heart as a gesture of appreciation but also to make sure it's still beating. "That's so thoughtful of you."

He tries to keep from blushing. "It's cool. I mean. You know." He glances sideways.

Awww. I smile. *He's nervous.* I think it's kinda cute.

"I'm saying." He squares his shoulders and looks me in the eye. "I want you to come see me play tonight."

I stare at him confused.

"Yeah," he says, grinning and sizing me up.

"Actually." I turn to Jen for help. "I think we have work to do."

"Do we?" questions Jen, obviously ignoring my plea.

"Don't tell me y'all are *all* business? What's the pleasure in that?" He rubs his left arm, which I can't help but notice is dark, muscular, and littered with tattoos, and then flexes it.

Bianca Williams

Have mercy.

"Come on. It will be fun." He purses his lips then licks them like LL Cool J. "I guarantee it."

I give up. "Excuse me." I leave them and grab a bottle of water from the pantry. I can't drink it fast enough.

Jen laughs at my reaction.

Shane blushes.

"Alright ladies. I should go. But I really hope you make it out. I'll be looking for you in my section." He tugs on the brim of his hat, hikes up his pants, and initiates a fist bump.

"Can't wait!" Jen shoots me a smile before walking him out.

"Jen!" I cry as she locks the door. Then I realize he's probably still within earshot. I run to the window and am relieved to see that he's entering his truck.

"Preparation plus opportunity equals success!" She spins in her doorway, snaps her fingers, and starts dancing the two-step. "We just landed a freaking whale!"

"I think I'm sick." I hold my stomach and keel over onto the floor. "I don't know. Do you think we can really do this?"

"There's only one way to find out," she giggles. "By the way, nervous Nelly, you need to get some professional help for that." She points at me sprawled on her new shag rug.

"Whatever. I have good reason to be anxious. Did you see the show he just put on?"

"I didn't want to interrupt." Jen raises her eyebrows. "I saw that LL lip action he was giving you."

"Oh my God!" I laugh, covering my eyes. "I can't believe this!"

"Believe it!"

"Well, we gotta watch him." I point to the door even though he's long gone.

"It was harmless flirting." She shrugs her shoulders. "I saw your face as soon as he did it. You looked a bit pale. But who cares? It doesn't matter." She turns and walks away. "Unless you like him."

"God no!" I shout. "He's an athlete. Besides, I told you that I Googled him."

"Then why haven't you stopped smiling?"

"What do you mean? We just signed our dream client!" I dust myself off, rise from the floor, and join her in the dining room. "That's why I'm still smiling. I assure you."

"Umm hmm." Jen rolls her eyes and grabs the stack of hundreds from the table. "You say you're not interested, but clearly he is. I mean the man's not blind. I fully expected him to be attracted to you. You're short with big boobs and long hair. What dude isn't? I really don't want to talk about this. Thanks."

"Fine, but what about the 'no fraternizing with clients' rule? I'm just saying."

"Never mind that. We've got six weeks. I'm going to need you to get your mind right." Jen splits the stack of bills and hands me half. "Now go get dressed."

"We're going?" My eyes widen.

"Yes!" she shouts. "And *this*, my dearest friend, is just the beginning."

For some strange reason, I have a feeling she's right.

At seven o'clock we head downtown to M&T Bank stadium, home of the Baltimore Nighthawks. It's located in a sketchy part of the city. Surrounded by warehouses and abandoned buildings, it's the perfect backdrop for a mugging. To make matters worse, the distant parking is scarce, expensive, and frequented by dancing junkies begging for cash. I know this because I've been to a few Nighthawks games (mostly by winning office draws for corporate seats).

They were fun, but none of them measure up to tonight's.

The skies are clear and the air is crisp, perfect for Thursday Night Football. It's a sold-out televised game and, thanks to Shane, we've got premium parking *and* our front row seats are on the 50-yard line.

The stadium is on fire. All the fans, dressed in every combination of Nighthawks colors—blue, black, and white—are on their feet. Drunken men dressed as birds complete with face paint, beaks, and blue spray-painted spiked hair. Dancing women in pink jerseys and cobalt-blue tinsel wigs. A row of teens with nude chests bearing the letters N-I-G-H-T-H-A-W-K-S, which when I look again, reads NIGHTHWAKS.

I excuse myself as we squeeze past cheering fans to our three empty seats. Leaning on the railing in front of them is a tall man. He's attractive and extremely well groomed (I think even his sweat pants are professionally pressed).

"Bryn." He grabs my hand. "I finally get to meet you. I'm Terry, Shane's assistant."

"Hello." I free myself from his grip. "This is Bailey." I pat my daughter on the head. "And there's Jen."

"Hi Bailey, how old are you?"

"Eight!"

"You are so beautiful. Has anyone ever told you that you look like your mom?"

"Yup," says Bailey, plopping into her seat. In fact, she hears it all the time. She really is a mini version of me with her naturally sun-kissed skin, long dark wavy hair, and bright round eyes.

Terry looks over my head at Jen. "Hello Jen, I'm Terry. Can I get y'all anything? Drinks? Candy? Shane wants me to make sure y'all are good before the game starts."

"I'm fine Terry, thank you." I wave and take my seat.

"Alright. I'm going to be over there." He scoots by us into the center aisle and points to the next section over. "If you need me, just wave and I'll come right over."

When I look in the direction he's pointing there's a girl with red hair staring back at me.

"Mom! Mom!" shouts Bailey, getting my attention. "There's Shane!" She points to the center of the field at the coin toss. "It's game time."

It's the battle of the beltways and it's not until the referee gives the two-minute warning that I realize we've been on our feet, cheering, all four quarters.

'WILL YOU PROTECT THIS HOUSE?' blares from the stadium's speakers as the Nighthawks defense takes the field.

"I WILL! I WILL!" roars the crowd in unison. Fireworks shoot into the sky. The marching band beat their drums in preparation for battle, as the defense line up to execute their infamous blitz.

"DE-FENSE!" I wail, pounding on my plastic seat. I bang and bang until the ball snaps, soars between the legs of the quarterback, and bounces freely onto the field behind him. "Oh shit!"

"Mom," whines Bailey.

"Sorry. Quarter in the swear jar."

Pure chaos erupts all around us, in the stands and on the field. Referees sprint from every direction towards a massive pile that's forming. Each time a player is tugged from the stack, another one jumps in. The Nighthawks' head coach, now red in the face, rips off his headset and charges onto the field.

Flags are flying everywhere. Three of our guys and two of theirs are throwing blows and wrestling for the football. Referees are shouting and trying to pull them apart. When they finally separate, the Pro Bowl linebacker and our newest client, Shane Smith, surfaces with the football secured in his arms. Fans go insane as he dances to *Got Money* by Lil Wayne playing on the loudspeakers.

"Girl, what an ending." My voice is hoarse from screaming.

"Bryn. This is freaking *awesome!*" We start high-fiving each other and the college students, reeking of Natty Bohs, jump around wildly in the seats behind us. When the music stops, Shane runs towards us with the ball raised high above his head and tosses it to Bailey.

I cover my mouth in shock. And just when I think it can't get any better, the cameraman finds my baby, bouncing and proudly hugging the ball. Enjoying her few seconds of fame, she keeps jumping and screaming as the Nighthawks offense take a knee and secure another win for the city of Baltimore.

Bailey is beside herself. Giggly, silly, and full of joy.

"Do you know Shane Smith?" An excited fan taps her on the shoulder.

Jen knocks his hand away. "Excuse me, do not touch her."

Nighthawks fans are known to be slightly insane so I grab my jacket and motion for Bailey to exit in the direction we came in. On our way up the stairway I hear my name being called.

"Come on!" It's Terry, waving us over with his lanky arms. "Follow me. Shane wants y'all to wait for him."

Bailey grabs my hand as we follow Terry across the stadium through a sea of people to double glass doors flanked by security guards. "They're with me," says Terry to the older one who shamelessly undresses me with his eyes. *Yuck.* I'm used to second glances and flirtatious looks, but this is blatant gawking. I cross through the doorway, pulling Bailey to the opposite side and avoiding Mr. Creeper McCreepy.

Inside what appears to be the Nighthawks' family waiting area, I overhear praises to sons, cousins, and brothers for their performance on the field, and watch them embrace their beloved Nighthawk as they exit from an elevator. Bailey's face lights up as the famous players pass her, but being in here makes me realize that they are just people with ordinary families like us.

Everyone *appears* normal until a six-foot, pale-skinned, pregnant girl with fire-engine-red pixie-cut hair and a toddler on her hip flings the lobby doors open. She huffs, switches the little

Bianca Williams

girl to her other hip, and storms towards the elevators, where Shane finally emerges.

Shane swaggers out of the elevator dressed in a mousy-brown three-piece suit, complete with a knee-length jacket (like the preachers on Sunday's Best). Meanwhile, the girl—his wife? girlfriend? or just baby mama?—catches up with him. She strokes his arm and tries to steal a kiss. Shane brushes her off and lifts the little girl from her arms.

"Where they at?" He scans the crowd with a frown and finally locks eyes on Jen. "Go home and get dressed. We are celebrating tonight. Y'all need to see how I like to party."

2

MISS INDEPENDENT

Jen races to Betsy, the silver Honda Accord I've had since college, cackling like a silly schoolgirl. She's not ashamed of her behavior at all. "What is wrong with you? We *are* going tonight."

"Seriously? It's a school night."

"Suck it up and take one for the team." She signals for me to hurry and unlock the door.

"I—"

"I don't want to hear it. I'm cashing in that IOU for my services as Bailey's chauffeur last summer."

"Shame on you. You're her godmother." I unlock the doors and we all hop in.

"Call it what you want. Let's go." She loudly claps her hands.

"I secretly hate you, you know?"

I call my mom and convince her to watch Bailey as I race home. Breaking the speed limit the entire way, we arrive safely at our duplex in thirty minutes, which leaves us fifteen to get ready.

"What are you wearing?" Jen runs across the lawn to her front door. "I'm wearing a dress."

"Not sure yet. I can't think." *If it were left up to me, I'd be in jeans.* I nudge Bailey to wake up. She's curled up with her arms locked around that ball. "Let me get her settled and I'll call you." I tap Bailey a few times, calling her name, but she's out cold. I climb in the back seat, pull her out, and struggle to carry her all the way to my front steps, where she conveniently awakens.

"Do you have to go?" Bailey pouts and bats her long lashes.

"I don't. But I think I should. I'll tell you what, come and help me pick out a dress."

She perks up as I unlock the door.

I shower, moisturize, and apply my make-up at top speed. Next, we pick out a champagne-colored, BCBGMAXAZRIA dress with matching five-inch, nude, peep-toe Dior pumps I snagged half-off at a sample sale. They match perfectly. Standing in front of the mirror, I let my hair down and comb it with my fingers until it falls into place, reaching the small of my back. *Hmmm, not bad for twenty-eight.*

I check the time again and see I'm right on schedule. I apply another layer of mascara and my doorbell rings. I drop the tube on the bathroom counter and scurry over to my bed. "You can sleep in here tonight." I give Bailey a kiss on the forehead and grab my cell from the nightstand to call Jen.

"Please tell me you're ready?" I say as soon as she answers.

"I know how to tell time," she fusses.

"If you say so," I say, out of breath from hurrying down the stairs. I disconnect the call and open the front door. To my pleasant surprise, my mother arrives at the same time as Terry.

"Hey hey, hey," she says in her best Dwayne-from-*What's-Happening* voice. She bops through the doorway and hands me her favorite oversized knockoff Louis Vuitton handbag to put away for her. "You look gorgeous." She gives me a kiss on the cheek.

"Terry, this is my mother, Ms. Joan, and Mom—"

"I know, we already met. Where's Jenny Jen? I want her to see my latest find." She points to her over-the-knee leopard-print boots.

I stare with raised brows.

"They're my September issue. Just came in the mail today. I gotta get you on, *girl.*"

Lately, my mother, a freckle-faced debutante from Long Island, has been acting as if she's from the hoods of Baltimore. I'm not sure why. For as long as I can remember, my younger sister and I were constantly reminded about how to act like proper ladies.

"You look incredible." Terry admires my dress before reaching for an embrace.

"Thanks." I give him a side-hug.

"Y'all ready? Because Shane is waiting in the truck."

"I believe so." I bang on the adjoining wall of our duplex. This is Jen's last warning before we walk out the front door.

When Terry and I get outside, Jen appears on my doorstep with her pashmina dragging on the ground. "Why must you always do that?" She shoots me an annoyed look and discreetly adjusts her Spanx. "You look good though." She points to my shoes. "Great choice." Then she looks through the screen door. "Hi, Ms. Joan." She waves, still shimmying in her dress.

"Alright, Ms. Thang," my mother answers. "How you doin'?" she says, impersonating Wendy Williams.

Embarrassed by my mother's behavior, I quickly shut the door. Jen struggles to hold in her laughter. She knows I want to shrivel, but the feeling dissipates as I approach Shane's shining black Range Rover parked in my driveway.

Shane gives Terry an irritated look as he hops into the driver's seat. "What took y'all so long?" He turns to the back seat to eye the two of us. "I bet Jen wasn't ready." The spotlight is on her. "Were you?"

"I was ready!" she shouts back.

He gives her a look of surprise and turns his attention to his two cell phones that are simultaneously sending alerts. He flicks through both and then grabs his iPod. "So what's up? Y'all find my venue yet?"

I give Jen a pissed look.

"Yes. We have a walk-through tomorrow afternoon."

"Bet." Shane starts thumbing through his iPod. "Did y'all listen to TGS's new track yet?" Without waiting for a reply, he pushes play and after a few notes, starts belting out the lyrics, "Girl, you know you want this."

Shane's so-called dancing and spontaneous outbursts continue during our ride to D.C. He finds it amusing to repeatedly disrupt the conversation Jen and I are having about his group's album release party. His silly behavior continues until we pull up to the valet in front of the nightclub an hour later.

Shane's the first to jump out and get the doors for us. He motions for Jen and me to walk in front of him. I take the lead and stop at the security booth. A hostess is waiting for us and takes us inside to a reserved area sectioned off by red velvet stanchions.

The space is small but decorated beautifully with velvet sofas, leather benches, and chandeliers. Splashes of amber up-lights against the fuchsia walls create an intimate glow. I take a mental note of the decor and sit on a purple loveseat. Jen scoots me to its edge to make room for Shane, and Terry sits on a gold tufted ottoman bench across from us.

Almost immediately, a young blonde hostess wearing a black bustier, booty shorts, and fishnet stockings sashays up to Shane and hands him a menu. He checks out her ass as she sets our table. Eventually, he realizes we're watching him.

"My bad," he chuckles. "What would y'all like to drink?" He leans in. "If you don't mind, I want y'all to try my favorite. It's pink and I want lots of this at my party—excuse me," he clears his throat and adjusts his collar, "my event." He places an order for a few bottles.

Terry orders a Sprite.

When our waitress returns, other girls parading in similar sexy black attire, each carrying a bottle with lit sparklers attached, follow her lead. They form a semi-circle and seductively dance with the bottles held high until the sparklers burn out. Then she opens a bottle of Nuvo and pours the first round of drinks.

Shane turns to Jen and me. "Cheers." He raises his glass. "To new partnerships."

"Cheers!" Terry joins in last minute with his soda.

"Now," he continues, "I signed with y'all cause y'all business minded. People always trying to get me to do stuff, but I can see that y'all are the real thing. With that said, the Squad will be here in a few weeks when they get out of the studio." He finishes his drink in a huge gulp. "Yeah, I can't wait for this event. It's going to be hot! Baltimore's not used to anything like this."

Jen chats with Shane while I people watch. The club is packed, and the DJ has the party jumping. Gradually, a variety of women make their way over and surround our section. I can only assume they're here waiting to speak with Shane since they're treating Terry like he's invisible. I'm slightly bored by it all until the DJ starts playing my song, *Miss Independent* by Ne-Yo. *Perfect timing.*

I hop up and tip-toe over to an open space in our little sectioned off area. "Miss In-de-pen-dent," I sing, dancing the two-step. Out of the corner of my eye, I notice Terry making his way over to me. He's awkwardly boogying to the beat and getting closer and closer to me. *And stop right there.* "Hey Terry." I wave to him innocently, trying to play it down.

"You know what? I was talking to Shane and we think you're a bad chick. And we bring you to D.C. and you are still the baddest chick in here. When I say bad, I don't just mean your body." He eyes me, cringing and biting his knuckles. "Girl, damn. What I'm trying to say is that you've just *got it.*"

I smile awkwardly, not knowing how to respond, but at the same time thankful to the person who created shape-wear.

"You want to dance?" He opens his arms wide.

I hold my hands up in front of me. "Thanks, but I'm going to rest my feet for a little bit." I leave Terry and head back to the table to refill my champagne flute.

"You like it, don't you?" Shane's beaming, proud of his drink recommendation.

"I do. I really like it." I give him a friendly smile.

"I'll have some of that!" a woman shouts over the music. She shoves a glass in front of my face. "How are you?" She positions her flute for me to begin pouring.

I hand her the bottle instead.

"I hear you're working for Shane. How long have you known him?" she asks in a nasty tone.

I instantly become defensive. "Actually, we just met a few weeks ago." I return lots of attitude. "And yes, you're correct. We're planning the event for his group, The Gentleman's Squad."

"That's Jen?" She points and flicks her long, obviously fake, golden tresses towards Jen.

"Correct again." I smile and end our little chat. I can tell she wants more information, but instead she bites her tongue and scoots onto the sofa on the other side of Shane.

Good ol' Terry seizes the moment and finds his way back to me. "What did she say?" He laughs wholeheartedly. "That's his girl, you know?"

"That's *not* the same girl I saw earlier at the game, the red hair, piercings, and all."

"No." He leans in close and whispers, "That was Carice, his baby mama. That, over there, is his girl. Well at least one of them. Man, he can't go anywhere in D.C. without her knowing about it." Terry holds his stomach and tries to contain his laughter. "She's probably asking who you are because she knows that you're his type."

Shane's 'girl' glances over at me but I don't pay her any attention. If I felt so inclined, I would have told her I didn't want his ass and the only reason I was here, and *not* in my bed, was because he was paying me thousands of dollars.

I'm kinda over it all and I guess Shane can see it on my face. He checks his watch and signals to Terry that he's ready to go.

Terry is kind enough to leave ahead of us and retrieve the truck from valet, sparing Jen and me the cold wait outside. I'm so happy I could kiss him, but I wouldn't want to give him the wrong idea. I give him a brief pat on the shoulder instead. "Thanks Terry."

"You're welcome, B!" he replies, puffing out his chest at the attention.

I lean back onto the warm leather seat, cuddling my faux-fur wrap, when Jen grabs my shoulder and whispers, "Shane says Terry really likes you."

"You don't say." I cover my mouth to hold in the laughter.

"Wait, let me finish." She shields her mouth and tries to whisper in my ear. "I told Shane that you don't date the man standing next to the man. I told him that you only date alpha males." She giggles loudly into my ear. "He said, 'Like me?' I said, 'Yes! Like you!' I could tell he got excited." She falls around the back seat laughing hysterically.

"What's so funny?" barks Shane.

"Oh, nothing," replies Jen.

"Stop this." I hit her. "You better not have given *him* any hope." I laugh so hard my nose starts to run and I'm fresh out of tissue. I tap Shane on the shoulder. "Do you have any napkins?" I ask, slightly embarrassed.

He checks in his glove box and then the center console. "Nah." He looks out the window. "Terry, pull over." He points to a fast food drive-through.

Shane jumps out and knocks on the window. The lights are out. Regardless, he taps again. An older heavyset woman wearing a red headscarf appears behind the glass, but doesn't acknowledge him. He taps harder this time, getting her full attention, and points to a pile of napkins leaning against the glass.

She shakes her head no.

"Please," begs Shane, clasping his hands.

She stands motionless for a moment, looks left and right, and then cracks the window, handing a few napkins through. The next moment, Shane peels off three $100 bills. We hear the window fly back open.

"Did you see that? Did you see what just happened?" Jen, in disbelief, pinches my arm.

"Yeeeeessssssss." I try not to show any reaction.

"Here you go." Shane hands me the napkins before pulling his door shut.

"Thank you very much." I attempt to blow my nose as silently as possible.

"Girl!" Jen nudges me on the shoulder. "Those are some $300 napkins you're blowing your nose with!"

3

OFFICE SPACE

On my eighteenth birthday, I traveled to Trinidad for Carnival, and from Saturday morning until Ash Wednesday, participated in lots of underage drinking. I partied constantly, and after four days without sleep, even a single thought was painful. My head throbbed, my eyes burned, and my entire body ached. This morning, ten years later and after only two hours of sleep, I feel similar.

Wincing with every step, I trek down the hall of offices towards my desk, hidden in a maze of tall, gray cubicles in Merchant Bank's finance department.

"Morning, Imani." I yawn as I pass her office. Imani is a senior analyst and the fashionista of the department. She keeps her hair short and sleek and her attire is always runway ready. Her office is adjacent to our manager's, Alex, whose lights are still off. *Yes, I beat him into the office.*

"Hey girl." Her expression is perplexed. "You alright?"

"Girl, exhausted." I hope it serves as an excuse for my lateness and my sad wardrobe choice for today, wrinkled khakis (cringe: I should have ironed them) and a mint-green Merchant Bank logo polo given to me at a re-gifting party—it's simply pitiful. Even Bailey didn't want me walking her into school this morning. Oh well, it's casual Friday.

As I round the corner to my desk, I feel as if a large, black cloud is hovering over me. The proposal for Shane's event has taken over my life for the past two weeks. Beside my normal stacks of work papers there are fabric samples, catering menus, and venue floor plans. I stare at it all in despair, toss my laptop directly on top of all the mess, and pull my chair out. Someone's put a copy of today's paper on my chair. Shane, in full color, graces the cover. Feeling a surge of giddiness, I plop down, clear space for my feet and attempt to read the article.

"Aww man, that game was awesome last night. Shane was a monster." Brian, my young and impressionable junior analyst and football fanatic, pokes his head over our shared cubicle wall. He's so excited his face is flushed, blending in with his golden-orange hair. He widens his green eyes. "Did you go?"

"Yes, and guess what? He officially signed the contract yesterday."

"Sweet!"

"We hung out afterwards," I add on purpose.

"I'm so jealous." He slinks away, sulking like a five-year-old kid about to have a temper tantrum. When he returns to his senses, he comes back and I share the story of the most expensive napkins in the world.

"I would have flipped out. You're so lucky!" He walks to the main hallway and I hear him shout to someone, "Bryn went to the game last night and hung out with Shane Smith afterwards."

He marches back with Colin, our new payroll assistant. "That's pretty fantastic." Colin, dressed in a tailored suit, leans on the wall as if he's modeling for GQ. "King Smith! Man, he's one ugly dude. That scar!" he belts. "But he's a beast on the field. He kind of scares me." He shudders.

I try for a quick comeback to his insult, but am too busy staring in horror at the amount of product in his hair. He has the nerve to talk about somebody while he's walking around the office looking like Christian Bale in *American Psycho*.

"Come on now, that's not nice," I say in my best rendition of June Cleaver, when instead I want to snatch the silk hankie from his front pocket and shove it down his throat. "Shane may seem scary, but he can also be very sweet."

"Shoot. His money is sweet," Colin adds with an arrogant laugh.

I ignore this comment. I could come up with a few choice words, but I refuse to let him get to me. My head hurts too badly already.

"He likes you, doesn't he?" Brian laughs and gives Colin a shove to his shoulder.

"That came out of nowhere." I struggle to keep a straight face.

"I bet he does." He stares me down, taking a sip of coffee from his 'F***Off, I'm a Ginger' mug. "Everybody likes Bryn."

"We work together, *Brian*." I exaggerate his name. "I'm a professional. I don't mix business with pleasure. Besides, there's a 'no fraternization' clause in his contract."

"Aww man, come on, screw that. You should get with him," chuckles Brian. "I would *love* to meet Shane. Hell, I'll date him." He and Colin laugh together.

I make a face at them. Colin smirks and follows Brian out.

Exhausted from my headache, I pop four Advil and walk over to Alex's office to see that he has arrived. Leaning on his doorframe, I wait for him to acknowledge me.

"Morning." His eyes stay focused on his computer screen. "Come in. Close the door."

"Alex, you know Susanne hates it when we're in here with the door closed." I giggle. Imani taps the paper-thin wall to let us know we are too loud. Alex and I laugh even louder. Susanne, our CFO and office pit-bull, is bitter, self-righteous, and on an ongoing mission to destroy anything remotely fun. Most days she can be found pacing the floor dressed in her ankle-length khakis, turtleneck, and brown loafers (most likely purchased from JC Penney's), accessorized with a dumb looking nautical neck scarf (I think it's called a neckerchief). If she loosened it, she might be able to relax and remove that fake grin plastered across her face.

"Check this out." Waving me over to his computer, Alex turns his monitor towards me and points to the Orrstown, Pennsylvania police blotter. "Look at this. A woman called 911 because a *cow* knocked down her mailbox."

"You are so stupid. I come in here to talk about work and you want to show me a story about a cow." He is such a country boy. Standing about six feet, he's slim with blonde hair and vivid blue eyes, impressive for a forty-year-old. Most guys his age let themselves go, are half-bald, and have huge beer bellies. I wouldn't be surprised if there was a six-pack hiding under the button-up shirt tucked into his slacks. If he wasn't married, I'd be willing to find out.

"Bryn, stop being so loud and obnoxious," he jokes. "In fact, open my blinds. I want her to see you in here when she walks by."

"Alex, I need to take a long lunch. Do you need anything from me today?"

"Fine. Leave. I'll email you. Watch out for Susanne!"

"I—can—hear—you," warns Imani, enunciating each word.

I leave Alex's office, return to my desk, and open a complex spreadsheet to appear busy before the warden passes. I check my cell and see five missed calls from Jen. I punch some buttons on my keyboard to act like I'm working and call her back. "What's up? I missed your calls."

"I've got great news," she whispers. "Oris Odili, the designer I was telling you about, is going to design a custom suit for Shane." Her whisper turns to a squeal. "Finally . . . finally, I get him out of those big Ed Hardy jeans and long shirts. I can't have him play himself like that. He's got a hot body and I'm going to teach him how to show it off. I'm so excited! Hold on, there's Shelly again." She turns me over to piano music while I wait. Shelly is her manager who has concerns about Jen's side business. Jen has been tardy, ineffective, and borderline disruptive (due to her emotional outbursts) in her office since she launched Platinum Events. "Sorry about that, she just handed me one of Shane's receipts I accidentally printed on the main copier. Dang it! I meant to get it, but got distracted. This is the third one she's found after my warning last week."

"Yeah, that sucks. Especially since you just got caught yesterday. Now, so we both won't be in the unemployment line, let's get some actual work done. I'll see you this afternoon." I disconnect the call and stare at my monitor. I don't have the desire or the energy to focus on anything, let alone a budget for Merchant Bank. The only thing on my mind is sleep and this walk-through in a few hours.

I sneak out of the office a little after twelve o'clock and drive towards my dream venue. It's a new high-rise located on the west side of the harbor. I found it during an online search and became obsessed about booking it after taking the virtual tour. I called a bunch of times and the owner took forever to call me back. When he finally did, he told me the building was still under construction, but he was willing to pull some strings since he's a huge Baltimore Nighthawks fan. Today, I finally get to see it.

When I pull into the lot, I look in the rearview mirror at the concrete and glass building and see that it's raining. I know Jen will use it as an excuse for being late, but I'll call her anyway. "Hey," I say, watching Shane's black Range Rover speed past me into an empty space a few spots over. "He's here."

"Well, go and talk to him!" she shouts. "I'll be five minutes." She blows her horn and shouts nonsensical names at other drivers. She's famous for honking if she thinks a car wants to move into her lane.

I hang up, grab my pocket umbrella, and walk over to Shane's driver side window which is tinted the blackest black. As the window descends, a tired-looking Shane gives me a blank stare.

"Hi," I smile. "Jen is on her way. She shouldn't be more than five minutes." I lie. I know she will be much later but I don't want to upset him. I've already learned that he detests lateness.

"You want to get in?"

"Umm." I spin the umbrella and look towards the building, not knowing what to say. "I'm fine."

"I won't bite." Shane grins from ear to ear.

"Ahhh. That's nice." I look up, away, anywhere but at him.

"You would rather stand in the rain and get wet?" He looks down at my feet. The bottoms of my khakis are soaked.

"I'm okay," I assure him and turn my umbrella to shield my face from the rain.

"Have it your way." He shrugs his shoulders.

I look around, hoping Jen will appear and try to think of what to say next. "I think you're going to like this place." I point in random directions. "You know, from what you said you were looking for, I envision you here."

Shane looks around then focuses his attention at a mound of dirt, gravel, and a ghastly hedge wire fence. He looks apprehensive. I can tell he needs convincing.

"Just trust me. I know you'll love it. Wait until you see the inside."

"If you say so." He gives me an impartial look before turning his attention to his phone. "So, how long have y'all been doing this?" He glances at me. "You know, planning parties?"

"Unofficially, for some time now. A few milestone birthday parties, social gatherings, a sweet sixteen, and a wedding." *Would I ever forget Bridezilla?* Jen and I vowed never to take on another wedding because of her. "But Jen officially launched her company with a big charity fashion show a few months ago. I even suffered an injury." I point to my right foot. "One of the bases from our pipe and drape fell on my foot. It caused a nasty gash and I was wearing a boot for a few weeks."

"I didn't know event planning was that dangerous." Shane sets his phone down. "You know what I want?" He sits up from a slouched position.

I raise my eyebrows.

"I would be so happy if y'all could get Majestic or Houston to come."

Those reality vixens? Really? I hope my face doesn't mirror my thoughts. I haven't mastered the art of masking my emotions. "That is something I can definitely look into." I give him my rehearsed smile.

Our exchanges end in an awkward lull. Seeing Jen pull into a parking space gives me the opportunity to walk away without feeling like a complete idiot.

Inside the lobby, I ask for the owner, Nick. He comes right out. I lead the introductions and as we exchange handshakes, Nick, handsome and sporting a five o'clock shadow, rakes his hand through his sandy-blonde hair before handing us each an orange hard hat.

"You guys are going to love it." He leads us to the elevators and presses the thirtieth floor. "Awesome view, best in the city. I've been working on this project for the last four years. I've been up here every day just taking in the view."

We step out of the elevator and I stay close to Nick listening to him ramble on about the amazing building and construction details, past and present. He continues until we reach the end of the hallway and does his best to make a dramatic entrance, slowly opening the door and allowing only a small peek before flinging it wide open.

I'm the first to enter the space, which has twenty-foot floor-to-ceiling glass windows, a few steel and concrete columns, and a flight of exposed wooden stairs. "I love it."

"You haven't seen the best part yet." He reaches for my hand and walks me over to a large window ledge, which also functions as a door, onto the balcony that wraps around the entire building. That's when Shane appears from nowhere and grabs my other hand and assists me outside.

"Chivalry isn't dead yet." Shane takes my umbrella and opens it.

"Thank you." I nod.

"My pleasure."

I look for Jen but she stays inside. Nick walks out in the rain.

"Like I was saying, you can throw some heaters out here and you've got yourself an awesome party with a spectacular view. You can practically see all of Baltimore." Nick chuckles. "Look, the two buildings over there, that's Towson."

"This is *hot*!" Shane blurts.

Back inside, Jen and I take our time checking out the space and discuss design plans as we head back to the elevators, where Nick is standing holding the doors open for us. "Now—there's one more space I want you guys to see."

"What?" Shane's bark echoes down the empty hallway.

"The Penthouse." Nick gives me an 'I've-got-things-under-control' gesture. He presses a card key against a digital screen and the elevator takes us to the top.

"Nick," I whisper. "I thought this was the only space that's nearly complete?"

"It's okay. Seriously, it's fine," he says under his breath.

The elevator doors open and everyone's faces light up. Even Nick looks like he's seeing it for the first time and from what he's shared, he's seen it a thousand times. A sound of collective 'oohs' and 'aahs' fill the space. The forty-foot glass walls spanning hundreds of feet, steel columns, and an exposed ceiling are the focal points. From this view, we have front row seats to the expansive Baltimore skyline.

"Ladies and gentleman, I give you . . . The Monarch." Nick spreads his arms wide and bows. "It's seven thousand square feet and the space is lined with floor-to-ceiling windows. It's the length of the entire building. And did I mention the three-hundred-and-sixty-degree view?" He laughs at himself.

"I want it. How much?" Shane pats his pockets. "I'll write the check right now."

"It's twelve million, but I'm sorry, it's already sold. If we can get it completed in time, you can have the event here before we turn over the keys."

"Nick, I'm speechless. This place is phenomenal." I walk towards the windows and watch the rainfall. Nick joins me.

"This is where I come to escape, especially when it rains," he says.

"It's so romantic." I blush and regret that it's casual Friday.

"I want my party here!" barks Shane, startling me. "Make it happen." He gives Nick and me the evil eye.

I walk back to the parking lot completely stressed out. *Thanks a lot, Nick.* He just made my job a lot harder. Not only that, but when I check the time I realize I'm running very late. I rush to my car and call Jen. She doesn't give me a chance to speak.

"Don't stress. Nick is a businessman. He has no choice but to get it done. Remember, Shane's a Nighthawk so we've got leverage."

"I understand. Thanks for the reminder."

"But onto other more important matters . . . Shane wants to know if you have a man."

"I'm starting to feel like you are encouraging this. Why? No, I'm not interested. You could have told him that. Actually, I think I like Nick."

"I didn't peg Nick as your type. He's short. White . . ."

"Well, Shane certainly isn't my type. Besides, I read he's married or something."

"I don't know about that."

"Listen, I've read how he gets down. The women. Girl, please," I say in disgust. "No offense, he's a gentleman and all but nothing, and I mean *nothing* about Shane and his host of women is attractive to me."

Jen laughs until she cries.

I don't understand why she keeps bringing it up. Shane isn't my type. And from what I've seen so far, I'm even less his.

I manage to sneak back to my desk without running into Susanne. When I pass Brian, he rolls his eyes at me.

"You were with him, weren't you?"

I laugh and stick my tongue out at him. What I really want to tell him is that his instincts are right. Shane does like me. But I'll never admit it to anyone. They'll think it's the only reason we landed this contact.

Thinking about our coveted agreement reminds me I have to scan it for my file. I dig in my laptop bag and retrieve it. It's a mini hike over to the copier room, so I hide it from my nosy co-workers between work papers. I place the contract on the top tray for scanning and hit go. Simultaneously, a nasally voice behind me almost makes me jump.

"Bryn!"

The warden. I turn around to see Susanne staring down at me with a clipboard tightly pressed against her chest. "Yes?" *Just shoot me now.* I maintain eye contact while removing the contract from the bottom tray.

"I'm not a fan of the colors you chose for the budget template so I've emailed you a sample of the hues I would like to see. Can you get an updated copy to me by close of business?"

I match her grin.

"Sure. No problem." *Whew.* I wait for her to clear the hall.

4

THE MEETING

Shane will be here any minute and we're in a state of panic. Today is our first 'weekly' meeting with him since he signed the contract. Jen, Bailey, and I are trying to get Jen's house in order. I'm cleaning the kitchen, Bailey's vacuuming the living room floor, and Jen's upstairs in her office kicking her printer.

"Jack-Scrabbit!" I hear her scream, followed by a huge thud. "I can't take it! It stopped on the last one! The LAST one!"

"I don't need one," I call up to her. "Seriously. I'll look at your copy." Honestly, I don't *want* to look at anything. I'm not a fan of meetings. I loathe them. They bore me to death. At work, I have a terrible habit of falling asleep and so I try to avoid them whenever I can. Just last week, in the financial review meeting,

Imani said she tried to keep me awake. She said my chin fell to my chest and stayed there throughout Susanne's presentation. *Supposedly*, every now and again I lifted my head and let out a guttural moan. At one point, she thought I'd woken up. She said I sat straight up before leaning forward, grabbing my pen, and starting to write. But apparently, seconds later, I drew a long diagonal line before slumping onto the table. That's when she kicked me, hard. I remember that. I'm sure that's another reason Susanne hates me.

"Okay." Jen jogs down the stairs out of breath. "Are you almost done?" She runs her fingers through her hair, giving her bob hairstyle a lift. The emerald sheath dress looks radiant against her dark brown skin.

"Were you wearing that earlier?"

"I just changed."

"I thought so. I like that color."

"Thanks." She places an agenda on the table in front of two of the chairs.

"I feel underdressed." I'm wearing pink sweatpants, a white tank top, and fuzzy socks. My hair is in a high bun. "Should I go and change?"

"We're not going to have that discussion. Where are the bottled waters?" She runs into the kitchen.

"Right here." I hand them to her.

"Bailey, are you almost finished? Can you light a few candles?"

"Yes." Bailey turns off the vacuum and runs to grab a candle.

"I'll do it. I don't let her touch fire."

"Whatever, the lighter is in the kitchen drawer." She paces, touching things but not moving them. As I light the candles, the doorbell rings and Bailey runs to the door.

"Hey, Sweetie," belts Shane's deep voice. He picks her up and gives her a huge bear hug. "Good to see you again, Bailey baby."

"I made you something." She reaches into her book bag and pulls out a sheet of blue construction paper. She blushes and hands it to him.

"Read it to me."

"I love Shane Smith #50."

He smiles. "Bailey, I love it. I'm going to hang this at my house." He pats her on the head and walks towards Jen. He stops and points to me. "I love her. That girl is awesome."

"Thanks," I say and wave hello.

"Hi Shane," says Jen. "Just you today?"

"No, Terry is coming. He's outside inspecting my rims. His blind ass hit a curb on the way over here."

"Bailey. Upstairs," I say, signaling to Jen's office.

"Sorry, Bailey. Earmuffs," whispers Shane.

Bailey holds her ears as she runs up the steps.

Shane plops down in the chair and scans the agenda. "Bryn," he calls. "Terry says he sent you a friend request on MySpace. He said you ignored him."

"When was this?" laughs Jen.

He tried to holla at me through MySpace?

"Hey, Bryn." Terry walks in. "Hey, Jen." He joins Shane at the table.

"I was just asking Bryn why she didn't accept your friend request?" laughs Shane.

"Yeah, she broke my heart." Terry takes out his phone. "I'll show it to you."

"Stop." I wave my hand "You two are silly. There's no need."

"We're real friends now so you have to accept both of our requests." Shane picks up his phone. "Let me find you right now."

"Bryn. Can you join us over here?" Jen taps her agenda.

"Sure." I leave the kitchen and join them in the dining room. Jen wants to be formal, I guess.

"Thank you all for coming. If you will refer to your agendas we can get started. The first order of business today is design."

Shane leaps from his chair and walks into the kitchen. Jen goes silent. "Oh, you can keep talking." Jen rambles on about something while Shane stares at the photos on her refrigerator. He zeroes in on a photo of Jen and me at our high school ring dance. "Who's this?"

"Bryn and I," she says. "As I was saying . . . we're bringing on a designer, Christian. Would you like to meet him?" She stares at Shane, waiting for an answer.

"I don't care," he says in a monotone. "Where are y'all at in this one?" He points to a photo of us at Maracas Beach.

"Trinidad," she snaps, letting out a theatrical sigh. "Okay, never mind. Let's move on to guest lists."

"Who's she?" Shane's large finger presses the middle of someone's face.

"That's my sister."

"What's her name?"

"Taylor."

"Where is she?"

"She's home with her mother. Why?"

"Because y'all look alike. I thought she was your daughter."

"Are you saying I look old enough to have a sixteen-year-old?" She stands with her hands on her hips.

Shane laughs and then opens the refrigerator door wide and looks around. "No Orange Fanta? Gatorade?" He slams the door shut. Then he walks to the pantry and rummages through it. "Nothing sweet? Your food is boring."

"Shane. I'll add those items to my grocery list."

"Don't worry about it. Go on . . . go on."

"Guest lists." Jen takes a deep breath. "I've invited—"

Shane starts rapping and dances his way into her living room. I hold in my laughter and look over at Terry, who's not paying attention to anyone. He's busy playing Tetris on his phone.

Jen leaves the table and follows our silly client into the adjoining room. "How about models?" Jen's jaw tightens.

"There is something horribly efficient about you."

Jen returns a blank stare. Terry laughs. I guess he *is* paying attention.

Shane starts laughing hysterically. "You know where that's from?"

"*Quantum of Solace*," shouts Terry.

"That was perfect, wasn't it?" Shane looks at me to agree. At this point, Jen is the only one who isn't laughing. "Jen." He rubs her shoulders. "Lighten up, babe. This is going to be fun."

"Shane, I just want to keep you up to date with everything that we've done so far. We've gotten a lot accomplished in a week."

"I know. If it will make you happy, I'll sit down." He takes a seat and scoots his chair so that his abs are flush against the table. "Continue," he gasps. I laugh this time. Shane gives me a wink and pushes his chair back and balances on the two back legs. If looks could kill, he'd be dead. Jen's a boiling pot of water.

"Okay, I'm ready." He sets his chair on all fours and stares at Jen with his elbows resting on his knees. "You were saying?" He gives her his undivided attention.

Jen looks at her agenda. "I guess the most important thing you need to know is about—"

Without warning, Shane reaches down and yanks a stiletto off Jen's foot.

"SHANE!!!!" screams Jen.

He points to her toes. "Terry, look!" Shane laughs so hard that his eyes fill with tears.

"Do you take anything seriously?" she screeches, snatching her shoe from his hand.

"Nope. Not really."

5

<u>MATTER OF TIME</u>

"I thought event planning was fun?" Michael lifts his plate to his face and takes a deep inhale. "Yum. Glad I'm not on a diet."

"It's been a rough week." I sigh and look out the seventeenth-floor window of the Legg Mason building. It's where I enjoy taking long lunches on stressful days like today. My favorite booth overlooks the Baltimore Harbor and even though I know the water's rancid and murky green, from this height, it shines a calming blue. "By the way, I need to come and see you in your office so you can walk me through creating a custom report. Susanne's requesting actuals from commercial banking and during my last attempt to run the report, it came out blank."

"You don't need me any longer. I thought you were quitting. Since you're a big-time celebrity event planner now. Have you put your house on the market yet? Did you put a bid in for a high-rise in Manhattan? NYC for Bailey, right? From here on out, life is good for you." He eats a few scoops of mac & cheese.

"You're so NOT funny." Unfortunately, at some point in his life, someone told him he was witty. The sad part is I don't think I've laughed at a single joke since the day he jumped into my cubicle on Halloween wearing a Michael Myers mask. He welcomed me to the company and asked me out to lunch. I'm still not sure why I agreed, but we've been hanging out ever since.

"Maybe I should become an event planner. Can you ask Jen if I can join? I'll be your assistant," he laughs.

"Lately it hasn't been a walk in the park. This new client is a lot of work. In the last twenty-four hours, Shane has called Jen three times changing his mind about stuff. I mean we had things locked in and now I've got to scramble and change it."

"You're big-time now, so what's the problem?"

"It's three weeks away. You can't keep changing orders at the last minute. Regardless, I'm just feeling frustrated today. We don't have a response to his last-minute catering changes and our meeting is at six o'clock tonight. I'm behind, so I'm sure it's going to be a long evening."

"I still don't know how y'all got his business." Michael shakes his head. "Couple of ordinary county girls, hooking a Nighthawk? He's got enough money to hire a professional event planning company. Why y'all?"

"We put together a kick-ass proposal, that's how."

"Whatever. More like, Shane wants to sleep with you, that's how."

"I am so sick—you know what?" I set my fork down. "Never mind, it's not worth wasting my breath. I'm sure I'll need it one day. You're wrong. Moving on."

"Why wouldn't he want you?"

"Like I said, I'd appreciate if you could help me with that report." I ignore the topic of Shane and finish my salad.

"Then again, he probably knows you're too good for a guy like him. That's it. That's probably why he hasn't stepped to you."

"Yup. Whatever you say."

"Yeah." He wipes his mouth with a napkin. "You don't want to get involved with a guy like him. They've got lots of women."

"Agreed. Now can we change the subject?"

"Cheer up. You'll find a man soon enough." Michael reaches across the table and pats me on the shoulder.

"I tell you what . . ." I push his hand away. "You worry about your love life and I'll worry about mine. Comprende?" *Ha, love life? Who's got time for that? My plate is full. I have zero time or tolerance for drama.*

My phone rings. It's Terry. I hush Michael and take the call.

"Hey B!"

"Hi Terry. Is everything okay?"

"Shane wants to cancel tonight's meeting."

"Sure, no problem whatsoever." Whew. I can relax. This is wonderful news. "Jen and I need to wrap up a few tasks before we meet again anyway."

"Well, he was canceling so he could take his baby mama and daughter to the game but now he says he wants y'all to come instead."

"Umm . . ."

"He says we'll pick y'all up at seven." Terry disconnects the call.

"Fuck!" My shoulders stiffen as I disconnect the call. "That was Terry." I set my phone down. "He says the meeting is canceled and we're going to a basketball game tonight."

"I told you. It's just a matter of time before he makes his move."

"Trust me. It's all work." I roll my eyes when my phone chimes. It's a text from Terry.

`Shane said tell Jen no agendas`

As promised, Shane and Terry arrive at our duplex at seven. I'm surprised I don't have to harass Jen to get out of the house. She's ready and waiting when I walk out of the door.

"Is Bailey at your mom's?"

"Yes, and Joan's starting to complain that I'm going out during the week."

"What are you, twelve? She needs to get over it. We're halfway there."

"I know . . ." I grab the back-door handle.

Shane jumps out of the front passenger seat. "Let me help you with that." He opens the back door and lifts me into the seat. For a minute, *Shane* makes me feel like I'm twelve. It feels weird. "I just got bigger rims," he explains.

"Oh." Now it makes sense. I was about to say, 'I'm short but I'm sure I can get into a truck on my own.' "Thanks."

Shane jumps back into the passenger seat and Terry drives off.

"So, any updates? Is everything wrapped up? Y'all ready?" Shane smacks his dashboard for effect.

"There's plenty of work still. I don't have any updates since I spoke to you last night." Jen starts to look through her phone.

"You don't?" Shane yells. "What am I paying you all of this money for?"

"I can try to call the caterer but they're closed for the evening. When I spoke with her earlier she mentioned she would review the amendments and call me back."

"Yeah, she's tripping. I'm not paying that kind of money for food. Fuck that!"

"I'll get it straightened out. Please keep in mind that I need to use her because it's last minute."

"Whose fault is that? I gave you six weeks."

"I mean . . ." Jen looks perplexed. "You're right."

I can tell she's caught off guard by his behavior.

"Damn straight, I'm right." Shane turns the music up. "My shit better be on point."

Jen gives me an evil look. "I thought you said he said no agendas?"

"That's what Terry said." I show her the text.

"I was unprepared for that. Gosh." Jen is pissed and starts working from her phone. "I could have stayed home for this."

"What did you say?" barks Shane. "Here you go again talking under your breath. Is there something you need to say to me?"

This is awful. I feel sorry for her being in this position. What makes it worse is the two of them look like they want to fight.

"I'm saying I have work to do and y'all have me going to a game!" Jen shouts.

"Lighten up. We are gonna have a little fun tonight. Always so uptight. Chill Jen, chill."

The energy in the car relaxes for the remainder of the ride to D.C.

At the Verizon Center, Terry drops us off at the front and leaves to park the car. Jen and I follow Shane to the Will-Call window where he picks up the tickets. He leaves one behind for Terry and then motions for us to follow him through security and down a gazillion steps to a row of black leather seats located in the front row under the basket.

Jen and I take our seats but almost immediately Shane makes us stand. "Switch," he says, plopping down onto the seat between us. "This way I can talk to both of y'all."

"That's cool. I have a better view of A.I.," laughs Jen.

Allen Iverson makes a three-pointer and everyone cheers, even the so-called Wizard fans.

"You like Iverson?"

"We went to school in Philly," says Jen.

"Don't tell me you like him too?" Shane bumps me on the shoulder with his bear-sized arm.

"Like who?" Terry appears in the seat next to me.

"Y'all want something to eat or drink?" Shane pulls out a stack of twenties and reaches across me to hand it to Terry. "Go get us some snacks. I want Twizzlers."

Terry leaves us again.

"Like you were saying . . ." Shane stares down at me waiting for a response.

"I don't like him like she does." I point to Jen.

"Well, who do you like?" Shane leans back in his chair and crosses his feet.

"I don't know. I'm not really into sports like that."

"It can be a regular guy. When was the last time you were on a date?"

"I don't know."

Shane crosses his arms and purses his lips.

I feel like I'm on the stand and I need to plead the fifth. "I don't know . . . like six months ago." Goodness. Talk about pressure.

"Six months!" He sits up in his chair. "What happened? Was he a loser?"

"I'd say so." I nod. "I found out I wasn't the only one he was seeing."

"Oh." Shane turns his attention back onto the court. "So you don't date." He pouts. "It has to be like . . . exclusive?"

"I don't share. It's that simple." I flash a tight-lipped smile.

"That's wack!" Shane cheers and claps wildly at a play on the court. Then he leans over to me. "Now back to what I was saying. "What if—"

"What on earth are y'all talking about?" yells Jen.

"Stop being nosy and keep your eyes on Iverson." Shane shoves Jen with his shoulder before turning his attention back to me. Right before he can form his next word, Terry returns.

"What did I miss?" Terry gasps, carrying a tray full of junk.

"Not a thing, Terry." I help him with the snacks and hand them to Shane. "Trust me."

"Oh good." Terry makes himself comfortable. "Do you like basketball?"

"It's okay."

"I love it." Terry's face lights up.

"Who cares," barks Shane. "You can't play."

Terry shakes his head.

"I can play basketball and football," brags Shane. "In fact, I should be on the court right now."

"It sounds like you're a jack of all trades but a master of none." Jen laughs, keeping her eyes on the court.

"Shit—I dominate everything I touch." Shane glances at me.

I sure as hell don't care. I don't bother to respond. Instead, I take a handful of Terry's popcorn and ask him about a play.

Shane takes the hint and starts to aggravate Jen. I hear them arguing over nonsense. They fuss through half time and into the third quarter. They go back and forth so much even the cameraman thinks they are a couple. When it's time for the kiss cam, they zoom in on the two still fussing. Jen shrieks when she

Bianca Williams

sees herself on the Jumbotron and practically throws herself on the floor to get out of the frame. When the entire arena is screaming with laughter, Shane throws up a peace sign.

Hours later, when we head back to the truck, Jen and Shane are still at each other's throats.

"I hate you, I hate you, I hate you," Jen fusses as she chases Shane around the parking garage.

"You love me," teases Shane, ducking and darting through moving traffic to get away from her. "All women love me."

I follow Terry to the truck shaking my head at the two of them. The night started out rough but it seems like they've made up.

"They fight like brother and sister," says Terry, unlocking the truck.

"Truly. Shane has a way of getting under her skin." I hop into the back seat.

"Shane, I don't know how anyone puts up with you!" Jen slams her door.

"I don't give them the choice." Shane jumps in the passenger seat. He looks into the back seat. "Even my side chicks have to be faithful."

"Is that right?" Jen shoves the back of his chair.

"Yeah—'cause I know how to fuck."

I blink. *Wow! He just said that aloud.*

6

FRIED CHICKEN IN A
PAN

"I think he was trying to send you a message."

"Gross. It's been a week. Please change the topic."

"Fine. About today's meeting—"

"This shit sucks," I cut in. "I shouldn't be the one to tell him."

"Bryn! I can't be there. Just stick to the script."

"You know Shane is as crazy as a bag of cats!"

"It's not like he's going to attack you."

"You won't be here to find out."

"I gotta go." Jen hangs up.

I'm pissed. Today, our weekly meeting starts any minute and thanks to Shelly, Jen's boss, *I* wait alone in Nick's sales conference room. Shelly chooses today, of all days, to give Jen an ultimatum. And to make matters worse, I have to deliver bad news.

My anxiety increases as I watch Shane open the main doors. He's looking left and pointing right. He stops and waits for Terry before darting towards a gigantic Plexiglas blueprint Nick has suspended from the exposed ceiling.

I feel cold sweat drip down my sides as he finally reaches for the conference room door handle.

"Where's Jen?" Shane's booming voice echoes in the barely furnished room. Terry trails him. Shane snatches a water bottle from the center of the table and then drops onto the chair to my left. He winks, twists the top from the water bottle, and chucks it at Terry. The top hits the side of Terry's head and falls into his lap. He looks slightly irritated, ignores us, and continues to pick at his cuticles.

"HELLO! Earth to Bryn. Where's your boss?"

"She . . . she couldn't make it today." Jen told me exactly what to say and I've rehearsed it a thousand times, but it's all for nothing. Shane manages to cause all my thoughts to muddle. "But, here . . . here is your contract I need you to sign."

"What's this? A contract?" he growls.

"Contract. Catering contract, remember?"

He flips through two pages and smacks the table. "Didn't I tell y'all just last week that I don't want food?"

"Yes. But, in order to have the amount of liquor you're requesting, the law requires a certain amount of food," I explain.

He slaps his hand on the contract and slides it towards him before picking it up. His body tenses. He's seething, like a ticking time bomb ready to explode.

"Man, fuck this!" He smacks the table again. "Just throw some fried chicken and fries in a pan and they can eat that. $50,000? Fuck that!" Shane leaps from his seat and storms out.

Reacting from pure adrenaline, I run after him, but by the time I reach the sidewalk, his truck is speeding out of the parking lot.

"B, wait!" shouts Terry.

Tears fill my eyes as I walk back towards the building.

"B, I know you're really upset," says Terry, out of breath. "Just give him time and we can go back to him. This is how he is. He doesn't like having his back against the wall. You always have to present him with options, even if the options aren't what you want. Trust me. I know," he says, rolling his eyes.

"He didn't have to yell like that—like he's a fucking ogre—agh!"

"He doesn't mean it. That's how he acts sometimes when he's under pressure."

"Fried chicken? Really Terry? I'm done! He wants to serve fried chicken in a pan at an exclusive event? I'm going back to work. I promise you. I AM DONE." I gather my belongings, get into my car, and speed off.

I'm still pissed when I get back to the office and couldn't care less who notices me walking in late. I can barely contain my

Bianca Williams

emotions and as soon as my butt hits the chair, tears begin to fall. I'm not sure I'm cut out for this. I call Jen at work.

"I. Can't. Do. This. Any . . . anymore," I manage to say though a clenched jaw, feeling as if I'm holding back a mini army inside.

"Bryn. What happened?"

"I . . . I . . . I . . . am . . . done . . . with . . . this . . . shit." I feel like, any minute now, I may hyperventilate. "Fffuuuck him! He's fucking crazy! He's yelling at me. Cursing at me. I didn't do anything to him. I quit! I'm not doing anything else for him or this fucking event!"

"Are you bleeding?"

"What kind of question is that?"

"I understand. It's stressful. We're up against tight deadlines. He's bi-polar, stubborn, and a host of other things. But he's our client."

"Are you seriously taking up for that bully right now?" I go quiet as Jen tries to talk me off the ledge, but it's no use. I've made up my mind. She rambles on and I zone out, listening again only when she mentions my name. Then my phone chimes. It's Terry. I cut her off. "Jen, why is Terry calling me?"

"I don't know. Find out, but I've got to go." I hang up the receiver to my office phone and answer my cell.

"Hello?"

"Are you alright?" Terry sounds concerned.

"No, I'm not. I quit. So you need to call Jen for everything from now on." I hear silence. "Hello?" I hear shuffling followed by Shane's voice.

"You mad at me?" he laughs egotistically.

I remain silent and imagine my fist connecting with his eye, making it swell to the size of a lemon, bloodying his face, like Lennox Lewis did to Vatali Klitschko in their 2003 fight in Vegas.

"Cat got your tongue now, huh? Terry told me what you said after I left. He said you were upset, yelling 'fried chicken in a pan'," he says in an exaggerated girly voice. "I hope you weren't really upset?"

Look, you asshole, is what I want to say. "Well, the death stare wasn't nice and you CAN'T serve fried chicken and french fries in an aluminum pan at a formal event." *Jerk.*

"What did Jen say?"

"She says it's your event, so you can have anything you want."

"Is that right?"

"Yes." I hear nothing but silence. "Hello?"

"Bryn?" says Terry. "Yeah, sorry. I think he's talking to Jen. Look, just give it time."

"Terry, we are two weeks away . . . time is something we don't have."

"I got you . . . just . . . be patient."

"I'll try." I hang up Terry and search the Internet. "How to deal with crazy client . . . enter." Then my office phone rings. "Yes, Jen. How may I help you?"

"I lost my job. Shelly just called me into a conference room and gave me notice."

1

<u>TGS</u>

I enter Jen's home and find her seated at her dining room table with her head in her hands.

"Hey." I kick off my shoes at the door. "I'm sorry. I come bearing gifts." I hand her a brownie sundae from Baskin Robbins.

Even though she doesn't hesitate to take the bag, she smiles with disappointment. "Thanks, but I shouldn't be eating this. I'm still seven pounds away from my goal weight."

"So, what's the deal? What was Shelly tripping about this time?"

"I'm not going to say it was *totally* your fault, but I did call Shane and curse him out while I was still at my desk."

"What?"

"Yeah, I know. I went off on him. I could have, well should have, got up and called him from outside. When I called him, I snapped. And now I'm unemployed." She stands and walks into her kitchen. "With that said, you can't quit."

"Jen—"

"Hold on. Let me finish. I called Shane back when I got to my car. I told him what happened . . . and . . . he's coming over tonight to sign the catering contract. And he's bringing TGS."

"Jen, I don't know what to say."

"Say you'll get this freaking bottle of wine open and you will finish this job so I can get another." She gives me a serious look, hands me a bottle of Cupcake Moscato with a corkscrew, and returns to the kitchen and grabs two bowls and spoons. "I'm not making excuses for him, but he claims that he had drama at work. Unfortunately for you, the catering contract was the straw that broke the camel's back."

"That's no excuse. He doesn't have the monopoly on drama at work."

"Yeah, tell me about it. But if I'd been there . . . maybe this wouldn't have happened." She sets two wine glasses in front of me. "Then again, I'm kind of glad it happened. I mean not what happened to you, what happened with my job. The corporate environment is hindering my creativity."

"What about money?" I pour the wine.

"Yes, money. Thank God she offered me a package to leave quietly." She drums her fingers on the tabletop. "I'll be fine." She forces a smile, opens her laptop, and begins to type. "Right now, I just need you to relax while I put the finishing touches to the agenda. Besides catering, is there anything that you need to cover?" She raises her eyebrows and eats a spoonful of ice cream.

"Besides my foot in Shane's ass?" I grin at the thought. Jen gives me an evil look. "No. The only thing still open are the flights for the celebrity guests."

"I'm so glad you said that." She jumps out of her seat and walks back into the kitchen. "Now that we're only a week out, everyone's calling me back with their availability. We need to narrow down who we're going to bring in. Xavier"—she's referring to Shane's publicist—"keeps sending me these *King* magazine models and D-list celebrities. What's the point of a publicist if he can't get the producers and record labels to his client's listening event? I just don't get that. What does he do? I'm supposed to be planning the event, not soliciting celebrities." She slams the cabinet door closed and tosses honey buns and Golden Oreos onto the table.

"Yeah, well, that's a conversation we can have later, after the event."

"Knock, knock!" roars someone in a deep voice.

I turn towards the door and see *him*, holding the storm door wide open for Terry and four other guys to enter.

"Roman, DeShaun, Zander, Qmar, meet Jen and B. Jen and B, may I present TGS."

"Hi," Jen and I say at the same time and then we laugh.

"Please come in, you can have a seat at the table if you like." Jen pulls out a chair.

I grab my glass and a bottle of wine and take it into the kitchen area. Everyone except Shane takes a seat.

"Jen, I was thinking . . . we should do introductions like they do in school. Make everybody go around the room and say something about themselves, ya know?"

Rolling my eyes, I mouth 'oh my goodness'.

"Roman, you first. Stand, tell them something about yourself," commands Shane, standing behind his chair.

Roman stands. He's tall, of average build, and has thick curly hair pulled back into a ponytail. "I'm the lead singer and creative director of the group." He sits, palms his face, and shakes his head.

I'm embarrassed for him.

"DeShaun," barks Shane.

"I love exotic looking women," says DeShaun (aka the Adonis), walking towards me. His lips, full. His eyes, a startling gray. His jaw, perfectly chiseled. His hands, strong. He reaches for my hand and flashes his perfectly white teeth. A wave of heat passes through me causing temporary weakness.

"Next!" shouts Shane, noticing DeShaun holding my hand a bit too long. "And remember, *no mixing business with pleasure*. Zander, you're up."

"Hi, Jen. Hi, Bryn. I'm Zander and I write all the music." He's adorable and looks like the youngest of the four. He's tall, thin, and has impeccable shoulder-length dreads. "Oh, and Terry is my cousin."

"Yeah, yeah," interjects Shane. "And this is Qmar, my cousin and the founder of TGS," Shane finishes. Qmar stands and smiles, revealing deep dimples. He's tall and thickset with dark chocolate skin just like Shane's.

"Thanks for speaking for me," says Qmar. Unlike Shane's scary, booming voice, his is deep and mild-mannered.

"Ladies. Let's make this short and sweet. I've got somewhere to be. I hope this shit is done 'cause I've got other things I need to take care of." Shane plops down onto the chair. He gives the table a huge smack, spilling Jen's wine onto her agenda. Managing to keep her composure, she lifts the laptop above her head before it gets wet. I run over with a paper towel roll.

"You up? I was trying to wake you." He leans back in the chair and opens a honey bun, cramming it whole into his mouth.

"Shane, please do not lean back in the chair." Jen points a roll of paper towels at him. "See those chairs over there facing the wall? They broke."

"Stop buying cheap chairs." Crumbs fall from his mouth onto his shirt.

"They aren't cheap. Chairs are designed for all four legs to be on the floor."

"Ain't I paying you enough to buy new chairs?" He laughs and looks over at the boys for support. They all join in except DeShaun, who's trying to eye-fuck me. I look back over at Jen who looks as if she's about to explode.

"That isn't the point, this was a set. And it was the *last* set."

"Man, bill me for it." He crumples the wrapper and tosses it at Jen. "I'll buy you some damn chairs." He pushes away from the table, skips to her counter, and rifles through Jen's unopened mail. "What's up? What do you have to tell me? Let's go! Let's go!"

"The venue is secured. Liquor is finalized. Insurance premium still needs to be paid . . ."

"How much?" He cuts her off.

"$450." She looks up at him for approval.

He nods. "Go on."

"Bryn. What else?"

"Surprises and flights," I chime in, "and the caterer's contract," I mumble under my breath.

"Surprises!" Shane's face brightens. "Tell me about the surprises." He smiles at me.

"Do you really want to know?" asks Jen.

He returns his attention to the guys. "What y'all think?" But instead of waiting for their response, he repeats, "Tell me . . ."

"Okay, we decided—"

He cuts her off again. "No! Don't tell me! I like surprises." He blushes.

"Now," Jen says, taking a huge breath. "Moving on to flights, we need to narrow your list down. Xavier's been sending me a bunch of D-list celebrities, video vixens, *King* models, and even a few popular strippers. But we have some producers and record label reps that are interested, so we'd rather bring them in."

"Wait! Strippers? Strippers are people too."

Jen looks at him with utter disgust. I know she's appalled at his response, but she must try harder at keeping a poker face.

"See, that's what I'm talking about. Chill, girl. Don't worry about Xavier. Terry will deal with him. In fact, cut off communication with him." He looks deep in thought as he starts to tug on the hairs of his goatee. "Obviously, we want to have the record labels there and a few producers so we can get these guys collaborating with some hot artists. So just get 'em here. I'll give you my credit card details tonight so you can take care of the flights and insurance. Anything else?"

"Yes, the contract you need to sign." She hands him the contract with a pen. "I don't want to keep you any longer because I can see you're in a rush."

He scrunches his face as he signs. "Alright." He jumps up from the chair, spins around, and grabs Zander by the back of his head, dragging him out of his chair and towards the door. "Are you happy now?" he asks me, as he hops down the three steps to Jen's landing. "Remember, there's no crying in baseball."

"Tom Hanks," shouts Zander, pointing at Shane.

"I love what I do. I'm just so darn good at it," says Shane, grabbing the door handle.

"Shane, it's your mom." Terry hands him his cell.

"Yeah? I said I had a meeting!" he yells into the phone.

Either she's yelling back or I have supersonic ears. I hear her fussing and clearly distinguish the words 'baby mama'. I'm not the only one, because DeShaun and Qmar are snickering.

"Yo, baby mama, man," says Zander, shaking his head.

"Look, I'll deal with her." He disconnects the call and continues to walk towards the door. "B, where's baby girl?"

"She's at home doing homework."

"Tell her I said hi."

Jen runs towards Shane as he opens the door. "Wait, I almost forgot. Your date, the mother of your children, does she need a dress for the red carpet? Should I set up an appointment with Oris?"

"Nah, don't worry 'bout her. *She* ain't my date." He lets out a boisterous chuckle.

I shut the door behind them. "He's such an ass."

8

<u>TRICKS & TRAGEDY</u>

I rub my temples, hoping my meeting with Jen is nearing its end.

"Are you sure we aren't forgetting anything?" Jen repeats herself for the thousandth time tonight. It's the eve of our big reveal and we've been checking and re-checking our to-do list.

"We must be sure. This is it. Do or die."

Straining my eyes, I skim through my list again. "Once I get these itineraries out tonight, I'm done."

"Fine then. I'll see you tomorrow. Remember, both of our necks are on the line," she says as her phone rings. "It's Christian." Christian, our designer, fashions large events effortlessly, so he was our number one choice considering the time constraints of this job. "Are you expecting a call from him?"

I check my phone. "Nope. He should be at Nick's setting up."

She answers the call and seconds later her Blackberry crashes to the floor. Her body convulses. "What? NO! NO! Oh, my GOD! I can't breathe!" Jen bolts out the front, letting in a gust of cold October wind.

"Jen!" My heart is pounding in my chest. I run after her, but she's already pacing the lawn, crying, and screaming to the heavens.

"Lord, have mercy! I'm ruined!"

What on earth? I call Christian.

"Christian, it's Bryn! What happened? Jen is frantic."

"Love, sorry to tell you, but we don't have a venue for tomorrow's event."

"I don't understand . . . we're twenty-four hours away."

"You girls better get down here."

"Viktor!" Jen runs towards me reaching for my phone. Viktor is our home improvement contractor from Russia and single-handedly turned our once all-white basic duplexes into homes that complemented our different personalities. She yanks my phone from my hand. "What's Viktor's number?" She scrolls through my contact list with tears streaming down her face. "Viktor! I need your help." She cries and babbles incoherently.

Within five minutes, Viktor, who lives around the corner, runs through Jen's front door as she falls onto her new linen sofa. "What is it?" He sits on the edge of the cushion and rubs her back.

"Viktor, the venue isn't ready." She continues to sob. "They haven't finished the work. You don't understand. I put everything into this company." She takes a huge breath and pushes her face into a throw pillow. "I lost my job." She continues to sob.

"I help. I get my guys." He rubs her back and then looks around the room before turning to me. "Does she have vodka?" He mimes taking a shot.

I grab a bottle of Ciroc and pour a double shot and hand it to him.

He nudges her. "Jen—take this." Without questioning him, she takes one gulp, tosses the glass across the room, and plunges her face into the pillow again. Once again, Viktor turns to me. "Bryn, what to do?"

I can only think of one thing and that is to call Christian back. "Hey, I've got an independent contractor who says he can help get the venue ready."

"Union workers only, darling," Christian snaps back.

"Fuck! That's it! We're dead. Shane is officially going to kill us." I need a shot as well. I hang up on Christian. We're screwed. I've spent thousands of Shane's dollars creating this event and he is going to sue Jen for every dime, plus punitive damages. We'll be broke, desolate, and the laughing stock of the city. That will be the end of Platinum Events. I grab my coat, purse, keys, and run for the door. "Viktor, watch Jen. I've got to work something out. I'll be back." I kick into high gear and race downtown.

I arrive at the venue in a record ten minutes. I'm stunned as I pull into the parking lot. It's beautiful. The unfinished lot with piles of dirt, rocks, and a ghastly looking flimsy privacy fence attempting to conceal a dumpster are now gone. Instead, the grounds are landscaped with lush green trees and shrubs, and the lobby building, once a gray slab with glass windows, is lit with a kaleidoscope of color.

The penthouse can't possibly be as bad as Christian described it.

I spot him as soon as I approach the main doors. He's dressed in his usual attire, a pair of dark blue jeans, a fitted black T-shirt, and black velvet loafers. He reminds me of a shorter, stouter version of Michael Kors. He's talking with Nick, who looks delicious, clean-shaven, and wearing a dark gray European-cut suit. Nick hands him a piece of paper, jumps into his silver Lotus, and pulls away. Christian folds it with his stubby little fingers and slips it into his front pocket without missing a beat. He looks up, sees me, and sashays over. "Bryn, darling." He hugs me. "Where's Jen?" He seems mighty perky for someone who just called with a crisis.

"Passed out. Jen's a wreck. Christian, this lobby is magnificent." Thirty-foot trees flank the doorway. Charcoal wood floors gleam under the long hanging lights. Asian inspired art is affixed to the walls. "Please tell me you're exaggerating about upstairs."

"I can do amazing things, but I have to draw the line. Upstairs is simply disgusting. I'll show you. Are you ready?"

"Now or never."

Christian swipes the access card and we take the elevator straight to the top. Before the doors open, Christian takes my hand. I close my eyes and squeeze his hand with all my strength. My heartbeat increases when I hear the doors open. Peeking through one eye, I step off the elevator into the space I was once captivated by. It now looks more like a dark, abandoned crypt lit by a single cannon up-light in a far corner. The breathtaking views are overpowered by the unfinished work of union contractors. Remnants of paint, drywall, and sawdust are everywhere.

"Wow." I cover my mouth. "I see what you mean." I walk over to the floor-to-ceiling windows and see handprints everywhere. "This is bad. This is really bad."

"He thinks this is acceptable, talking about the view—the view—all he cares about is the view." Christian's voice echoes, sounding like a bitter old divorcee.

I look out at the harbor skyline and the city lights twinkling in the water like stars. "I have to agree; the view is exquisite at night. But this place is nasty." I take a deep breath and close my eyes and try to think. There's no backup plan. I feel defeated.

"I can't simply build my masterpiece in this filth."

"What are we going to do?"

"I threatened Nick." Christian flashes a sinister smile. He pulls out the little piece of paper from his pocket. "Nick's signature. He's going to get professional cleaners in here tonight.

But—" He raises his finger and I hold back my excitement. "I need extra hands for set-up. Since we're starting late, my staff is fully committed to design."

"I'll make some calls."

I leave Christian and walk to my car alone. I need to call in a few favors.

When I return home, three people agree to help. I'm thankful and can only hope things come together at the last minute. As I start to unlock my door, I debate whether I should update Jen. I probably should.

She's fast asleep on her sofa when I unlock her door. "Jen . . . Jen, wake up." I shake her arm.

"How's the space? Is it okay? Is he going to fix it?" Tears start pouring down her face. She grabs at her chest and slowly inhales.

"Jen, I can't have you in the hospital. Breathe." I take a seat on the floor and continue. "It's a mess. I . . . I can't see how he can fix it in time but I've made some calls to get Christian some extra hands."

Jen stares at me, holding onto every word. I spare her the details of the disaster.

"What are we going to do if he doesn't?" Her voice quavers.

"Pray for a miracle." I hate to leave Jen sitting in a zombie-like state, but there's work to be done. I'm mentally and physically exhausted, but I'm going to force myself to finish our last-minute task items. I don't want to fail. Disappointing Shane will be horrifying, but nothing can be worse than ruining our reputation. I have no choice but to keep fighting.

I walk next door to my house and find Taylor, Jen's younger sister, sprawled across my sofa, asleep with her cell phone strategically propped near her ear. Under any other circumstances, I'd yell at her and shake her out of her sleep for squashing my favorite throw pillows, but since she's babysitting this weekend, I'll let it pass. Instead I hit the end button on her call, remove her shoes, and place a cover over her.

I set the house alarm, turn off the lights, and make my way upstairs to check on my little monster. Shockingly, I find her in her bed sound asleep. She's usually in my bed if I get home late. I kiss her on the forehead. *If only she knew.* I creep out, pulling her door halfway shut, and head straight to my room. I'm in need of a hot shower.

The warm water always relaxes me. I towel myself dry, put on my PINK tank short pajamas, grab my laptop, and jump into bed. I check my cell for any missed calls and am thankful there are none. I toss my phone aside and power up my laptop for the millionth time this week. A loud chopping sound, like a helicopter, emerges from the bottom of the laptop. I flip it over and discover the fan is jammed. *Great, perfect timing.*

I must have fallen asleep because I awaken, spread-eagled on the bed, to the faint sound of my cell phone vibrating. "Hello?" I answer.

"B, it's me," slurs Terry.

"Is everything okay?" I shut the computer and push it to the edge of the bed.

"Yeaaaahhhhh. What are you doing?" Terry's cranking up a weird laugh.

"What do you mean what am I doing? I'm trying to sleep. I need rest for tomorrow. My laptop crapped out. I've got a huge fire to put out . . . but it's not worth staying up to talk about."

"Bryn, I'm drunk. I had my first drink of that pink stuff y'all drink. Shhhhh."

"Okay . . ." Are you kidding me?

"You won't believe where I'm at."

I don't care where you are. I can hear a bunch of talking and music in the background, I assume he's at a party.

"They're collecting their money in trash bags. TRASH BAGS!"

"Huh?" He really must be drunk. "What are you talking about?"

"Strippers. These strippers Shane got. We're kicking off the weekend right. There are naked strippers everywhere! Some are even fucking."

"Whoa! You mean—this is happening in front of you?"

"Nah, in the other room. But this dude is right next to me getting head."

"Why are you calling me?" I'm fully awake at this point.

"I don't want to be here. I don't drink like that and I don't do strippers. I told you girl, I'm looking for the one."

I stay calm and try to forgive him for waking me up with this foolishness. But as I snuggle under my covers, Shane comes to mind. "WAIT! Where is Shane?" I'm not sure why I asked. I'm not even sure why I care, but my heart starts pounding in my chest. "In fact, he better not be the guy fucking with one of those strippers!" I yell at the top of my lungs.

"I don't know. He's around here somewhere."

I hear a thunderous roar in the background.

"B. For real though, this chick just sat on a baseball bat!"

"What do you mean she just sat on a baseball bat?" I ask unsteadily, feeling a migraine coming on.

"She just took a Louisville Slugger and sat on it. Half of it disappeared. These chicks came here ready. They're much better than the ones we saw last week down at Norma's. Those girls looked like they had bullet wounds."

"Bullet wounds?"

"Yeah, like scarred dimply skin. I don't let them touch me."

"Ewww. And men pay to see this?"

"Yo, B, his teammates came in here with backpacks full of money and there is so much money on the floor, at least a foot deep. They're scooping it up in trash bags, butt naked. Yo, B, you there?"

"Terry, I don't know what to say. I think I'm about as shocked as you are." I now have a headache.

"Don't tell anybody," pleads Terry.

"I won't." I'm lying. If he's got an ounce of sense, he knows I'll call Jen first thing in the morning. If she didn't have a full-court breakdown tonight, I would wake her up right now. "You be safe." I hang up the phone.

You couldn't pay me to date an athlete.

9

SHOWTIME

When my alarm sounds, I leap out of bed and jump in the shower and out again in five minutes tops. Hurriedly, I apply moisturizer and instead of feeling silky smooth, my body feels pasty. The fine hairs on my arms are standing straight up. *What the hell?* I take a second look at the moisturizer and realize it's shower gel. I jump back into the shower and rinse the sticky substance from my body.

My breathing is rapid and my heartbeat chokes me. I stop moving and let the hot water run over my face. *Breathe. You can do this.* Despite my growing anxiety, I manage to collect my thoughts. If I don't get a grip now, I won't be able to make it through the day, or the night, for that matter.

I slow down a little, pack a bag, give Bailey a hug and a kiss, and head out the door.

At the venue, the parking lot is full and I'm sure I'm the last to arrive. I park, throw on my shades, and jog towards the main entrance.

"Hey diva, I'm loving the look." Christian waddles towards me and eyes my mismatched sweats and brown Born slip-ons. He gives me a hug and flicks my messy ponytail. "I won't worry. Style is like the clap. You've either got it or you don't. I know you clean up nicely." He laughs then blows kisses in the air at both my cheeks.

"Thanks, dear. I'm a bit slow today. The boys had me up late last night. Any updates for me? Did you talk to the people I sent to help you?"

"We've been here all night." He rubs my back. "I've got it all taken care of. We *must* do this again."

"Christian dear." I yawn. "We haven't gotten through this yet. This client of ours is full of madness." I chuckle as we take the elevator to the penthouse again.

"I have something magical to show you." When the doors open, I step onto faux marble floors.

"Marble floors, Christian?" My jaw drops. The windows are spotless, and the ceiling and columns are pristine white. "I didn't know there was a ceiling." Christian's crews are hoisting forty-foot white sheers. The wind flowing in from the open balcony tosses them about.

"Poof. It's magic. You just turned into a ball of glitter."

I don't know how he did this in less than twenty-four hours.

"*Farmer's Almanac* says tonight is going to be the coldest day in October." Christian leads me to Shane's designated VIP area, fashioned for a king, and takes a seat on the white leather tufted banquette.

"Christian. You are amazing. It's beautiful. I love it. It's hot. Shane is going to LOVE it!"

"Listen, did you bill for crazy money?" He examines the seam of the sequin throw pillows. "By the way, I made these." He tosses one to me.

"Nice." I fluff the pillow and ask, "What's crazy money?" peering at him over my shades.

"Crazy money, my dear, is an upcharge you build into your fee. That way, when your client goes nuts, and they always do, it's a perk for dealing with their insane asses." I toss him back the pillow. "Shane pays us well."

"I hope so. A job like this . . . you should be clearing at least twenty-five grand each."

"Christian, I'm leaving you to finish creating your magic. I'm not messing with you today. If I let you, you'll tie up all my time. I'll keep that crazy money concept in mind."

"Yes, make sure you tell Jen. I called her, but I'm getting her voicemail."

"She's tending to Shane's out-of-town guests." I wave as I walk away.

Managing set-up all day leaves me with hardly any time to get dressed. I'd be screwed if Nick hadn't given me a corporate suite to change in. I grab the complimentary white fluffy robe, plop down in a chair, kick my feet up, and close my eyes. Everything we've done leads up to tonight. The endless days and sleepless nights, the twenty-four-hour on-call, anything you need, you want it and I'll get it done. It's all finishing soon. I just hope it's smooth sailing from here. I don't know if my mind can handle any more glitches.

I zip my dress and wish I'd bought a different one. I hate it. I only purchased it because Jen begged me. "It's perfect for this event. Trust me," she said. I trusted her fashion sense more than mine, but I'm thinking she got it wrong. With my hand, I cover the Little Ms. Prissy crystal pendant at the side gathering. I want to rip it off but I can't. My saving grace is that it fits my body like a glove.

I spray a little Givenchy Amarige on my neck, back, and wrists. I save my shoes for last. Oh, how I love my sparkly Jimmy Choo strappy sandals. They were purchased specifically for tonight. As I lift the lid of the shoebox, the smell of expensive leather fills my nostrils. It's exhilarating. Paying half price for them makes it more intoxicating. They look gorgeous on my feet. "Here goes nothing, it's show time!" I hit the lights and walk out the door.

I see Jen when I get downstairs. She struts down the center red carpet aisle wearing a custom black mini dress and a killer pair of Stewart Weitzman's. Christian prances beside her all in white. "Dorothy, lose the dress but keep the shoes," he says.

I flash him the back of the dress and roll my eyes at Jen. She knows I hate the dress.

She laughs. "You could have worn something else."

"A bit late, don't you think? But you look great."

"Thanks." She hands me a headset and walkie-talkie. "Alright Christian, show us what you've got."

"Don't talk, you're spoiling it." He waves his hand and we follow. At the entrance, the carpet is lined with female fire-eaters dressed in nude body suits with shimmering iridescent strips of fabric strategically blowing over their privates.

"The men will love them. Next," says Jen. We continue past them and stop at the elevators. Runway models from NYC, who look fabulous in their floor-length Cavalli gowns, greet us. "Ladies, you are responsible for our VIP guests. Please stay focused," says Jen.

We step onto the elevator and the attendant, wearing an all-black tux, takes us up. As we near the top, I can feel the bass of the music.

"Brace yourself, bitches." The elevator doors open. "Welcome to Wonderland!" screams Christian.

I may faint from excitement as we exit the elevator and walk through a tunnel of white flowers, passing platinum body-painted girls posing on elevated ceramic platforms. A contortionist inside a clear bubble sits at the entrance into the party. Her silver pasties sparkle in the strobe lights.

Christian dances through the room, passing the white leather tufted benches, sofas, and ottomans. He stops at a TGS ice luge and refills his glass before leading us through another maze of white-flower walls towards the designated performance area.

"It smells like vanilla in here!" I shout over the music.

"Electronic aroma diffusers."

I inhale again. It smells wonderful. Christian taps me and Jen on the shoulder and points up. Two fabric aerialists spiral down from the ceiling, stopping short of the floor. I know Jen's thinking what I'm thinking. *Where are the mermaids?*

"Now!" Christian shouts to his assistant. "He wants tanks? Let there be tanks!" Christian raises his hand, a wall-size screen lights up, and we see the silhouettes of our mermaids swimming in their tanks.

Our surprise turned out perfectly. He's going to love it.

Jen radios security and lets them open the doors. The place fills at a pace we could never have anticipated.

An hour later, I get a call. TGS and Shane Smith have arrived. I work my way through the crowd towards the elevators. While waiting for the doors to open, I notice in the reflection my once straight Cher hairstyle now looks like Diana's in her 'Endless Love' video. I'm horrified and try to press it down but it's useless. The doors open and I flash my credentials, taking a fast, non-stop ride to the front entrance.

Downstairs a fleet of sports cars, Ferraris, Lamborghinis, and Maseratis are parked in valet. The car doors open in unison and the boys step out looking like new money. Tailored suits, designer shoes, bling, dark shades. And of course, Shane has an all-black baseball cap to match.

The ladies go wild and create a barrier between the door and me. I can't get to Jen, but I can see her at Shane's side doing karate-chop moves, along with security, to escort him in. Frustration overwhelms me as I'm pushed from side to side. It's hot and stuffy in this unrelenting crowd, so I backtrack to the red carpet where I know they'll be next.

At the carpet, it's just as congested with celebrity guests and male and female groupies alike. The velvet ropes are minimal protection for Cindy, Baltimore's local news correspondent and her cameraman, who are waiting patiently for the guys.

With the help of a few strange men, I flash my badge and get a lift to the front.

I'm relieved when they reach Cindy. Shane's commanding presence attracts all the attention and with a smile, he confidently poses for the paparazzi. TGS, however, stand next to him in their suits and shades. "Shane, over here!" a voice shouts behind the continuous flashes. Shane throws up a peace sign. I manage to get Cindy's attention and motion for her to go over to him. If she doesn't do it now, they will be here all night.

"Wow Shane! What an event!" she yells through the continuous shouts, moving in closer and placing her hand on his back. "What do you have to say about this turnout?"

"I'm just flattered. I'm really honored and flattered. Everybody put in countless hours. It was really frustrating at times planning an event this big. I'm amazed. I haven't even gotten into the party yet. I'm at the red carpet and it's crazy out here. I'm flabbergasted. I appreciate everything and everyone that had something to do with behind the scenes. I truly appreciate Jen and Bryn. They were my event planners. You know, I'm just overwhelmed. Terry, my personal assistant, Xavier, my publicist, they did a really good job. Everybody is out here. We are going to have a great time tonight."

"There are a lot of beautiful people that came out for you guys tonight. Congratulations on your new group. Looks like you're bringing more to your city than just football."

"Well you know . . ." He turns on the charm, giving her a half-smile. "I support my city that supports me. This is the least I can do." He winks and reaches for her hand. "So Cindy . . . I hope to see you on the dance floor tonight." She turns red with excitement. I'm not sure if Shane realizes he's on live television so I cringe, embarrassed for the two of them. Shane moves over so Roman can speak. However, as soon as he opens his mouth, the place erupts again. The remaining Nighthawks, including the star quarterback and our future hall of famer wide receiver, start to file onto the carpet.

I manage to grab Shane's hand and escort him to the elevators. TGS follow.

"This is bananas, Bryn," says Zander.

"Is it like this upstairs?" barks Shane.

"Just trust me," I say, grinning.

The elevator doors open and from Shane's expression, I can see he's mesmerized by what he sees. He's speechless as he walks into the main party area. It's packed with beautiful people smiling, drinking, and dancing. It's perfect.

At four o'clock in the morning, I walk out onto the balcony and look up at the stars. *Thank you, Jesus.* And I exhale.

"It's nice, huh?"

I turn around and Nick embraces me.

"It looks great. I was just backstage talking to Rovensak."

"Roger Rovensak? The owner of the Nighthawks? He's here?"

"Yeah."

"Yeah, and I swore I saw Diddy in Shane's VIP."

"Really? If so, that's MAJOR. He's in D.C. this weekend for Howard's homecoming. We'd hoped he'd stop in. If that's true, I know Shane'll be ecstatic."

Nick is standing next to me, leaning on the balcony. "I'm in love with this place."

I'm in love with you, I think.

"You girls did an awesome job. I was a bit worried at first. Since you were fairly new at this. But I'm glad I took a chance on you."

"Yes, and I appreciate your honesty. It was a lot of work. Nothing this great happens without a lot of fires. Thanks for getting the place ready in time. Thanks to this amazing space, I've got a satisfied client."

He smiles and looks through the glass walls at the contortionist in the clear bubble. "Who thought of that?"

"Crazy, isn't it? Research. You'd be shocked at some of the acts I've come across." I look up at Nick with dreamy eyes and let my imagination loose. And just when I want to kiss him, I hear Shane's voice.

"Excuse me, sorry to interrupt."

You aren't sorry, I think. Still, I bite my tongue and play the part of the faithful event planner. "Shane." I smile. "Having fun?"

"Yes, it's almost over and I had to save the last dance for the most beautiful woman here." He looks at me then at Nick.

"Ha. Ha. You're a funny man tonight."

Shane waits with his hand extended. I don't want to leave Nick, but I can't possibly say no to Shane. I smile graciously and take his hand as he leads me through the crowd to the dance floor. He extends his arms in a ballerina's third position. I laugh and reach for his leading arm.

"By the way, thanks for the compliment even though my hair looks crazy."

"So what, it's yours isn't it? Besides, I'm not worried about your hair. Your beauty shines through. And ..." he leans in to whisper in my ear, "you're wearing my favorite color."

"You're such a flirt." I laugh.

Shane spins me around. "Sweetie, I haven't even gotten started." He takes me down for a dip.

10

WE DID IT!

I hear Jen's voice say, "I have Bailey and Taylor. Wear your cream pantsuit; it's hanging in the closet. Terry will be here in thirty minutes." Then my bedroom door slams.

I open my eyes and I don't even know what day it is. "Ugh." My head weighs a ton. I push myself up and notice I must have jumped in the bed face first. I'm still wearing my cleaning clothes from yesterday. I spent my entire Saturday helping Christian take things down.

I crawl out of bed and walk into the bathroom. I look like I've been in a fight. Hair disheveled, puffy eyes, and ashy skin. I don't bother to try and fix anything. I remove my clothes, jump into the shower, and stand like a statue under the shower head, letting the scalding hot water rush over my face.

After the shower, I slick my wet hair into a smooth bun. For make-up, I add a simple light bronzer and a nude lip. I keep my neck bare, but add my classic diamond studs. I'm almost ready to put my jeans and T-shirt on when I hear a knock at the door. It's Terry. I grab my robe and run downstairs.

"Hey Bryn. You ain't dressed yet?"

"Almost. Five minutes."

"We've got to get to Shane's before he leaves for his morning meetings."

"Okay, okay." I leave him at the front door and bolt upstairs to finish getting dressed.

I cut Terry's wait time down to two minutes. He smiles as I lock the door and walk over to a dark blue H2 Hummer parked in front of my house. Terry opens the passenger door.

"Got a new truck?"

"No, this is Shane's." Terry revs the engine, pulls away from the curb with force, and makes an illegal U-turn in the middle of the road. I grab onto the door handle to brace myself. He slams on the brakes once he reaches the main road. Taking off again, he zigzags across the huge intersection into a neighboring community of single-family homes. He takes a sharp right, pulling into a small cul-de-sac, and parks in front of a traditional family home, complete with a wicker wreath hanging on the door.

"Shane lives across the street from us?" I ask, laughing and a little shocked.

"Yup." He rushes over to help me out. We walk down the narrow sidewalk past bunches of plastic flowers partially shoved into mulch, a mini black Cadillac Escalade parked next to a real one in the driveway, and large empty planter pots strategically placed on the half-brick porch.

Terry lets himself in the front door. "You can have a seat." He points to a black leather sofa in the middle of a colossal stark white living room. I look down at a tiny pair of pink sneakers next to the door and reach down to remove my shoes. "Don't worry. We'll only be a minute," says Terry, tapping me on the back.

I'd die if I scratched his gleaming hardwood floors with my heels, so I decide to wait by the door motionless. Shane's voice is booming from upstairs. Thank goodness Terry quickly returns with Roman. DeShaun runs down the stairs behind him.

"Beautiful Bryn." DeShaun smiles. "Did you enjoy our set last night?" He opens the truck door for me. "You can sit in the front."

"Thank you. And yes, I did."

"Thanks for surprising us with Majestic. I didn't know she could sing," says Roman.

"Where's Zander and Qmar?" I strap on my seatbelt.

"Let's just say Zander is incapacitated. Be on the lookout for a bill," laughs DeShaun.

"Should I really ask why?" I brace myself for an answer.

"He picked up one of your model chicks, took her in the bathroom and things got, ya know, *intense*. And they detached the sink from the wall," says DeShaun. "Who knew the kid had it in him." DeShaun belts out laughing.

An image pops into my mind and I want to vomit.

Roman cuts in. "By the way Bryn, I've been meaning to tell you. You looked lovely last night in that blue dress." Roman gives me a wink.

I smile. "Thank you. You all looked dashing in your suits." I turn around and playfully bat my eyes.

"You're always hearing about our love lives, who's the lucky guy in your life?" DeShaun stares at me. It's hard to keep a straight face admiring his striking gray eyes. I swallow and clear my throat to release tension.

"No one at the moment." I exhale.

"I don't buy that. There's no way someone hasn't locked that down." He bites his lower lip.

"Well, DeShaun, you'd be surprised." I shift in my seat. "The men I'm interested in aren't interested in me and vice versa." I feel all eyes on me, including a thinly masked hurt look from Terry.

"All you have to do is tell Jen to remove that clause from the contract and you've got a few options sitting right here in front of you." DeShaun's smile widens.

"Look, y'all know what Shane said," interrupts Terry.

"Keep your eyes on the road," shouts DeShaun. "When is the contract over? I can't wait." He blows me a kiss.

He thinks he's smooth but all I see is a big red warning sign. A younger, dumber, inexperienced Bryn would have run straight in thinking she could change him. But after kissing lots of frogs,

I'm in a different place. I'm paying more attention to behaviors and not just listening to the sweet nothings that come out of a guy's mouth. I need more than a pretty face or fat pockets.

We meet Jen, Bailey, Taylor, Qmar, and Zander at the main gates of the Nighthawks stadium.

"Bailey, Taylor, y'all go with them. I need to take your mom and Jen someplace." Terry hands Qmar six tickets.

"Bailey, y'all stay with Roman." I give her a hug and a kiss. "I'll meet you at the seats."

Jen and I follow Terry over to an older woman wearing a black Nighthawks jacket and with multiple lanyards around her neck. She walks up to Terry and gives him a big hug.

"Hey baby, look at you. You look so handsome. Give me some sugar." Terry scrunches his face as she plants two wet kisses on each cheek. "Hey darlings," she says, turning to Jen and me. "I've heard so much about you two. The boys have been going on and on about the party y'all did Friday night."

"Hi," I say, reaching out to shake her hand. She dismisses my hand and gives me a huge bear hug and rocks me back and forth. *I have no idea who this woman is and she's invading my personal space.* I can see Terry laughing at me from over her shoulder. Even he knows I don't like people touching me. She releases me, takes a lanyard from around her neck and places it over my head, then does the same for Jen and Terry.

"Ms. Mable is the team mom," Terry whispers in my ear.

"I get it now." I chuckle, fiddling with my all-access badge.

"Alright y'all, let's go." She leads the way down the concrete ramp below the stadium. We continue through a maze of

Bianca Williams

cement hallways, passing workers dressed all in black carrying boxes of programs. She waves to some guys driving golf carts. We continue past a few other guys in football pads, white uniform pants, and white T-shirts. They smile and wave at us.

We finally reach a long tunnel with the sunlight shining at the end of it. Jen grabs my arm and squeezes it so tight that it goes numb. "Is this what I think it is?" Her hands tremble.

Terry walks up from behind and wedges his skinny body between us, placing an arm on each of our shoulders. "Alright y'all, don't be out here crying. There're TV cameras everywhere." We walk out of the tunnel and emerge onto the Nighthawks playground. It's official. We're standing where the action happens every Sunday.

"Oh my goodness Bryn, we . . . we are walking on the field, girl." She holds her hands over her mouth and looks up with glassy eyes. The grass is so soft under my feet that it can't be real. I've never seen grass so perfect.

"This grass is so lush!" I shout over the cheering fans to Terry. He starts laughing.

"It's not real grass. It's turf." It feels surreal standing here on the sidelines watching the Nighthawks warming up. "Look up!" Terry shouts to us.

Right in front of me, flashing on the Jumbotron, is a message from Shane.

Thank you Jen and Bryn of Platinum Events – Job well done! Love, Shane Smith #50

I look over at Jen with teary eyes. "Aww, this is really sweet. It's going down in history."

"Y'all are so sensitive. I told him it would make y'all cry." Terry takes out his phone. "Turn around so I can take a picture." He takes the photo and shows it to us. "Y'all did it!"

"No. *We* did it!" I say, reaching out to Terry to pull him in for a group hug.

11

PTSS

I jolt out of sleep, believing I heard a door slam. Whatever it was makes me sit straight up in the bed. My house is dark and still. The only sound comes from the heartbeat in my ears. *Oh, shit! Jen is going to kill me.* I jump out of bed to get dressed, stagger into a dark closet, and feel for my dress on the back of the door. It's not there. Confused, I stumble into the bathroom and check behind the door. It's not there either. *What the hell?* Panicked, I dive onto my bed and toss my pillows around, frantically searching for my phone to tell Jen I'm running late. When I find it, I see that it's three o'clock Thursday morning.

The event is over.

I fall back onto bed and take deep breaths to relax because I'm tripping. Unable to fall back asleep, I stare at the ceiling. Memories of the event come to mind. Shane yelling 'fried chicken in a pan', Shane yelling nonsense at Jen, and Shane asking me to dance. I close my eyes and try to count sheep. I have to be up in three hours. When counting backwards from one hundred doesn't work, it dawns on me to call Terry. He's boring as hell and sure to talk me back to sleep.

He answers on the first ring. "What up, Bryn? Is everything okay?"

"I think that I'm suffering from PTSS." I hear him chuckle. "Seriously, I just jumped out of bed and started running around my room. I was searching for my dress. I thought I'd overslept . . . and I was super late . . . and the event had started without me."

"Really?" He laughs. "You've got to relax, girl."

"I know, right?" I stand again and pace the floor. "But I keep thinking about it. I keep rehashing things."

"Girl, the event was a success. Shane is happy. The boys are happy. The city is buzzing about y'all. Get some sleep. Don't you have to work tomorrow?"

"Yeah, I do." I rub my forehead. "You're right, I shouldn't be keeping us both up."

"Nah, you good. I just want to make sure you are straight."

"Thanks Terry."

"Anytime, B. Goodnight."

He's right. It's ridiculous to keep worrying about the event. It's over. I straighten out my pillows and nestle under the covers. Tucking a wisp of hair behind my ear, I see the card from Shane sitting on my nightstand. *With Gratitude.* I reach for it. Running my fingers over the crimson embossed roses on the ivory textured card recalls fonder memories. I open it and re-read the handwritten message.

B,

All I can say is you did the damn thing sweetheart.
You took something as small as an album release party and
blew it up to the size of the world. This couldn't happen without you.
Y'all were the only women for the job.
Take a bow "B" cause now it's your turn to get pampered.

Great Job!!

Love, SS

The night he gave me this card, two weeks ago, he and Terry made a surprise visit to Jen's. They walked in carrying two of everything: pink roses, cards, and #50 blue Nighthawks jerseys. It was another sweet, unexpected gesture. Shane handed us the gifts and said we were officially part of his team. Jen and I were all smiles, eager to open the cards, but Shane asked us to wait. He didn't want us reading the cards in front of him. We thought it was adorable so we obliged. In addition to the beautiful message, inside were gift certificates to the Pearl Spa. And hidden in the two dozen pink roses were envelopes filled with twenty $100 bills.

Ever since that night things have been quiet around here, perhaps too quiet. Maybe that's why I'm still awake at this hour. I set the card back and grab my phone to text both Shane and Terry.

Missing you guys

Shane responds first.

Miss you too sweetie

Terry's message comes through moments later.

Meet us at the radio show tomorrow night

12

MESSAGE IN A COOKIE

Alex is holding me captive in his office. He's using me as a sounding board for an emergency meeting with the bank's executives scheduled for tomorrow. By the time he frees me, I'm starving and ready to meet Michael for lunch.

On my way out, I hear Susanne's loud complaining voice in the hallway. "Gabriel, I needed those reports yesterday!" She stands with hands on hips at the office door of our rate manager with Colin, her favorite brown-nosing flunky.

Her back is to me so I peek into Gabe's office. I can't tell if he's rolling his eyes at her (since he's got a lazy one) but he's aggressively ticking away at his whiteboard, which is filled with sticky notes and closely resembles a scene from *A Beautiful Mind*.

He scares me. He's a fifty-something single male who still lives with his mother and a shit-load of cats that he calls his children. One day he cornered me to sign a petition to allow employees to use sick days for their pets. I nodded and smiled until he freed me. Ever since then I'm always super nice to him. I'm afraid that if they ever fire him, he'll come back with a machete and take everyone out, starting with Susanne.

I arrive at Michael's office and find him typing an email. Without looking at me he raises his hand. "Give me five minutes."

I wait at his door looking around his office. It's so clean, unlike mine. Everything has its place. Even his pencils are perfectly aligned next to his stapler, tape dispenser, and paperclip holder. I bet even his junk drawer is organized. He probably doesn't have one. What kind of person doesn't have a junk drawer?

I look back at him and notice that he's staring intently at his screen. He bites his lip and clicks his mouse a few times, scowling.

"What's wrong?"

"Reading an email from my boss," he says, "I'll respond when I get back. We can leave." He closes out of the programs, locks his computer screen, and pushes his keyboard neatly under his desk.

We walk to a café on the corner of Lexington Street. Inside, I scan the specials on the day board and place my order for a salad. Michael gets the same and we walk up to a newly opened line. "I'll treat," I say.

"Alright. That's what I'm talking about. Mommy Warbucks!"

"Shut up. You treated last week. This is just repayment." I collect my change from the cashier who's getting a kick out of Michael's stupid comment. "Thank you," I say to her, dumping my change into my purse.

"You know, the streets are still talking about that event. It was hot. I didn't know you and Jen had it in you. And where did y'all find all those beautiful women?"

"Thanks. We used modeling agencies."

"Man, I wish some of them were on Match. They're running a special for three months free. You should sign up." He's been trying to get me to sign up to Match.com for a few months now but I'm not a fan of online dating. Probably because I know guys like him are sitting at the other end of the computer.

"There're a lot of creepy looking people on that site. I already don't trust easily, let alone having anyone around Bailey. Besides, I keep telling you I'm not attracted to anyone on there."

"You're not attracted to anyone."

"Nick!"

"See, your problem is you don't give regular guys a chance."

"Nick is regular."

"No, he isn't. He's a millionaire with a Lotus which means he's got a team of women."

"I've never seen him with one."

"Guys like Nick, Shane, and the host of other guys you surround yourself with attract lots of the wrong type of women."

"So, you're saying I should just date anyone who's interested in me?"

"I'm saying you've got to look beyond the surface. Get to know some of these hard-working guys out here."

"Like these crazy looking weirdos in here having lunch?"

"That's what I don't get about women. Y'all want to date the guy that's going to dog you out."

"I need chemistry, sparks, passion, and I shouldn't have to lower my standards to get it."

"Stay single then."

"That was mean."

"Anyway, how is business?" Michael changes the subject.

"Jen's networking trying to secure more projects."

"I wish her well because we're in a recession. Her clients need to be in the upper echelon because the average working person is not going to have extra money to spend on an event."

"We know. Hopefully something will come through for her, and soon."

He grabs our food and we walk out.

Michael holds the door for me as we re-enter our building.

"Hey Michael. Hey, umm . . ." the security guard says, squinting at a tiny box. "Bryn Charles?"

"Yes?"

"I thought that was you. I always wondered who the pretty little lady was who's always out with crazy old Mike."

"Oh, you think that's funny? Wait until this weekend," threatens Michael.

"Miss Lady, you've got a delivery." He holds up the clipboard for me to sign.

"Oh wow . . ." My mind fills with random thoughts of who it's from.

"Yeah, sucka! Calling me old! Wait until I see you on the basketball court this weekend. We'll see who the old one is," Michael says to the security guard.

"Michael, shut up," I say, signing for the package. The security guard hands me the little box and a single long-stemmed rose. *What on earth?*

"Oh, I see, you holding out on me. You're keeping secrets now? I thought I was your brother. You're supposed to tell me everything."

"Michael, please! I don't know what this is or who it's from. Go Michael, go. I've had my fill of you today." I take the stairs to my floor and leave Michael behind. I hear him fussing until the door shuts. *Who could have sent me this?* I examine the little square box no larger than my fist and cut the tape along the edges. Inside, there's a small object in a bubble-wrap pouch. Carefully, I open the pouch and shake out into my hand a little rhinestone-encrusted fortune cookie. It opens. I find a message engraved on a tag.

You can be part of my future. Terry.

"Oh my . . . No, Terry, no." I call Jen and hold my head. I feel a migraine coming on. "I just got a delivery . . . from Terry."

"I know. What is it?"

"A fortune cookie. A bedazzled fortune cookie." Jen bursts into laughter. "And . . . a long-stemmed rose."

"Awwww. He called me this morning asking for your work address. He told me he bought you something and wanted it delivered to your job. I'm afraid he thinks that the only reason you've been turning him down is because of the contract. Now that the event is over . . . well—"

"Whoa, wait a minute. I talked to him last night."

"You did? About what?"

"I was trippin'. I thought I was late to the event. I jumped up running around my room looking for my dress. I called him because I needed a distraction so I could fall back to sleep."

"Yeah, that's a bit much. You might need something to take the edge off, if you know what I mean."

"I sure could, but not Terry. Yuck. I just got a visual. Anyway, what will I say? I'm going to see him in a few hours."

"First, I would recommend that you thank him."

"The message reads 'you can be a part of my future'." Jen and I share a moment of silence.

"Ooh. That's embarrassing."

"Tell me about it." I rub my temples.

When we arrive at the restaurant, the first person I see is Terry, seated at a small table with Roman. I smile and wave. He stands and gives me a tight bear hug. "Hey Terry, thanks for the gift." I mention it now to clear the air.

"You're welcome Bryn. Y'all know y'all are late. The show is almost over . . . Jennnnnnn—" he scolds.

Jen shoves Terry on the shoulder. "I needed gas . . ." she tries to explain. Terry ignores her and walks over to a chatty group of ladies at another table.

"Who are they, I wonder?" Jen leans over to me.

"That's the girl I was telling you about who came over to me at the club that time."

"Oh, his girl or something?" Jen rolls her eyes.

Shaking my head at Jen, I reach for one of Roman's french fries. "I guess. One of them, according to Terry. I can't keep up. There were so many women at that party who said they were with Shane. I stopped keeping track and started letting them all in his section." I take another french fry. "Sir Roman. What are you doing here?"

"Visiting my family." He smiles and reaches for Bailey. "Hey little cookie." He lifts her up and sits her on a barstool. "I swear she looks just like my sister." He and Bailey have become the best of friends since they met.

"Where's Shane?" Bailey pokes Roman in the side while looking around the room.

Roman points towards a long table where Shane is sitting between the team captain and Nighthawks poster boy, Jason Ross, and our future hall of famer wide receiver Ezra McKnight. All three superstars are smiling and shaking hands as the radio show ends.

I start eating more of Roman's fries when two big arms wrap around my shoulders from behind.

"Y'all coming?" barks Shane, rocking me back and forth on the barstool.

Goodness, he's strong. I tap his arm for relief.

"Coming where?" interjects Jen with a look of interest.

"New York! Terry ain't tell y'all?" Shane steps to my side and uses my shoulder as an armrest.

"Nope," I say.

"I'll get y'all a room. Just ride up with Terry. I got to travel with the team." He looks for Terry and watches him walk back to our table. "You ain't tell them?" Shane narrows his eyes.

"They just got here!" Terry shouts back. "Y'all wanna come to New York for the game this weekend?" This is the first time I've seen Terry lose his temper, however slightly. I'm surprised; I've seen Shane do worse things to provoke a clash.

"When are you leaving?" asks Jen.

Pointing at his chest, Terry goes on to explain, "I'm from New York—so I may go up early to see family."

"I can't leave until tomorrow night. I've already taken off enough days," I say, clearing my throat to hint they're the reason I'm out of vacation days.

"We can just leave on Saturday. It's all good," says Terry, smiling and pushing a half-eaten plate aside and sitting down.

"Alright then, let's eat," says Shane.

"Um, Shane, can I? Can I meet Jason and Ezra? Please?" begs Bailey.

"I've got something even better, Bailey baby. They're coming for dinner with us now and you're invited." Shane takes her hand and leads the way to a sectioned off area of the restaurant. We pass Shane's 'girl' and I notice he doesn't even look in her direction. Instead, he gives Bailey his undivided attention.

Shane sits first with Bailey next to him. I take a seat next to Bailey and Jen sits opposite me.

"Order anything you want." Shane gives Bailey a bear hug.

As I review the menu choices, Bailey starts fidgeting in her chair. Her eyes are glued on Terry walking over with Jason, Ezra, and Roman. "Don't let anyone else back here," Terry says to the wait staff. The three of them fill up the empty seats next to Jen. Bailey's turning red and covering her mouth.

"The infamous Jennifer," says Jason, extending his hand to greet her. Jason's tall with muscular arms, smooth almond-butter skin, and dark facial features with slanted eyes. He resembles Bailey's father. "I've been asking Shane about you." His voice is kind.

"Hello, nice to meet you," says Jen, blushing.

"This is my business partner, Bryn." She points to me. "And her daughter Bailey."

"Hello, Bryn." He waves. "And nice to meet you Bailey. How old are you?" He has a gentle smile.

"Eight," says Bailey, looking everywhere but directly at Jason.

"I've got a four-year-old daughter. In fact," he says, "I want to throw her a big bash for her fifth birthday coming up. And my brother Shane's been very reluctant about sharing the contact info of his event planners." He places a napkin on his lap. "How about you take my number," he says to Jen, "and we'll schedule to meet on Tuesday?"

Jen's eyes glisten as she nods yes.

13

<u>SO BEAUTIFUL</u>

I can't believe Joan is at the front door. I told her to come early, but she could have waited until sunrise. I let her in without speaking and crawl back to bed, pushing Bailey aside since she's sprawled across my bed taking up all the covers. It's our tradition that she sleeps in my bed on nights before I leave town. The thought is endearing, but not so much getting kicked and karate chopped most of the night.

At a decent hour, I wake up to get dressed. I packed last night as I listened to my mother give me shit about working too much. Even though I explained that this was for fun and generating new business, she's convinced it's a repeat of three years ago when she caught me at the office after midnight. Work will always be there, she reminds me. But this isn't work, I remind her.

Terry shows up a little after noon. I give Bailey a big hug and kiss, grab my bags, and shut the door. He waits at the truck for my bag.

"What's up, Pimp Daddy?" I joke. "I see we riding in style."

"Yeah, Shane gave me the Range to make sure y'all would be comfortable." He places my bag in the back.

"Road trip!" screams Jen, running out of her front door. "I'm riding the front."

I climb into the back and lie across the seat.

"We haven't been on a road trip in years."

"You're right!" I laugh. "We've come a long way since then." Jen's referring to our road trip up the Turnpike to Connecticut. We almost didn't make it there, or back now that I think about it. "Memories." I smile and let my thoughts take me back.

"Must have been some road trip by the looks on y'all faces." Terry raises his brows. "Tell me."

"I'd love to," I say. "Well, I'm a huge Lenny Kravitz fan. Huge. From like when I was a child. So just imagine how I reacted when he announced his US tour. And I bought the last ticket to his concert. Anyway, the night before the show, life happened. I don't remember the specifics but we didn't have any money and our chances of seeing Lenny were pretty slim."

"I wasn't worried," interjects Jen.

"But somehow between the two of us, we managed to pull together less than $200. We found a car rental online for like fifty bucks—"

"But they gave us a free upgrade to a truck," laughs Jen.

"And we found a cheap room at a Motel 6 for like $30."

"Motel 6?" Terry blinks.

"I would have slept in the truck. We're talking about Lenny Kravitz. Long story short, everything was starting to align. It was like we were meant to be there."

"Definitely. Same day of the show, I purchased a seat in the third row from the stage for $30."

"True story. So we got inside and when the lights went down, Jen pulled me from my seat in the back, dragged me to the front with her, and when the lights came back on, Lenny appeared on the stage."

"Now, fast forward to the good part," Jen rushes me.

"So he came out talking to the crowd and told everyone to come close to the stage. Jen and I pushed to the front, and for three hours straight, I got a personal concert from Lenny Kravitz. I have the shirt he ripped off his body, he signed my ticket, and . . ."

"He pointed to Bryn and said, 'so beautiful', and started singing his song, *Again.*" Jen claps, stealing my thunder.

"It was like a dream come true. Jen wanted to finish the tour with them. I mean she literally had one foot on the tour bus. I had no choice. I had to get home to Bailey. So instead of touring Boston, we traveled back to Maryland in our rental, singing along to all of his greatest hits."

"So beautiful!" squeals Jen. "I'll never forget it." She finds Lenny Kravitz on Pandora and we have a sing-a-long until we arrive at our hotel in Meadowlands, New Jersey.

As soon as we get into the room I turn on the television, change into my nightclothes, and start to unpack. And almost immediately, we hear a pounding on our door. Jen goes to investigate. I look for something I can use as a weapon. We *are* in New Jersey.

"Shane!" Jen unlocks the door and lets him in.

"What are y'all doing? Y'all not dressed?" he barks. He gives her the evil eye.

"We just got here. Dressed for what?" Jen prances around the room in Jason Ross' jersey #55, completely unaware of Shane's envy.

"Carmines, my favorite Italian restaurant." He turns to me, smiling and rubbing his stomach. "The car is downstairs, we are leaving now."

"But—"

"Unless y'all are ready in five minutes you gonna have to meet us down there." He reaches out to mush Jen in the head and misses.

"No, please don't leave us." I jump out of the bed, adjusting my tank top straps and shorts, and dart into the bathroom.

"I got one of my teammates waiting! Hurry up. I'll give you ten."

It doesn't matter how fast I get dressed. It's going to take Jen much longer to get ready.

It takes us twenty minutes to arrive in the lobby. I walk outside praying that he's waiting for us, but no luck. An older Hispanic gentleman dressed in a black suit steps out of the driver's seat of a black E Class Mercedes Benz parked in front of the hotel. He walks towards Jen and reaches for her hand. "Are you Jen? I am Miguel, your driver for tonight."

She turns to me and gives me a fascinated look. He opens the door for us and she enters the back seat of the car grinning like a kid in Disney World who has finally found Mickey Mouse. "Bryn . . . this is the life I'm supposed to live. You know how I dream of having a driver."

"I know Jen. I know."

Chauffeured through the 'city that never sleeps' in our very own car, I can't help but stare out of the window in awe as we speed down FDR Drive. We arrive in bustling Manhattan and I can't get over the crowds, the taxis, the skyscrapers. As we drive through Times Square, the advertisements light up the car. I catch a glimpse of my reflection in the window and understand Jen's excitement. "This is pretty awesome," I whisper to Jen who's swaying to the music, grinning, with her eyes closed.

When we pull up to Carmines it has started to drizzle, and just like in the movies, our driver escorts us under an umbrella one by one into the restaurant. When I walk in, I see Shane, Ezra, and Terry standing at a crowded bar holding drinks.

"Jen, B. Y'all look nice," says Terry, finishing his drink.

"Thank you," I reply, posing exaggeratedly with one hand on my hip and the other on the side of my head. I am wearing a little black high-waist pencil skirt and a frilly top with a plunging neckline. I wave to Shane and Ezra.

"They don't have any tables," growls Shane.

"I'll take care of it," Jen says.

"Table for seven!" shouts Shane. Jen nods and walks towards the host standing at a podium near the dining area.

"You know, you always have to have a fit ready when you travel with Shane," says Terry, staring down at me.

"What's a fit?" I ask, looking up at him.

"An outfit," interrupts Shane in his mean voice while staring at his cell phone.

Jen returns in minutes with the restaurant manager, who violently shakes Shane and Ezra's hands and apologizes as he leads us to a large round table. It is hard for both Jen and me to keep a straight face.

We approach the table set for eight. "Perfect! Ladies first." Shane orchestrates the seating arrangements. He sits me directly to his left and Terry to his right. Ezra sits between two empty chairs. Before Shane's butt hits the seat, his hand is in the breadbasket. "I love their bread." He grabs a piece and shoves it in his mouth.

"So many seats?" Jen twists her face.

"It's perfect. Ezra has two friends coming." Shane starts slathering butter on the next piece of bread. "Order what you want but I should tell you, the plates are huge."

"I see it's family style," adds Jen, pointing to the gigantic chalkboard with handwritten menu items.

"Yes, Miss-Know-It-All." Shane picks up another piece of bread.

"Alright you two, not in front of company," I say as two females in tight sexy dresses, one black and the other red, approach the table and stand on each side of Ezra. He pulls the chairs out for both. "Isn't he a Casanova," I whisper to Jen. Ezra looks bi-racial, Italian and Black. He's got jet-black curly hair and amazing green eyes with thick lashes. He's got swag, but he's also got the reputation of a whoring dirt bag.

We dine on a few of Shane's favorites including penne vodka and chicken parmesan, and test the waters on a 2008 Hess Collection Cabernet Sauvignon. Throughout dinner, Shane owns the night, captivating everyone with his talk about football and his outrageous, inappropriate jokes, and teasing Terry. I have to fight to keep from spitting out my food.

As our waiter clears our table, I excuse myself to visit the ladies' room. On my way back, I catch a glimpse of Ezra slipping his hands under the dresses of both girls. The waiter, now serving dessert, is oblivious.

Their famous tiramisu smells like freshly brewed coffee. Terry is the first to dig in. Shane takes a whiff of his then pushes it aside. The girl in the black dress slithers her finger along the chocolate drizzle, pokes through its center, then sticks it in Ezra's mouth. He sucks her finger clean.

The table goes silent. I look at Shane and he looks like he's holding his breath.

"I've got a big dick," says Ezra nonchalantly and starts to eat his dessert.

Why do they share personal business like Public Service Announcements? I look at Jen and we share looks of shock while Terry and Shane simply laugh it off.

I'm finishing the last of my dessert when the girl in red stands. "For two of tomorrow's game tickets, I'm down for whatever." She eyes Shane first, then Terry, then me and Jen. At this point I almost choke on my wine.

Shane looks at his watch. "Yup, time to go. Ezra, we gotta get to our team meeting." He opens the guest check holder, Ezra removes his hat and tosses in his credit card and Shane follows suit.

"I'll do the honors," chimes in Ms-I'll-Fuck-for-Tickets. She stands seductively, swirling her hand around in the hat and eventually grasps a card. With a suggestive look, she raises the card above her head.

"Dinner's on you." Shane points at Ezra, stands and pulls my chair out for me. "Y'all coming to watch movies later?" Shane helps me with my coat.

"Doesn't matter, we're just chilling," I say. "And thank you for dinner."

"You're welcome. Text me when y'all get back to the hotel."

Shane hops into a limo with Ezra and the two girls and Terry. For a moment, I wonder if the woman in red will make good on her offer in the limo. I'm feeling slightly uneasy, offended maybe . . . until I see our personal driver waiting for us. There is nothing like walking out on the streets of New York City and having a car at your service. It's like Christmas morning. I give one look at Jen and we start with the giggles again. "Remember this moment," says Jen.

"By the way, Shane wants us to come watch movies," I say, giving a fake yawn.

"Let it be clear, Shane wants YOU to come and watch a movie, my dear." She crosses her legs and rests her head back.

"No. He said y'all." I turn towards the window so she doesn't see me smirk.

Jen ignores me, humming along to the smooth sounds of Sade playing on the radio. She's thoroughly enjoying herself and taking in the experience. "This is where we belong, Bryn . . . this is where we belong." She shakes her head and laughs.

Back at the hotel I debate whether to tie my hair up or not. Jen pins her hair, changes into her pajamas, and dives head first into the bed. "I'm going to sleep. I didn't sleep half the day like you."

I put my pajamas on but leave my hair out. Just in case. I prop the pillows behind me and start to channel surf when out of the corner of my eye, I see my phone light up. A text message from Shane.

WHAT ARE YALL DOING?

I didn't think he was going to reach out considering they left with the ticket girl. I guess I was wrong. I reply.

Nothing, relaxing and watching a movie

He responds immediately.

WHAT? YALL GOT A MOVIE WITHOUT ME? I THOUGHT YALL WERE COMING BY?

"Jen," I call out her name, waking her up. "Shane wants us to come up."

"He wants you to come up," she slurs, rolling over.

"Y'all." I prove her wrong by holding my phone in the air and waving it, as if she can read the text from across the room without her contacts.

"I'm tired." She turns her back to me." I want to lie down."
She rolls over and tucks her pillow under her neck.

"We can stop by to be nice. We don't have to stay long."

"FINE!" She leaps out of the bed.

I text him back. `We will come`

`Room 513. The door is open`

It's late at night, so I throw a Nighthawks sweatshirt over my pajamas, but I realize it's a bad choice when the elevator door opens to a Nighthawks security guard stationed directly in front of us. He looks up and doesn't say a word, not even hello.

"OMG, I hope he doesn't think anything," I whisper to Jen.

"Dressed like this? Really? Girl, move." She pushes past me and storms down the hall. Shane's room door is ajar when we arrive and we let ourselves in.

I can't believe the condition of his room. It looks like my cubicle at work. This man has his stuff thrown everywhere. His Louis Vuitton carry-on is open on the floor with white T-shirts, socks, and black Under Armour boxer briefs spewing out of it. His laptop, multiple sets of headphones, and iPods are scattered across the bed.

He looks at us unembarrassed, sitting on the edge of the bed wearing a white T-shirt, gym shorts, and his silly baseball cap. He has his right leg propped up and he's rubbing his knee. The clothes he wore to dinner are on the floor beside him. I know as soon as Jen sees them, she's going to go crazy. Now that she's been styling him, she'll be devastated to see Tom Ford on the floor.

"Can you massage my knee?" Shane clears the bed, and tosses a small hotel lotion at me. "Right here." He gently touches the upper part of his knee.

"Seriously?"

"Please?"

"Rub that knee," laughs Jen, plopping onto the armchair with a blanket. Shane tosses her the remote control.

I roll my eyes and squirt lotion into my hands and lightly smear it on his knee like I'm putting lotion on a baby.

"Don't be scared, you gotta really rub it!" Shane demonstrates for me.

"I've got this—give me a moment, okay?" What the hell? Why can't he do it himself? His big old knees, his ginormous legs, this dude is HUGE. This isn't exactly what I imagined coming up here would be like.

"If you're tired, why did you come?" he yells at Jen, throwing a hotel notepad at her.

"I came because you asked me to come. If that's a problem, I'll gladly leave."

"Bring your funny-acting ass over here and lie down. This bed is big enough."

Jen falls asleep as soon as her head hits the pillow. Shane relieves me of my knee-rubbing duties and allows me to get comfortable. He sprawls across the foot of the bed and scrolls through the in-room movie menu.

I know I've fallen asleep because I wake to Jen poking my shoulder.

"What are you doing?" Shane yells at her.

"We're leaving so you can get some rest for your game tomorrow."

"Don't touch her—don't wake her up."

What he doesn't know is I'm a light sleeper and I've heard both of their big mouths since Jen first moved. I stay motionless until their exchange ends with Jen rolling over and going back to sleep.

My beauty sleep is disrupted again. Shane is tugging at the covers trying to pull the little sliver of blanket available to him over his broad shoulders. He's lying straight with his arms at his sides on a few inches of bed. I feel sorry for him so I scoot towards the middle, turning my back to Jen to give him more room.

"Order a movie." Shane hands me the remote control with his face about five inches from mine. "Yeah, Jen was trying to wake you up and shit, I told her to leave you alone." He removes his hat and sets it on the nightstand.

Feeling slightly self-conscious being this close to Shane, I lie on my back and begin scrolling through the list of new releases. "Ooh, *Mummy III!*"

"It's wack!" He sits up, removing his T-shirt and exposing his bare chest.

My goodness, this man is built like a machine. His shoulders, arms, and back are finely chiseled. I can see practically every muscle. My eyes slide down his body to his abs. As much as I try to act as if I don't see anything, I can't stop myself from imagining him completely naked. *Umph. So beautiful.* Shit, I hope he doesn't see the little bit of drool escaping from the corner of my mouth.

Bianca Williams

14

THE ANNOUNCEMENT

We got back late last night so I'm surprised I made it into the office today. When my alarm went off I wanted to roll over and go back to sleep, get up hours later, and watch last night's episode of *The Amazing Race* to vicariously travel the world with Ken and Tina.

Unfortunately, I got an 'important' email from Alex asking me to arrive on time, but he's not even here.

"Meeting in fifteen minutes, top floor, board room," says Susanne, sticking her head in my cubicle. I keep a fake smile on my face until she turns her back, then stick my finger down my throat. I'm not in the mood for Susanne and her shit. I just got here and she's already infringed upon my morning entertainment.

My back-up plan to avoid work was to sit here and tease Brian for at least an hour about my weekend in the big city, the personal driver, the nosebleed seats for the away team, and the fact the Nighthawks got their asses spanked by the Giants. Jen keeps saying it's because Shane didn't get proper rest, but he's the one who didn't want us to leave. Even when the sun came up, he wanted us to stay for breakfast. Personally, I wanted to get as far away from him as possible. I barely slept. Shane removing his T-shirt has been on replay all night, throughout breakfast, and on the drive to work.

"Bryn, what's going on?" asks Brian.

"I don't know. I'm going to see if Michael knows anything." I hear Susanne making her way around the office, so I lock my computer and grab my cell phone. Sneaking downstairs to the mezzanine level, I slip onto a chair across from Michael's desk. He's on a call and motions for me to wait.

I wait, but before the receiver connects with the base, I'm whispering, "Susanne told me to be in the executive board room and I saw her telling others when I ran down here."

"Yeah," he says, leaning back in his chair with his hands folded over his chest. "I'm not surprised. Something is going on. I worked very late last night pulling reports for my boss. He was stressed about having a meeting with the CEO. When I left, it looked like outside investors went upstairs. That was close to midnight, so I'm not sure of anything. But I told my boss last night, the bank must address the losses related to these bad loans."

"Hmmm, I know Alex was stressing about the outcome of his meeting last week but I didn't think anything of it, because he always stresses over everything lately."

"Well, we'll soon find out," he says. "What time are we going to lunch?"

"I'll call you at 11:30."

I'm one of the first to arrive and I observe our CEO standing at the front of the room with his head lowered and his hands tightly clasped behind his back. He paces back and forth as the remaining fifty people from my department take a seat around the enormous wooden table or stand at the back of the room. His secretary, gray haired and wearing a Merchant Bank blue suit from the sixties, is the last to enter. Slowly, she shuts the large oak doors and gives him the cue.

He inhales loudly. "Merchant Bank is merging with USABankersTrust headquartered in Harlow, New York. All back-office positions will be terminated in three months. There will be a formal announcement following this meeting. HR will be sending out an email to answer all your questions. Thank you for your dedicated service over the years," he says in one swooping breath.

I hear a few gasps. The payroll manager, who's been here since high school, is in tears. My old boss, with thinning gray hair, is silent as she grabs her cane and wobbles towards the exit. Brian rocks in his chair smiling and talking with Colin. *They're young and clueless.* I'm trying not to react, but this is my first layoff.

Naturally, my mind starts calculating monthly expenses, savings, and 401K balances.

"This bank has been around for over a hundred years and we've been given notice in a moment," says Gabe. His good eye is twitching. The lazy one, I think, is looking at the CEO.

"A hundred years. I thought they'd never sell." I agree with Gabe and get the hell away from him. I don't want to be in here if he snaps.

I head straight back to Michael's office, stopping at his doorway when I see him on a call. I can tell by the look on his face that he just found out too. He slams the receiver down and looks up at me. "Let's go," he says, hurriedly grabbing his wallet off the desk and shoving it into his pants pocket.

"I've got to get my purse."

"I've got it," he says, locking his computer. "You can treat tomorrow. I'm sure I'll be needing it," he says seriously. I follow a silent Michael out of the building. I'm scared to say anything, because this is the first time I've seen him speechless. I know he's upset because he's walking to our favorite Jamaican spot for comfort food.

"I'll take the jerk chicken platter, tell her what you want."

"I'll have the stewed chicken platter . . . extra plantains please." Michael pays for our food and gets our number while I find a place to sit.

"This is really messed up." Michael rubs his thinning hair. "I haven't updated my resume in twenty years."

"You've been working here since I was in the third grade."

"Thanks for pointing that out."

"Wow, that's a long time."

"Tell me about it." He removes his coat and scarf, placing them neatly on the extra chair beside him. "And you know what? I've got to search for a new job while they all get to keep theirs."

"Who?"

"Greg, Lester, Hugh . . . all of them. They cut a deal to sit on the board of directors of USABankersTrust. Typical corporate bullshit."

"Oh wow."

"All the tellers, branch managers, loan officers, and back office will be replaced by USABankersTrust employees. All Merchant Bank employees will need to reapply and go through the interview process. This is crazy. Do you realize most people have been here since high school?"

"Do you think they knew this was going to happen? I thought it was rather strange when the treasurer broke out of here for a demotion at another bank when he was a few months from retirement."

"I don't know, but the losses we took on our last financial audit were strong indicators that we needed to do something." He slams his hands on the table and points at me. "You're lucky Jen started her business because the banking industry is shit right now."

My career as an analyst is how I support my lifestyle. The event planning money is a perk. It's no use trying to educate him. He's pissed, so I just let him unload.

After lunch, I grab my personal items and leave the office early. There's no need to invest additional time here since my days are numbered. I've got three months to find a new job. I want to call someone and vent, but if I call Jen, the glass is always full. If I call my mother, the glass is always cracked. I'm not in the mood for either. I'm looking for something else, so as much as I don't want to, I send both my mother and Jen a text message and call Terry.

"Hey Terry, you busy?"

"No, what's up?"

"My entire department, well technically everyone, got laid off today."

"I'm sorry to hear that. Don't worry. You're smart, so you'll find another job. You'll be okay." He says all the things I already know and don't want to hear, especially around the holidays. His kind words do not resonate now.

He continues to talk about random things as I drive to Bailey's school. I'm not paying attention, but his voice is calming.

I arrive in time to get Bailey at the front for regular dismissal. She likes the afterschool care, but I think she'd rather be with me. Thanks to Terry, I'm able to get control of my emotions.

"Thanks Terry. I'm here with Bailey."

"Anytime. Call me later if you need me."

Bailey hops in the car, bouncing around in the back seat. She leans forward and gives me a kiss on the cheek. She has no idea of the stress I'm under. She's just happy to see me.

"No dance class tonight. Let's play hooky."

"Yes. Can we play—?"

"No Monopoly."

"Aww."

I look at her through the rearview mirror and her bottom lip is protruding. "Let's make it a movie night."

"Ratatouille?"

"You got it."

Bailey's in la-la land without a care in the world before the movie ends. I want to keep her that way. It's not healthy to expose young children to adult problems. I slide out of her bed, give her a kiss goodnight, and shut her door.

I'm still wide-awake. I grab a small photo album off my bookshelf and thumb through it. I stop at a photo of my father waving to me on a beach in Trinidad. *I guess I won't be traveling to see him next year.* I reach for my phone to call him and update him on the latest news when I find a text message from Shane.

`How come you don't call me when you are having a bad day?`

He sent it hours ago. Strange. I don't know how to respond. I forward the message to Jen and immediately follow up with a phone call to her. "Did you get my text?"

"Hold on. I got it."

"How should I respond?"

"I'm sorry—what? You want to respond? It's too late." She pauses. "Don't say anything to that man tonight."

"Just ignore him?"

"Okay. Stop. It's 10:18 p.m. and you're going to reply? How about you don't reply at night? I don't talk to people at night that I'm not attracted to. If you're not attracted to him, talk to him tomorrow."

"I've been busy all freaking day and I—"

She cuts me off. "Right, I understand, it's your down time, but to him it's prime time. You can't talk to someone at prime time if you're not interested in any horizontal time. So I would say no."

"Where did you get that line from?" I laugh.

"My brain, I'm talking to you, I'm not reading quotes."

I laugh so hard I begin to cough. "I've never heard of that before."

"What would it look like me calling Nick late at night? 'Hey, what's up'? No, no . . . it's ten at night. He could be doing something *or* somebody. Now is not the time to be hitting up pals, that's not what's happening this time of night."

"But I talk to Michael at night," I say, trying to argue the case.

"It has been *established*. Michael knows it doesn't matter if you call him at 2 a.m. It ain't nothing happening, captain. In Shane's case, you know he's attracted to you. He's always been attracted to you. There is nothing you need to say to him tonight. *Nothing*. And the fact you didn't respond to him today . . . well . . . it's pretty bad."

"I was busy," I explain, filling the kettle to make chamomile tea.

"Right. That's what you say *tomorrow*. 'Sorry I didn't hit you back yesterday, I was busy'."

"Yeah, well . . . what I didn't want to start was a daily conversation."

"Right, so don't respond tonight. Actually, you don't ever need to respond since you violently don't like him. But if you're bored and need something to do . . ."

"I don't," I interject.

"Well, don't reach out to him. It's fairly universal, after ten o'clock—no," she reiterates.

"I mean, I think he's cool and all. I just want to be careful not to give him the wrong impression. Especially after seeing him strip practically naked."

"Excuse me! What?"

"Girl, bye!" I hang up the phone remembering I haven't told her.

15

MOMENT OF TRUTH

I took the week off work because Alex couldn't care less. I spent Monday with Jen at Starbucks making the final changes to Jason's proposal. We met with him on Tuesday and he signed the contract. He couldn't have signed at a better time. Even though I smile and act like everything is fine, I'm scared of getting laid off during a recession.

Jen got tired of my nervous energy, as she likes to call it, so by Wednesday she staged an intervention. Since she's on a mission to get me laughing again, she organized a game night with Shane and Terry. Even though she volunteered to cook, bring games, drinks, and desserts, it's Friday, game night, and

I'm returning home from the grocery store with everything she forgot to pick up.

Terry arrives first with his two boys in tow. "Hey B. Hey Jen," he says, letting himself in. "B, your house smells like fried chicken." He takes a whiff and removes his shoes.

"By the way, just so you know, Jen tricked me into frying chicken. Technically, I'm a baked chicken kind of girl. I'm trying my best."

"B, you are so funny. What else y'all make?"

"Caesar salad, my Aunt Jackie's mac and cheese, and asparagus," sings Jen.

"Oh, I see how y'all do. Y'all only made Shane's favorites," says Terry, hanging up his coat in the hall closet. "Boys, go give them a hug."

"Terry!" shouts Jen as she removes her macaroni and cheese masterpiece from the oven. "It's not like that. You know we love you too."

"Well, if that's the case, how come y'all didn't make any fish?"

"You know Shane hates fish," I tease, dipping the last boneless skinless chicken breasts into the flour mixture.

"Hey honeys," says Jen, squeezing the cheeks of Terry's boys. "Terry, there's a dessert table downstairs just for you, Pimp Daddy," she says with a snicker, referring to his MySpace name.

Terry makes his way downstairs and the boys run after him. I'm glad Jen thought to bring sweets, because he's right, we unconsciously cater to Shane because we're used to it. *Speak of the devil; here he comes through my door without warning.*

"Bonjour, Sir Shane. Welcome, come in. Please . . . don't knock . . . make yourself at home," I say, waving a floured hand in the air.

"Shane!" squeals Jen, as she runs over and gives him a huge bear hug. "I miss you. How was your Halloween?"

"Fun. Miss y'all too. What up? Where Bailey? It's nice in here, Bryn."

"The little ones are downstairs with Terry," I say.

"Oh yeah, that sucka ain't answer his phone. I wanted him to come get me."

Within seconds of hearing the bass of Shane's voice, Bailey flies up the stairs and leaps into his arms. It's funny to see her so attached to a guy. I've never seen her enamored of anyone besides me.

"Come Bailey, help make the plates," I say, putting everything on the serving dishes.

She quickly makes up the plates for the boys and takes them downstairs. I tell her to hurry, because I'm not sure when Shane will start spewing inappropriate comments. Jen has a Ciroc and lemonade already made. He'll be swearing within minutes.

"Who fried this chicken?" yells Shane, dangling the faintly breaded tenderloin in the air.

Jen immediately points over at me. *Freaking Benedict Arnold.* I start to feel warm as I await the thrashing that will soon fall from Shane's lips.

"Where da skin?"

Bianca Williams

I look over at Jen, confused. "I don't eat chicken with skin on. They're boneless skinless chicken breasts. They don't come with skin," I utter.

"Ick!" he shouts, staring at it cautiously before stuffing it in his mouth. "My bad, Jen. I forgot. She doesn't know anything about mayonnaise sandwiches." He laughs with a mouth full of food.

"Or Al Green," chuckles Jen.

"Or rice with sugar."

"Wait a minute. Wait, that's disgusting. You put sugar in your rice?" I ask Shane.

He jokingly rolls his eyes.

"She ain't from the jets, Shane," says Jen.

"What are you trying to say?" I ask Jen, slightly offended.

"You're not from the projects. That's why you don't know how to fry chicken. That's why you get angry when I blast Aretha in the car," she explains.

This is awesome. He insults my cooking in my own house and Jen is supporting him. *My bad. I didn't think to buy chicken on a bone or with skin.* I'm sure I will never live this one down.

Shane picks through his plate, not letting the asparagus touch the mac and cheese, which required a separate plate from the chicken. *Is he serious?* Terry finishes his plate without a word and is already working on his second chocolate chip cookie.

"Well Shane, once you finish eating we'll start playing the games."

"What y'all got?"

"Bryn went and found eighties Trivial Pursuit."

Shane bursts into a boisterous laugh. "We were born in the eighties. We ain't gonna know none of that."

"You are right." Jen places the box on the chair next to her. "Next, we have Moment of Truth."

"What's that?"

"It's like a truth or dare, except it comes with a little hand-held lie detector device."

"Let's do it," says Shane, slapping both hands onto the table.

I pull the first card. Going clockwise, I ask Terry a question. "Have you ever parked in a handicapped spot?"

"Uh, yes."

I place the card at the bottom of the pile and hand it to Terry.

"Jen. Do you care about the environment?" Terry leans on his arm and yawns.

"Yes." She reaches for the pile and pulls the next card. "Shane, have you ever driven in a carpool lane while alone in your car?"

"What is that?" Shane snatches the card out of Jen's hand.

"A carpool lane is designated for cars with two or more occupants." Jen grabs it back.

"This is stupid!" shouts Shane.

"Come on. Give it here." I take the pile from Jen and shuffle through the questions because the ones we're pulling are sending everyone to sleep. "There's a modified version we can play. According to the rules, we can substitute a word with one of our choosing."

"I agree," says Jen. "And let's go counterclockwise because I don't want to ask Shane questions."

"Good, cause that means I get to ask you!" shouts Shane.

Jen smacks her forehead. "Gosh-darn-et!"

Shane pulls the first card and clears his throat. "JEN! Do you have a . . ." I can see him thinking ". . . a sugar daddy?"

Jen looks at me then looks away.

I almost spit out my drink.

Terry points at her. "Tell the truth," he says, laughing.

"I mean, I . . ." She lets out a huge exhale and looks to me for help.

"Why you looking at her? She can't help you. Answer the question." Shane bangs on the table.

"Yes. Now give me the cards." She snatches the deck from Shane. "You make me sick!"

Shane jumps up from the table and high-fives Terry.

Jen rolls her eyes. "Let's move on. Terry, have you ever . . . taken credit for someone else's work?"

I know where that question is coming from. Terry's always calling in favors from Jen for Shane. She wonders if he tells Shane where he gets the answers from.

"I don't think so."

Jen raises her eyebrow. "Sure about that?"

"Yeah Terry. Is that your final answer?" snaps Shane.

"If I did, it wasn't like it was on purpose."

"Yes or no?" Jen squints.

"Yes." Terry looks deflated.

"I thought so," says Jen under her breath. "Moving on." She pushes the cards over to Terry. Instead of pulling the next card, he reaches to the middle of the pile.

"Bryn. Have you ever had . . . a one-night stand?"

"Nope."

"That was quick," barks Shane. He smacks the table again, causing our drinks to shake.

"Because I've never. And don't start breaking furniture like you do over at Jen's."

"Well, excuse me," says Shane, giving me attitude.

"Okay, Mr. Diva Star. You're next. Terry, give me those cards." I reach for them and shuffle. "Let's see . . ." I pull a few cards and put them away.

"You're cheating. I quit. Cheater!" He points to me. "She's cheating."

"Shane, hush." I want to find the perfect card, something really embarrassing. It will be refreshing to pick on him for once. The next card I pull is the perfect set-up. "Shane . . . have you ever told a lie . . . regarding a certain body part?"

His body stiffens, so different from his normal rowdy state, and he calmly replies, "No."

In unison we all scream, "Liar!"

"Take the test!" shouts Terry, throwing the lie detector at him.

Shane picks up the little hand-held device that looks like a computer mouse and places his fingers in the metal grooves. "I *never* lie about my baby-maker," he says in a steady voice.

The device starts to chime indicating a fibbing Shane.

"Game over! This is phony." Shane chucks the lie detector into the adjoining living room. It crashes into a photo frame, knocking it onto the glass side table.

"That's not very sportsmanlike," I snicker.

"Shit, I ain't gotta lie. Not about that!"

"Glad to hear, how about Taboo? It's my favorite. Shane, you can be my partner." Jen runs over to the counter and brings back the game box.

"I've never played it," says Terry.

"It's really easy. I'll show you." Jen empties the contents and prepares a card for Terry. "Your goal is to try and get Bryn to guess the word at the top. Except you can't use the words on this card when you describe it. You get it?"

"I think so. I can't say any of these words." Terry points to the card with a confused look.

"Correct. Let's do a practice run. Don't forget to be creative. You'll have one minute." Jen flips the plastic hourglass.

He turns to me with a lost look on his face. "Umm. Umm. It's dark."

"Night?" I guess.

"No. It's very, very, very dark . . ." His eyebrows are inverted.

"The devil?" I shout. Jen starts to laugh hysterically.

"It comes every once in a while," Terry says, staring at me as if I know what he's talking about. "It's very, very, very dark."

"The Grim Reaper?" I guess again. Jen is in tears waving her arms wildly.

"Stop! Stop! I can't take it. The word is shadow. Shadow."

"No, Terry can't be my partner. No. He can't play."

"Good. I'm ready to play cards," says Shane. We forgo the board games and Shane plays his iPod and chats about TGS while we play cards.

Later in the night, Bailey walks upstairs, curls up on the sofa and falls asleep. Terry looks at his watch.

"Alright, that's my cue," he says and leaves the table to collect his boys.

"Bryn, I'm falling asleep on myself listening to this slow music. I'm going home." Jen stands to leave. "Will you be okay?" Jen raises one brow.

Shane is the only one still bright-eyed and ready to play cards. With his drink, his cards, and his music he's in his element. I can't possibly disappoint. "Of course." I wave.

"I'll call you in the morning." She lets herself out.

Shane and I continue to play cards and talk. He tells me about his week at acting camp when he was fifteen. How he played the archangel in the nativity play. He wore a king-sized sheet because he was too large for the costume. He tells me about his participation in the student government association at his high school and their visit to the White House and the Capitol all the way from Indiana. On the bus ride, even at seventeen he needed two seats. He tells me about how his sisters used to hide his pet hamster, King, in different places before he got home. The last time he saw his fuzzy friend was in the clothes dryer. Someone didn't look before adding the wet clothes. *Traumatizing.* He rambles on about random things like shoes, juice versus soda, and greatest movies of all times. I use this chance to cut in.

"Anything with Leonardo DiCaprio or The Rock are my favorites."

"Leonardo DiFaggio?" he teases. "Nah, just kidding. He's a phenomenal actor. I would love to meet him one day."

"I didn't jump on the bandwagon until *Blood Diamond*."

"That movie was hot. You think he's cute, don't you?"

I giggle. "Yes. He's on my vision board. I want to meet him."

"You like Dwayne 'The Rock' Johnson, huh? I'm not as handsome as The Rock."

"No one is as handsome as the Rock, my dear." It's my turn to deal.

"Is he on your vision board too?"

"He isn't. Believe it or not, I'm afraid to ever meet him. I'm so infatuated with him I think if I met him in person I would lose consciousness right there on the spot. I hyperventilate when I watch his movies. I had to stop watching them. Him in *The Game Plan* . . . mmm hmm." I start to fan myself. "My heart is fluttering just thinking about him."

Shane's 'give me a break' look doesn't go unnoticed.

"What *else* does Bryn like?"

"That's such a broad question. What do I like? Hmmm. I like lots of things. Can you ask a more specific question?" I take his Ace with the Joker. He must be distracted.

"What makes you smile?"

"Seeing Bailey light up when she sees you."

"You don't light up when you see me."

"We're always happy to see you, Shane."

"I'm just fucking with you," he says, looking down at his hand. "This one is about to be over really quick." He organizes his remaining cards. Somehow, he wins.

Around 2 a.m. I feel myself fighting sleep. I struggle to keep my eyes open.

"Go to bed!" roars Shane. For the first time, he doesn't startle me.

"Oh gosh, I'm sorry. I'm so sleepy all of a sudden." I take the last gulp of my watered-down vodka. "You know what? You're not exactly what people say you are, like all the time."

"Oh yeah. What do they say?"

"That you're mean, scary, kind of a jerk."

"Yeah, well. I like to play the bad guy. People love to hate the bad guy."

"But you're great at what you do."

"I kinda have to be. I mean, for people to accept me?" He points to his scar which has become unnoticeable to me. "I ain't the pretty face that you're going to see on 95. I'm not Jason Ross." He goes silent.

"Well, Jason isn't you. You're like a big kid. You believe in fairytales and Tinker Bell." I laugh.

"What's your favorite Disney movie?"

"Aladdin."

"Give me some." Shane gives me a fist bump. He makes me laugh.

"Tonight's really been fun." I collect the cards and put them into the sleeve.

Shane stands and stretches.

"And sorry about the chicken," I say. "I'll get chicken on a bone next time."

"Yeah, your chicken was wack."

"See, you just hurt my feelings again."

He stops in his tracks. "I will never hurt your feelings," he says. "I mean that."

Somehow his words feel truthful.

"Alright Bryn, I gotta get out of here. Goodnight."

"Auf wiedersehen," I say, following him to the door.

"What about her?" He points at Bailey lying on the sofa nuzzled in her fluffy blanket.

"I'll carry her to her bed."

"You can carry her?"

"Umm. I'm short, but not weak." I flex my minuscule bicep. He squeezes it, deflating it, and then laughs so loudly he startles Bailey.

"You want me to carry her for you?"

"Be my guest."

Effortlessly he lifts Bailey, carries her upstairs, and gently places her in her bed. "Well . . ." he says as he makes his way back downstairs. He starts to hum *Come and Talk to Me* by Jodeci, an old-school love song.

As he nears the door, he stops, grabs the side banisters, and leans towards me. "Maybe I can come over one day and play you some more music."

"How about you just give me your playlist?" I ask, pointing at his chest.

"Nope," he says, exaggeratedly puckering his full lips. He raises his chin, facing me at eye level, and lifts his arms for a hug.

I pout. "Well, you should reconsider, because I really want it," I say, batting my eyelashes as I pull away.

Our eyes lock.

"I'm looking at what I want," he says confidently.

Then unexpectedly, some atmospheric energy surge zips through my body and I'm lost for words.

16

<u>SLEEPING BEAUTY</u>

I'm lying on a beach in a netted hammock between two palm trees, staring up at the stars. The air is warm and a soft breeze blows my hair across my face. Nick appears, looking dreamy, and hands me a glass of champagne. Then I'm alone, floating in the Caribbean Sea staring at the full, brilliant moon. I hear sweet steel pan melodies playing me a lullaby. The rippling sea rocks me peacefully. I close my eyes and my body sinks to the shallow bottom and then I come to the surface again. I stand and Nick appears, smiling. Then he morphs into a dark-skinned and naked man, standing tall and strong in front of me. Softly, he caresses my face.

Suddenly, I'm in deep waters. My feet can't touch the bottom. I panic and tread water. The small ripples are now large waves. I try to float on my back, but a riptide is forming next to me. I'm being pulled into deeper water. Yards of black tulle wrap heavily around my waist. Waves crash wildly around me and the wet skirt weighs me down. I'm exhausted.

I sink. Underwater, I look up and the moon is still shining brightly. Then a hand plunges into the water, grabs my arm and pulls me up to safety. I wrap my legs around a set of hard abs and my arms around a strong neck and lay my head on a carved chest. I'm carried ashore. I feel weightless again. It feels so right. I've waited forever for this moment.

"I want you, now," he says. His voice is melodic. His large hand trails my spine. He turns his head to kiss me. I feel excitement building inside me as I turn to kiss him. Our eyes connect.

Shane????

My eyes snap open.

"What the fuck?"

17

THE FLIRT

I had a dream about Shane. *Shane? Really Bryn?* I want to tell Jen, but I'm afraid if I give it energy, it will manifest. I was once told that if you ignore something long enough, it will go away. But as much as I try to focus on prepping for this upcoming job interview, I can't. Thoughts of Shane are relentlessly coming to the forefront.

"What are you working on?" shouts Alex. He walks into my cubicle and sits on the edge of my desk.

"Excuse me? How rude of you. I'm in the middle of preparing for a job interview I have lined up this week. Wanna see?" I turn one of my monitors to face him.

He points his finger at me. "You're not allowed to leave before me. Remember that. Seriously, we need to time it so that we're both gone within twenty-four hours of each other. I don't want to be here without you and I *know* you don't want to be here without me. Timing. It's all about timing." He taps his titanium watch.

"If we're so lucky. I hope Susanne loses it. I've got a new name for her, *The Eye*," I say enthusiastically.

"Yeah." He rubs his forehead. "Funny you should choose that name. I'm over here because she's implementing a new timekeeping policy. The IT guys should be around today to install it on your laptop. It's sort of an attendance tool for the computer. Every time you log onto your computer you have to sign into a message board. If you leave your desk, you need to say you're away and add a reason code."

I stare at Alex with my mouth wide open. "You know I'll sign out right now. Does she realize she's lowering morale? Why does she even care anymore? We all just got laid off. This is exactly why I need a new job."

"She's a miserable hag," says Alex as he walks away.

I send Jen and Terry a text message.

```
The crazy bitch has lost her mind. I
can't wait to quit
```

I take a deep breath, say a small prayer, and immediately get back to taking notes because I'm now determined to be the first one out of here. The thought of handing Susanne my two-week notice brings me joy. If I could afford it, I'd write 'I quit' in fireworks in the sky, or do something dramatic and unexpected. Like hire a hip-hop Barney to rap sixteen bars about me leaving.

A call interrupts my joyful thoughts. "Yes Michael," I answer.

"Would you like to come out and go drinking with us tonight?"

I'm sure he's thinking about hanging out in Canton. A local beer on tap, iced cooler drinking, pool table, foosball, standing in a huge crowd, bar. "I don't know. I could use a drink these days. Who's going?"

"Just a few of us from work. I know it won't be like hanging out with your celebrity friends."

"Shut up."

"Come on, you may meet your future husband."

"Whatever. I'm free. Bailey is going to a Cheetah Girls concert with Jen tonight. You need to drive, because I plan on having a drink."

"Sure. Pick you up at ten."

The bar is crowded. I've been pushed, stepped on, even poked with a pool stick but when Michael turns to check on me, I just smile. I don't want to complain. I continue to follow him around the bar and somehow, we manage to find me a seat. "I should be fairly safe here." I squeeze in at the end of the main bar.

"In that case, I'm going to dance." Michael leaves me on my own.

"Have a blast." I wave to a few of his co-workers looking in my direction. Bored already, I look at the televisions hoping to catch a basketball game at least, but all that's showing is baseball.

"What are you drinking?" In my peripheral view, I see my inquisitor waving at the bartender.

"No thank you," I say without looking in his direction.

"How about a Heineken?"

"I'm not into beer, thanks."

"Bryn, will you let me order something for you?"

I spin my entire body around. "Nick." I'm blushing. "What are you doing here?" *I had a dream about you.*

He smiles a beautiful smile. "This is where I hang out. Well, technically." He leans towards me. "I own the place."

"This is so funny." I laugh a silly valley girl laugh and twirl my hair. "I'm here with co-workers. Well, soon-to-be-ex co-workers from the bank. We've been laid off."

"Wow, I'm sorry to hear that. Now you really have to let me buy you a drink."

"Sure. Since I know you and all," I laugh. "I'll have that drink."

He runs his hand through his blonde curls and hands me the cocktail. I take a sip and it goes straight to my head.

"Another!" he shouts. "Whatever this wonderful lady wants for the rest of the night is on the house," he says to the bartender.

Every now and again Michael looks over and gives me a thumbs-up. I raise my two glasses letting him know I'm okay.

"How about some shots?"

"Sure. Lemon shooters?"

He smiles, raises two fingers to the bartender and shouts, "Lemon Drops!"

"Extra sugar, please," I request.

"Extra sugar," he adds. The bartender also brings a small plate with extra lemons. "Thanks," says Nick. He hands me the shot glass and the plate of lemons. I place a lemon between my teeth. "To finding a new job." He raises his glass.

"Woo-hoo." I suggestively suck the lemon, lick the glass, throw my head back, and pour the warm liquor down my throat. "Wow. That was strong," I gasp.

"Another round?"

"Let's do it!"

We do four rounds of shots.

"Let's dance!" Nick takes my hand.

I'm going to rock his world! I try to stand but slide off the barstool and onto the floor and bang my head on someone's kneecap. I've lost my legs.

I swim around on the floor trying to get to my knees and Nick lifts me up by the arm. Michael comes running over because of the commotion, I'm sure.

"Nick, you're soooo hand—" I reverse burp. "Ugh. Gross." I lean on the barstool. Nick brushes my hair back, tucking it behind my ears.

"Bryn! What the hell?" Michael grips my arm.

"Hi, I'm Nick. I'm so embarrassed. This is my fault." He shakes Michael's hand.

"No . . . Nick. You're hot. I mean it's not. You *are* hot. But I know my limit is two drinks."

"I can't bring you anywhere." Michael looks at Nick. "She's a lush, ya know." He laughs at his own joke. Nick laughs to be polite and smiles at me. He's looking sexier by the second. "The least I can do is drive you home."

I let out a loud belch. "My God!"

"Don't worry about it, Nick. I've got her." Michael throws my other arm over his shoulder and leads me away. I'm too ashamed to wave goodbye.

I collapse onto the passenger seat and then Michael slams the door.

"I'm going to start calling you Drunk Debbie." I ignore him and check my cell for missed calls from Bailey. As I dial her number, a text pops up from Shane.

How come you don't call me?

I let out a loud "HA!" and read his message again. I type back. I don't know.

What are you doing?

Riding home

Why don't you call me to talk when you are having a bad day?

He really wants an answer to this question. I text back.

I don't know

I want you to call me instead of Terry next time

Why? I think of a nice reply but my thoughts are swirling.

Shane texts back.

I've been thinking about you lately

I giggle as I type.

Same here

"What are you doing?" shouts Michael. "You're looking devious."

I check my expression in the visor mirror. "Mind yours."

"Are you drunk texting? I hope you aren't texting anyone. Stop stalking Nick!" My phone chimes.

You've been thinking of me?

"Embarrassing, disgraceful—you should be ashamed! Wait until I tell everyone at work tomorrow. Out here about to give Nick the cookies. I need you to sober up." Michael laughs and my phone chimes again.

Hello?

I roll my eyes at Michael and respond to Shane.

Yup! I had a dream about you

Oh yeah, what was it about?

"No worries Bryn. I'll take care of you. I'm calling AA tomorrow morning. I'm going to tell them I need to enroll a good friend Miss Debbie a.k.a. The Drunkard."

"Slut up!"

"You can't even speak! How many drinks did you have?"

I ignore Mike and check my phone. Shane sends another text.

I'm waiting

I reply.

I can't share

"What would your celebrity friends think of you now? You better be thankful you're with me and not them. Nick was going to scoop you right up if I hadn't intervened."

"I was perfectly fine with Nick scooping me up." I check my phone. It lights up again.

You can!

I quickly type back.

I can't. Goodnight

"Michael. You get on my nerves."

"You'll thank me one day, Debbie."

I lay my chair back and look at my cell, which has a series of new messages.

You can

You will

If you don't

I'm going to come to your house

Knock on your door until you answer

And make you tell me to my face

"Oh shit!" I yell. I type as fast as I can.

It was filthy

Be more specific

I cringe as I type.

We were together   ·

WHHHHHOOOOOOOOOAAAAAA!!!!

I THOUGHT YOU WERE GOING TO TELL ME WE
WERE ON A JUNGLE ADVENTURE AND WE WERE
FIGHTING BAD GUYS TOGETHER.

He's an idiot. I try and clarify any confusion.

No together, together. I woke up wet

Oh my God

I touched myself afterwards

I need a cigarette

You're funny

Can I come over? Please?

I gasp and a reverse hiccup-burp burns in my chest.

"What did you just do?" shouts Michael.

My eyes shift and I turn off my phone.

18

FIRST DATE

When I wake up the next morning, I head straight to Bailey's
room, passing Jen in my guest bedroom with her laptop. "She's
downstairs."

"Okay. How was the concert?"

"Why do you look like that?"

I look down at my robe. "I just woke up."

"I'm referring to your face. It has guilt written all over it."

I smile. "I don't know what you're talking about."

"You can't hide it. You're up to something . . ."

"You're crazy." I laugh. "How was the concert?"

"How was last night?" She stops typing and looks up at me,
squinting. "I'm listening."

"It was fine." My voice cracks. "Just drinks." I clear my throat.

"You're LYING!" She jumps up.

"No, seriously." I laugh. "Oh right, I ran into Nick."

Jen remains silent and stares me down. "Oh right, really? Is that all?"

"Yes. He's the one who bought all the drinks."

"Is that right?"

"Yes." I nod. "Why are you acting like Inspector Gadget?"

She looks at me as if she already knows.

"Did you talk to Shane or something?"

"Shane?" Jen pulls me into the room and shuts the door. "Our Shane Smith? What have you done?"

"Well . . . like I said, I was drinking."

"Yeah, I heard that part."

I cover my face. "I drunk texted Shane and told him that I had a dream about him."

"I knew it. I knew it. I knew it. There's more. I can see it on your face."

"He wanted specifics. So, I may have sent another text saying we were together. And perhaps another saying something like . . . I touched myself."

"How did this happen? You saw Nick at the bar. Where did Shane come from? How did you two even start talking?"

"He texted me while I was on my way home. He wanted to know why I don't call him."

"And you decided to tell him you touched yourself?"

"It didn't quite happen like that. He said he was thinking about me. I said I was dreaming about him. Well, technically I dreamt about Nick but he morphed into Shane in the end."

"You could have said anything. Why did you tell him the truth?"

"I don't know because I don't even like Shane like that."

Jen holds her head. "I need a Vicodin." She adjusts her seat and stares out of the window as if in deep thought. "So, what's your plan?"

"Avoid him I guess."

"I'm not sure how I feel about this."

"Well, I'm good. So . . ."

She quickly turns back to me. "You just told him you masturbated. I don't know *how* you're going to be able to keep him away."

My phone chimes. "It's Shane." I bite my nails.

"OH, MY GOD!" she screams. "Who are you?"

I leave the room to read his text.

What are you doing?

I don't know what to say. I could respond, oh I was just joking around last night. Having a little laugh. Or I can just ignore him. I choose the later.

I go downstairs to check on Bailey. She's entertaining herself with her Wii.

"Hey babe, how was the concert?"

"It was the best. They are so pretty! I knew all the songs, so I sang with them. The girl next to me didn't know any of the words."

"Cool."

"It was cool. Aunty got us these cinnamon sugar pretzels and cream cheese."

"Ugh! Sounds gross."

"They were delicious. What are we doing today?"

"Cleaning."

"Awesome, can I sort the laundry?"

"You sure can!"

She tosses her controller and darts upstairs.

The day passes quickly. I spend the day repeatedly kicking myself in the ass. *I can't believe I told him I had a sex dream.* I could have said anything, duh, or nothing at all.

My phone rings. I glance at it and it's Shane again. Well, I can't ignore him forever. I pick up. "Hello Shane. How are you?" I say, taking the stairs to my bedroom.

"I'm great. And you?"

"I'm okay. Just lounging around."

"Would you like to join me for dinner tonight?"

"Umm."

"I won't bite."

"I mean. I don't know if it's a good idea."

"How about eight?"

"Umm."

"I will see you then," he says and disconnects the call.

"Agh!" I scream while texting Jen.

He's taking me out to dinner tonight

She replies immediately.

You are a grown woman

Even though Jen is disgusted with me, she takes Bailey over to her house while I get ready. I keep my attire casual. I throw on my favorite dark skinny jeans and a black sweater with a pair of black boots. I pull my hair into a ponytail and put on a pair of large silver hoop earrings. It's exactly eight o'clock and my heartbeat skyrockets when I hear a knock at the door.

Shane's all smiles as I open the door. "For you." He hands me a dozen red roses.

"They are beautiful. I absolutely love flowers." I motion for him to come inside.

"I know, I can tell you're the type of woman who appreciates things like this."

"I love them," I say, taking a huge whiff. "Let me put them in water." *This is so sweet.* I hurry into the kitchen, grabbing a vase and filling it with water. "Thank you, Shane, they're lovely."

"No lovelier than you." He helps me with my coat.

I chuckle. "It was very thoughtful of you." I grab my keys and lock the door.

Shane opens the passenger door and helps me into his truck. I guess he's fresh out of corny compliments. Things definitely feel awkward.

"How was your day?" Shane drums his fingers on his steering wheel.

"Pretty quiet. Caught up on cleaning the house. How about you?"

"Work," he says.

"Yeah . . . work. I know the feeling." My mouth is dryer than this conversation. I'm at a loss for words and feel plain stupid. I'm not even supposed to be here. And we certainly shouldn't be on a date. What was I thinking? I'm making a mistake.

We pull up at my favorite restaurant, Oceanaire, and the valet attendant recognizes Shane's truck and hurries over. "Keep it up front for me," says Shane, tucking a $100 bill into the attendant's hand.

A hostess is anxiously holding the front door waiting for us to enter. "You're my favorite Nighthawk," she says, blushing and grabbing two menus. She walks us to a booth set for two. I look at the old couples seated and the men in dinner jackets. I look at Shane in his sweater, jeans, and baseball cap. We are underdressed, but they don't care. He's a Nighthawk.

I take my seat first and Shane scoots in very close to me.

Our server stands a few feet from us, white gloved and at ease. Shane motions for him to approach and he pours us bottled water.

"So, what's up with that text?"

"Wow. We didn't even order."

"I'm a straight shooter. No pun intended."

"I mean, I was out drinking and just trying to be a little fun. That's all," I say, taking a huge gulp of water. "Let's just act like that never happened." I remove phantom lint from my eyelash.

Shane sits silently staring at me in awe. "Like, I can't believe you are here with me."

Not knowing how to respond, I nod and smile. I really can't believe I'm here either. "Just think of it as two good ol' friends having dinner. There's nothing wrong with that."

"Nah, too late for that. I want to date you. Like 'date you date you'," he says while adjusting his cap.

I sit speechless.

"I want to seriously date you, like tell Bailey and everything."

"Shane, don't you have a girlfriend and aren't you about to have a baby?"

"I'm single. I'm completely single. I date who I want and I want to date you. Exclusively date you. Like you said at the game. No sharing. I don't want you seeing anyone else either."

"Let's order. I'm hungry." I grab the menu and hold it as close to my face as possible to hide the shock.

Shane orders a bottle of his favorite wine, a Chateau St. Michele Riesling, while I review the menu to decide between scallops and salmon. When I settle for the seared scallops with a side of lobster mac n cheese, I'm not surprised to see Shane's repugnance at my choices. It's endearing he brought me here because he hates seafood, but he knows it's my favorite. He orders his usual New York strip with a side of steamed asparagus.

"So back to what I was saying." He takes a huge gulp of his wine. "What happens after this?"

I remain silent and he begins to make his case. While I'm listening to this guy who normally intimidates so many people, I can't help but be touched by his vulnerability. Even though all I can do is smile, it's enough encouragement for him to divulge the details of his life.

"Tell me. What are your dreams?" Without losing eye contact, he reaches for my hand. "I want to know."

"Most of my dreams are for Bailey. I just want all of her dreams to come true."

"I completely understand. That's great, but what about dreams for you?"

I can't believe I'm having a hard time answering this question. I haven't given it much thought. *Do I respond with a cliché? The husband, kids, and the big house complete with the white picket fence?*

"I'm waiting."

"You first."

"No. You know enough about me. I want to know everything about you."

"Hmm . . ." I can't stop blushing as I try to come up with something. "My dream is to find happiness, love, and have peace of mind. A loving family wouldn't hurt either."

"I want to be the one to make you happy." He squeezes my hand before letting it go.

"Is that right?"

"I'm up for the challenge," he says, pouring the last of the wine into his glass.

19

MRS. SMITH

Shane and I've been inseparable all week and we haven't even had a first kiss. A moment doesn't pass without Shane reaching out to me on email, text message, or phone. So far, his favorite dates are the movies. We've gone at least three times this week. He likes to cuddle, wrapping his big arm around mine, and after about five minutes, my poor arm is asleep. It's adorable, but I prefer dinner dates. That way I can look him directly in the eyes and pick his brain. I like getting to know the real Shane.

He sounded disappointed when I told him I couldn't meet for an early dinner tonight, but Bailey had dance class. She comes first. Besides, tonight I need a break and I just want to relax. My head still hurts from a grueling interview I had today.

It went well, but I have to prepare for some other promising ones that I've set up for next week.

Bleep, bleep, sounds my cell, alerting me to a new message from Shane.

Hey sweetie, what are you doing?

Lying in bed, reading a book

What book?

Eat, Pray, Love

By who?

Elizabeth Gilbert

Never heard of her

Okay lol I type back. *I'm not the least bit surprised.*

Want to see a late movie?

I had a long day. I think I'm just going to relax

Where's Bailey?

In her bed asleep

Want a massage?

I burst into laughter. I'm sure women across the world have been asked this question a million times.

No thank you. Only licensed hands touch this body

You should let me. I've got skills

I delay my response and weigh my options. It's obvious we're getting closer but I'm not sure if I want to get *that* close. Jen thinks our closeness is unacceptable. She avoids conversations that involve Shane and usually cuts me off to talk about Jason's project. She constantly reminds me Shane is still a client.

My phone chimes again.

You took too long. I'm on my way

How do you figure?

Shane rules 101

I laugh. He's determined as always and certainly confident. I must admit his confidence is alluring. I leap out of bed towards my closet and grab a pair of sweatpants. I already know telling him not to come will only encourage him. It wouldn't surprise me if he's already sitting in my driveway. *This man is just out of control.*

Shane arrives in minutes with a huge smile on his face and leans in to embrace me. "I love it in here," he says, looking around.

"Thank you."

"You gotta give me the name of your painter," he says, taking off his size thirteen white Nike Airs and setting them neatly by the door. So . . . where we going to do this?" He rubs his hands together in anticipation of touching my body.

"We can go upstairs. I don't want Bailey waking up and seeing you massaging me on the sofa."

His face lights up, "Can we tell her?" He pulls his hooded sweatshirt off, exposing his ripped abs, and tosses it on the bannister then straightens his white T-shirt.

"No, tell her what?"

"Does Jen know?" He takes three steps at a time up the staircase.

"She knows we've been hanging out."

"Does she approve?"

"No. She has her reservations. As do I."

"Tell her the contract is over."

"She says you're still a client."

"I'm her client. I'm not *your* client."

"We're business partners."

"That's for y'all to figure out."

As he walks into my bedroom, I watch him slowly start to case the place like he does Jen's kitchen. Stopping at the foot of my bed, he stares intently at my Gustav Klimt *Tree of Life* painting spanning the length of my headboard. He glides his hand across the faux fur throw. "I'm anti-fur."

"It's faux."

He silently nods before walking to my nightstand and picking up a gold-framed photo of Bailey and me when she was a baby. "You look young," he says and begins to poke through a stack of my favorite books: *Memoirs of a Geisha*, *Running in Heels*, and *Interpreter of Maladies*. He runs his hand along my wall light. "It's like a spa in here." He places the photo back in its place. "Got lotion?"

I walk towards him and open the drawer. "I've got massage oil. It smells wonderful too, it's vanilla," I say, placing the bottle in his hands.

He twists the top off and sticks it to his nose, making a face. *He's such a child.*

I lie across my bed, lifting the back of my tank top to my shoulders and exposing my bra strap.

"Red!" He touches the strap. "You *are* going to take that off?"

"Do I need to?" I ask, looking over my shoulder at him.

His eyes widen. "I mean, if you want your shoulder and back rubbed, you should."

"Fair enough." I pull my shirt back down and unstrap my bra from underneath, pulling one arm out at a time then tossing it aside. I remove my tank top and cover my chest without him getting a peek.

I sink into the mattress as he straddles me with his knees. Butterflies fill my stomach and at the same time, my mind fills with doubt. *Girl, are you crazy? He's the client! He's a dog. Bryn, you are stupid, you should know better. He's an athlete and all athletes are whores. He's going to dog you out. He has more women than he has cars and you know about three, at a minimum.*

"Wow, you're tense," he says, giving me a tight squeeze.

I try my best to quieten my mind. The pressure from his massive hands melts away my worry. *He's so gentle. Maybe he's different. Maybe he isn't like the rest of them. Maybe he's—*

I realize I should enjoy this moment and address the particulars later.

The next morning, when I roll out of bed, I feel refreshed. Then I recall last night. Shane was a complete gentleman. I was pleasantly surprised that he had such skillful hands. Most guys claim to give great massages, but end up squeezing the area between your neck and shoulders to death. It was amazing and lasted for about an hour.

I take my time getting dressed and head downstairs. In the kitchen, I find Bailey dressed and ready to go.

"Morning honey. If you had a magic wish, what would it be?" I ask playfully. She doesn't respond, but gives me a nod accompanied by a weird look. Immediately, my neurosis kicks in. *Oh no! What if she heard Shane's bass voice coming from my room?* I've spent the last few weeks perfecting the art of opening and closing the front door without a sound.

"Ready to rock and roll?" I screech, playing an air guitar. My behavior is both pitiful and awkward and is probably making her more suspicious. I'm sure this is just my paranoia and she doesn't know a thing. I check myself and try to act normally on the drive to her school.

"Mom, don't forget I get out early today. We have standardized tests all morning and my stomach hurts."

"Awww baby, you're just nervous. Drink some water and say a prayer. Au revoir, my love," I say, waving. "You will do great. I believe in you."

At work, I walk to my desk with a new attitude. I'm so happy I may even speak to Susanne. "Hey girl." I wave to Imani in passing. She smiles and waves back.

"Aren't you chipper this morning," she laughs.

I let out a loud laugh as I pass Alex's office.

"You! Come here," says Alex, motioning me in. "I want to tell you first."

"Shit Alex. You make me sick." I know what he's about to tell me.

"I just gave that devil my notice. I told her I'd give her three weeks and she told me that I can leave today. You'll be reporting to Chris now. Be glad you don't have to report directly to that witch, like Imani does."

"I hate you," I whine.

"One more thing, I promise I will do your evaluation before I leave."

I frown and give him a hug. The news is bittersweet. I'm happy he's the first one to escape. I'll cut him some slack since he promises to complete my performance review. I've been really looking forward to this evaluation so I can have a higher starting salary someplace else.

I try to make him feel guilty by sulking to my desk. I'm motivated to intensify my job search. I've got to cast a wider net. The economy is getting worse daily. Jobs are scarce and qualified candidates plentiful.

I log onto my computer and hear Michael's boisterous voice in the distance. It gets louder as he approaches. "Hey Superstar!" He barges into my cubicle with a Sharpie and a piece of paper. "Can I get your autograph?"

I give him a stern look. "Shut up, what time are we going to lunch?"

"Wow, I can't believe I'm in your presence. I think I'm levitating."

"Whatever," I snap and continue to fill out an application for an analyst at a small bank. "Alex is leaving."

"Oh, he is?" he says, taking a seat. "That lucky son of a bitch."

"Yes . . . yes, he is, because I've been searching every day and I'm coming up with the same lame jobs. I'm about to start applying for everything in a minute, customer service if I have to."

"You've got to give it a rest for a few days. Besides, why are you looking? You can work for Jen and get rich off your new celebrity event planning business."

"Shut up, Michael. It's not the time for jokes. This is serious," I say, rolling my eyes.

"Well, I'm just waiting to hear what my package is going to be like and I'm going to live off that for a while. I'm not in a rush to jump ship."

"I'm not management, so I'm sure I won't get much."

"You'll be alright. You've got that Shane Smith and Jason Ross money now."

"Leave my desk before I throw this stapler at you," I say, holding it up poised to throw it.

"So sensitive today." He snatches the stapler from my hand.

"I just told you I can't find a job. You don't have a child like I do."

"Don't stress Bryn, you will be fine."

Michael irritates me so much that later, I duck him out for lunch. I tell him something has come up and I brought take-out to my desk.

I take out my cell phone to play a game and see a new message alert from Shane.

WE DID IT

We did what? I reply but he doesn't respond. I call Terry but he doesn't answer. "Ugh," I let out, kicking my feet up on my desk.

"What's going on back there, Bryn?" Brian shouts over the wall.

"I'm trying to decode this text I just got from Shane. It says, 'we did it'."

"What did you do?"

"Brian, are you kidding me? I just said I'm trying to figure it out."

"Oh yeah, right," he says, along with a goofy chuckle.

I laugh at his stupidity and check to see if Shane or Terry has responded. Nothing.

"What are you yelling 'oh my goodness' about?" Chris strolls into my cube with his hands neatly tucked into his pockets. "Did you hear the news?"

"Yup, you're my new manager. Susanne is an idiot. Don't let her know that we are cool," I warn. "Anyway, look." I show him Shane's text.

"You know they're announcing the players who made it to Pro Bowl in a few hours?"

"No I didn't. Chris, you are a genius. That would be freaking awesome." I grab my cell to text Jen.

"Are you going to Hawaii?" screams Brian, poking his head over the banister.

Later in the evening I get a call back from Shane. He tells me that he's going to Hawaii.

Bianca Williams

"Congratulations," I say. "The honor is well deserved."

"Get dressed. Let's celebrate. Bring Bailey and tell Jen. I'm on my way."

Bailey screams when I tell her the news and runs around when I tell her Shane's on his way to get us. She loves being around him. She says he's like a big brother.

An hour later, we pull out to Kobe's, a hibachi grill. Shane jumps out of the truck first and then helps us out. Jen walks ahead. Terry is at the door with his boys. "I asked for a private table," he says, holding the door.

"Good. You're learning," says Jen.

As promised, the hostess gives us our own table instead of filling it up with additional guests. We appreciate the special accommodations, although she requests an autograph before his ass hits the seat. It's sad fans don't realize they are imposing on the family as well as the athlete.

"After dinner," he mumbles.

Once we're seated and drink orders have been taken and served, Shane stands up. "I have an announcement." He clears his throat. "I first want to say, 'thank you' to everyone at this table. I know y'all worked hard on the voting campaign for me. I know, especially you, Bailey baby. Jen told me about you staying up past your bedtime to vote for me a bunch of times. I want y'all to know that I'm going to find a way for y'all to go to Hawaii with me."

The table erupts in cheers from the kids. Bailey's all smiles and red with excitement. I smile and look up at Shane, who appears to be getting emotional.

"And . . . one more thing," he says, blushing from all the attention. "TGS has been asked to open for 92Q's back to school jam. So, we are going to do it again. Jen, draw up a contract."

"Awww man, Shane. I thought you were going to announce the birth of your son yesterday," blurts Terry.

The lively voices hush as Shane gives Terry a steely stare. Jen and I exchange awkward looks. Even the chef senses the tension and tries to lighten things up by doing a few wild tricks, flipping knives and utensils, making an onion volcano, flaming smiley faces, and a zucchini steam engine. I clap politely and play with my chopsticks as a distraction.

Dinner ends and the kids have fun trying to catch the shrimp in their mouths. The waitress comes with the check and informs Shane that a long line has formed in the front bar area. "I'll be right back." Shane excuses himself from the table. *I guess it comes with the territory.*

It doesn't take long for Shane to return. "That was quick," says Jen.

"The more you do it, it's like walking." He helps me put on my coat and does the same for Bailey and then leads the way out of the restaurant.

"Goodnight and thank you, Mrs. Smith. Hope you had a wonderful time," says the hostess. Completely caught off guard, I look around and then realize she's speaking to me.

"Umm, ahhh, yes, thank you. Thank you. Umm," I say, not knowing if I should correct her or not. "You too," I blurt and rush towards the exit.

"You hear that, Shane?" shouts Terry, holding the door open for him. "She just called Bryn, Mrs. Smith."

Shane takes Terry's place as I walk through. "I think I like the sound of that," he says with a big grin.

20

ALL I WANT FOR

CHRISTMAS

Today, Baltimore gets its first sight of flurries. I can't help but hum 'it's beginning to look a lot like Christmas'. Bailey and I decorated our tree a few weeks ago, but there's still nothing beneath it. I haven't officially started Christmas shopping yet, but I have a few gift ideas in mind. Tonight is a great time to start, with Bailey over at her aunt's house babysitting her younger cousins.

I stop by Marshall's on my way home to see if I can find a great deal, but after circling the parking lot a few times, I give up and head home. When I open the door, Jen is sitting in my living room in front of the tree with a cup of tea, flipping through my holiday issue of O magazine.

"The furnace guy didn't come yet?" My furnace sounds like a drum roll when I turn up the heat.

"You're here early. I thought you said you were going shopping."

"There wasn't any parking, so I said forget it. I'm tired anyway." I never need an excuse to come home and stay here. I drop my laptop and head towards the kitchen to make a cup of mint tea and join her in the living room. I plop down in the big chair, throwing my feet up on the ottoman and sliding my bare feet under the chenille throw. I stare at the crystal ornaments on the tree twinkling in the white lights. This is exactly how I like to spend my evening after a long day at work.

"Yeah, he came, but so did your issue of *Oprah*," she says, holding it up. "So I decided to stay."

It's not long before Jen and I start swapping the daily office fiascos and having an enjoyable laugh.

"So, enough about work. What's the deal with Shane?" Jen sets the magazine down.

"I told him you don't approve of our friendship." I reach for *O*.

"Well, what did he say? Don't hold back now," she says sarcastically, tossing the magazine over to me.

I start flipping through the pages, looking for new items to add to my vision board. "He says that he's still your client, just not mine."

"How does that work? He's got us planning a new event. Are you telling me I have to replace you?"

"I guess. I don't know. I don't think it's going anywhere. Honestly, we can stay like we are, friends."

"Shane and I are *friends*. You two got something else going on. I don't know who you think you're fooling. Y'all have been spending a lot of time together."

"He wants to date."

"Do you realize how ridiculous this sounds? No offense, but you're normal. Nothing about Shane's life is normal. Sorry. Us, sitting in front of the tree . . . is normal. He's probably out drag racing, popping bottles, or better yet, chilling in the strip club."

I exhale loudly. "Jen, we've been out almost every day for the last month. That's not normal enough for you?"

"Exactly, you just used the word, out. Shane's got ADD. Test my theory and invite him over. See if he's capable of relaxing by the tree like we are doing right now. See how he acts in your world. Let Shane experience NORMAL with Bryn in an everyday setting. You two can just . . . talk."

"I'll text him and see what he thinks about that."

`You want to come over and chill?`

He responds immediately.

`Yes`

I show Jen his text, stick my tongue out at her, and run upstairs to change into something more comfortable.

When Shane rings the doorbell, Jen collects her things. "On that note, I'm going to bed. I'll talk to you in the morning." She opens the door and gives Shane a quick hug.

Shane stands in my doorway in his usual winter attire, a hooded sweatshirt and basketball shorts.

"That was fast." I watch him look around before taking a seat.

"I don't put my tree up until Christmas Eve," he mentions arbitrarily.

"We're making our personalized ornaments this weekend so you have to come over and make one."

"Awesome." He dashes into the kitchen searching through the refrigerator and all the cabinets. "Oh yeah, and Christmas is for kids," he huffs after his third time in the same cabinet. Finally, he finds his treasure, golden stuffed Oreo cookies, and shoves a few in his mouth. I hate seeing him stuff his mouth like a four-year-old. "Where's Bailey?" He wipes his mouth with the arm of his sweatshirt.

I hand him a paper towel. "Bailey is with her aunt." He takes the towel and sits it on the counter.

"Thanks, did Bailey make her list?"

I'm distracted by his crumbs. I want to hold the towel over his mouth.

"Yes," I say and look away, hoping to forget what I've just witnessed.

He opens the refrigerator again, grabs the full container of Cran Grape juice, and removes the top. He takes a whiff. "What is this?" he says and frowns. "Are you getting everything on Bailey's list?"

"Grape juice. There's Fanta in the cabinet for you, and no, I'm not getting everything. You should see this list."

"Oh yeah?" He retrieves the Fanta from the cabinet and chugs it. "Give it to me, whatever you don't get, I'll get." He winks and takes another swig and wipes his mouth with his sleeve despite the paper towel lying next to his hand on the counter. "Aaahhh," he exhales. "What does a woman who has everything want for Christmas?"

I smile, pointing to myself questioningly. He nods.

"Me? Oh . . . I don't know. An experience . . . I guess. Surprise me," I say coyly. "How about you? What does a guy who can get anything he wants, want for Christmas?"

"Something I've never had before," he says very sensually.

"Hmmm, something you never had before," I repeat as I walk away from the kitchen and head back into the living room area. He thinks he's slick, always quick on his feet. I start looking around the room for a distraction. I see a pack of playing cards on the edge of the side table. "Cards?" I offer.

He reaches and takes the cards out of my hand. "Sure, what's your wager?"

"Oh no, I don't wager on any type of game. I've had a bad experience. I got swindled once."

"Oh yeah, ha, ha . . . tell me," he says, shuffling the cards.

"Jen and I took Taylor and Bailey to the Poconos for Bailey's fifth birthday. On the first night, Jen and I were playing pool in the lobby. You might as well say I was playing alone because Jen doesn't know how to play. She couldn't hit one ball, not one. So, this guy walks over to watch and she stops attempting to play and asks him if he wants to take her place. He tells her that he's just 'okay' and only knows the concept of the game. That was all he needed for her to hand him her stick. He and I finished the game and I won. And I think twice more after that. All the while, he's complimenting my game and getting me all excited about my skills. And then he was like 'can we play just one more game'? I said, 'yeah, sure' and he was like 'okay, let's make it interesting and bet'. I said 'what's the wager? What's at stake here?' He said that if I won he had to do anything I asked him to do and vice versa. I was like 'oh NO—you're not trapping me.' I wanted to know exactly what I was getting into. He was like 'push-ups, on call push-ups.' I never heard of it, so I asked him to explain."

"On call is whenever he asks you to," he interjects and starts dealing the cards.

"Exactly. I agreed and he whipped my ass. I mean I don't even think I got the chance to hit one ball. He broke and knocked all the balls in and the game was over. I stood there in shock and horror and thank goodness it was only push-ups. I got hustled. All I could do was laugh. Over the next few days, whenever I saw him when I was running, working out, or doing yoga, he didn't bring it up. After two days, I figured he just forgot. Well, on the final night, the resort hosted a formal five-course dinner. Me, Jen, and the girls were seated, about to get our main entrée, when the waiter said that I was urgently needed in the front lobby. Since I'm a nervous nelly, I frantically excused myself from the table and darted towards the lobby. Jen was concerned too, so she followed me. I was thinking 'who on earth needs me in the front lobby?' When I got to the lobby, there was a group of about thirty guys in athletic wear. The guy walked over to me, gave me a big hug, and said 'drop and give me twenty'. I was beyond embarrassed and didn't want to do it. But I'm a woman of my word, so I did the push-ups in my dress. Jen stood behind me and laughed hysterically at the spectacle. From that day forward, I've never ever made any bets."

"He got you," he says with a half-smile, looking down at his hand.

"Yes, he did and it won't happen again."

Shane's beating me terribly and I'm starting to think he's counting cards. It's impossible for someone to lose as many times as I'm losing right now.

"Last one. All or nothing?"

"All or nothing." I shuffle the cards, allow him to cut, and shuffle again.

I lose, yet again.

"You really suck at playing cards."

"Jen says the same thing."

He collects the cards and places them back in their case. Then he snatches a pillow from my sofa and tucks it behind his neck.

"I don't know what it is, but I feel so relaxed when I'm over here. It's like I don't have any worries," says Shane, glancing up at the ceiling.

"Awww, that's a nice thing to say. I try to keep my home peaceful and drama free."

"It's not just that, I always have stuff constantly running through my mind and when I'm here it stops."

"Stuff like . . ." I nod, encouraging him to open up.

"My family. I'm pretty much responsible for everybody. I'm talking about every single person. They all depend on me for everything, not just money. I have to solve all their problems. I feel like it's always about what I can do for someone and it's never about what someone can do for me. Everyone is cashing checks, but no one is making any deposits."

"Oh Shane, that's got to be tough to deal with."

"Like, before you called me tonight, I had to break up a fight." He lifts his left elbow, showing me scrapes on his skin with dried blood.

"Are you serious? Why?"

"PlayStation. Madden NFL 08."

We both go quiet.

That is the stupidest thing I've heard today, but I don't judge him. I can't blame him for feeling slightly embarrassed. Family can be a blessing and a curse.

I look away, avoiding eye contact.

"You got any old pictures I can look at?" He changes the subject.

"I do. But I need your help getting them. They're in a large bin in my laundry room." He follows me downstairs.

He wants to see everything. I show him the highlight reel from my trips. Feeling up 'The Rock' at Madame Tussauds in London, sitting in the huge chair at Atlantis in the Bahamas, and holding a fake Oscar statue in L.A. He has questions for every destination. *What's the weather like in Trinidad? Why don't you wear your hair curly? Who did you party with in Vegas?*

"We should take a trip together." He gives me a bashful smile. Then he turns the page of the last photo album and a picture of me, Bailey, and her father falls to the floor. A shift in his mood occurs and I don't know what to say. He's withdrawn, unsure of himself. "I see you like them pretty boys." He chucks the photo into the plastic bin. "You look tired," he says, looking towards the tree. I can sense he's longing for something.

"Yeah . . . I am. It was a long day. I can't believe how late it is. It's way past my bedtime."

All of a sudden, he perks up. "You wanna chill and listen to my tunes?"

"Umm sure, do you have your iPod?"

"Why of course," he says with a smirk and pulls it out of his shorts pocket. Shane's been eager to play this playlist for me. I've turned him down a few times, but tonight I'll give him a chance.

"Where?"

"My docking station is in my bedroom."

"Ladies first." His grin is larger than the Cheshire cat in *Alice in Wonderland* as he follows me to my bedroom.

I dock his iPod and Tyrese's *Sweet Lady* begins to play.

Shane's confidence returns. Making himself comfortable, he stretches out and props three pillows behind his head. *What am I going to do with him?* I crawl onto the edge of the bed and lie on my back with my arms directly at my side. One wrong move and I'm on the floor.

"What color is this paint?" He moves closer to me.

"It's Moroccan Spice."

"And the walls?"

"I believe they are Warm Vanilla." I point to my Klimt above the headboard. "This was the first thing I bought for my house and I used it for inspiration."

"I like it," he says, turning on his side to face me. He slides his arm under my pillow and pulls me closer to him. I turn my back to him. "Your bed is so comfortable," he whispers.

"I agree." I close my eyes and fall asleep.

I wake up to Janet Jackson singing *Any Time, Any Place* and Shane flipping me on top of him. He's staring directly into my eyes. *Is he about to kiss me? Am I going to let him? If I do, there's no going back from here.* My mind's flooded with so many thoughts it goes blank. And then he kisses me.

What starts off as a simple peck quickly turns into a series of passionate kisses. We kiss for what seems like hours, although it's probably only ten minutes. I don't mind because there's nothing I love more than a man who can kiss.

Then he lifts me effortlessly, laying me on my back. Hovering over me on all fours, never breaking eye contact, he leans in for another kiss. I feel the intensity of the heat radiating from his body, but he restrains himself and just admires me. I take a deep breath, placing my hands on his face, then close my eyes and guide him in for another kiss.

He kisses my neck and shoulders, and eventually stops at my chest. His lips brush over the light material of my top. I stiffen as he lifts my shirt to expose my skin and softly licks my waistline. He continues to kiss down my side, reaching dangerous territory.

Instinctively, I grab my waistband. Quickly, but gently, he moves my hand and slides my pants down revealing my right thigh. I sit up and use my last reserves of willpower to resist him, but he lays his head on my pelvis, stopping me. *Oh, what the hell.* I'm enjoying this. Then, in one swift movement, my sweatpants are gone.

Bryn, what are you getting yourself into?

He brushes his face against my sheer panties. I'm doing my best to keep a straight face, but the music is right, the feeling is right, and his touch is right. Even though this isn't an ideal situation, I'm only human, there's only so much seduction one can take. Finally, I muster the strength to reach down and grab his chin, pulling his face up towards me. I shake my head no. He listens this time and flips me over on my stomach. I feel a delicate swoop of my hair to one side exposing the back of my neck. The kisses continue.

My senses are heightened and I feel like I'm going to pop as his hands gently run through my hair and down my spine. He reaches the curve of my back and flips me over and hovers over me, still staring. For a moment, he rests back on his heels. A half-smile flickers across his face. He lays my right hand against his chest, guiding it to his shorts, and presses it against a large, hard penis.

"I told you it wasn't small," he says, and abruptly leaps out of my bed.

"Oh, my." I'm sure my face is blood red. I've just been assaulted in a very lovely way. I collect my thoughts and stand up and grab my sweatpants. The only thing on my mind is the thing I just felt and how I want it unleashed on me. *I Care 4 You* by Aaliyah is playing when he stops the music.

I walk him to the door, not really wanting him to leave, but knowing that it's best. There're still lots of unknowns and so many questions to be answered. *What would Bailey think? How would she view me dating the man she looks at like a brother? She's eight. Would she really understand?* My mind races as we walk to the front door. He stops a few feet away from the door, leans down, and kisses me on the cheek.

Aww. My heart melts.

"Tell Bailey Baby not to forget about our movie date tomorrow." He opens the door and walks out.

"She'll be home by nine in the morning." I'm not sure if he hears me. I shut the door and look through the window, waiting for him to pull away so I can run next door to Jen's.

Once he's gone, I run out. Through a gap in her curtains, I see her lying on her chaise. I tap on the door and call her to warn her that it is me. She always thinks someone is going to break into her house. I don't get a response so I go back to the house and grab her spare key. I walk into the foyer and hit the light switch.

"AGH!" Jen screams and sits up in the chaise, desperately looking for her glasses on her chenille throw.

I plop down on the floor next to her elaborate white and silver tree. "It's me."

"Uhhhh," she groans. "What time is it?"

"It's about one."

"Y'all have been playing cards all this time? I left you around eight."

"Well, not necessarily. We did start off playing cards."

"Well, what have y'all been doing?"

"Talking, and oh, we looked at some old pictures from when Bailey was young, Bahamas, London, and a few old church photos."

"Hold on," she says, throwing her hand up to stop me. "Pause. Rewind. I better not have been in any of those old church pictures."

"Nnnnooooooo. I don't think so."

Jen is instantly wide awake. "Let me be clear. You better not have shown him any old church photos with me in them," she says, raising her voice.

"I said no. I don't think so. Anyway . . . I think he has a huge dick." I exaggerate and hold my hands shoulder-width apart.

"What?" Jen screams and sits up, tossing her throw pillows in all directions. "How did THAT happen?" she says, eyes wide.

"Well, he put my hand on it and said, 'I told you it wasn't small'." I laugh. Jen looks at me, confused. "Remember when we played the truth game and the lie detector thing said that he lied about his body part?"

"Oh yeah, that's right. You have a great memory. I forgot all about that. So, he just grabbed your hand and put it on his penis?"

"No, we were lying down in my room—"

She cuts me off. "Umm hmmm." With an unconvinced look, she says, "Start over. How did you get to the room? Tell me everything."

I tell her everything, leaving nothing out. Hearing about Shane having a sensitive side is hard for her to fathom. "Are we talking about the same Shane? We can't be."

"I know, right? But we are." I giggle, like a silly schoolgirl. "He's a completely different person when he's with me."

"Wait. Are you seriously considering dating him?"

"I—"

"Bryn, are you sure you're ready for this? You know he's an athlete and you see firsthand how he gets down. You can't afford to go into this with your eyes closed. You know he loves strippers, groupie girls, and those trifling reality chicks. Let's not forget the comment he made about how his side chicks have to be faithful. Dating an athlete is not child's play. If you do it, you better do it right. At least have a game plan."

"I know. I will." I feel the vibration from my cell in my robe pocket.

Goodnight sweetie. I'll see you when I fall asleep

21

GET ME BODIED

Christmas is a week away and the office is gloomy, unlike past years. No one has decorated their cubicles or handed out Christmas cards or stocked the kitchen with caramel popcorn or tins of delicious butter cookies. To make matters worse, I got an email this morning stating the annual holiday party is postponed indefinitely, so any hopes of seeing our controller dressed as Santa handing out bottles of vodka and Viagra again has been crushed.

This place used to be fun and I can't believe I'm going to miss it.

I walk over to the printer, grab a stack of plain white paper, and begin cutting paper snowflakes. *Merry Christmas everybody.* As

I tape them to my cubicle window, I hear shouting in the distance. *What the heck?*

Brian peeks over my cubicle. "Is that Alex?"

"I think so. Let me ask Imani." Before I can finish drafting the email, I see her name flashing on my caller ID. I grab the receiver before it can ring. "Hey girl, was that Alex?"

"Girl, yes. He just went off at Susanne," she says excitedly. "She came to his office complaining about you."

"What? Imani, you know what? I've had enough!" My anger level goes from zero to sixty instantly. "I'm going to punch that bitch in her face." I slam the phone down, kick off my heels, and replace them with the flip-flops stored under my desk. I leap to my feet, my chair slams against the back wall, and I charge into Susanne's office. Luckily for her, she isn't there.

"What did that bitch say about me?" I scream at Alex loudly enough for the entire floor to hear me.

"Come in and shut my door," he says with a red face. Calmly, he walks towards his office door and pulls the blinds shut. "Cruella comes to my office this morning asking why you haven't been here lately . . ."

As I listen to him speak, my left eye begins to twitch. Mentally, I start counting backwards from a hundred. A tap on Alex's door grabs our attention. When I reach for the handle, Alex stops me to first peek through the blinds, then he gives me the go-ahead to open the door. "Hey, I can clearly hear you through the wall, so I know they can hear you on that side," whispers Imani.

"I promise you, as sure as I'm standing here today—she's going to get fucked up. I'm tired of her shit. If she has a problem with me, she needs to bring it to me!"

Alex tries to hush me. "I told her if she has a problem with anyone using their personal time off, she should go to the HR department and speak with them about changing the paid time-off policy." Alex crosses his arms and leans at the front of his desk. "I mentioned your review and increase."

"And?"

"She shut it down. Said she believes that Michael's doing your work," he says, turning bright red in the face. "She's crazy."

"That's ludicrous."

"You know when I first interviewed you . . . she pulled me into her office and told me we needed to consider if you were a suitable fit for this position because you were a single mother who had a child out of wedlock. She wanted to promote Brian instead. Said he reminded her of her son and that he was young, vibrant, with lots of potential."

"Alex!" Imani yells, giving him a disapproving look.

My fists ball instinctively. "That's it!"

Imani jumps in front of the door, gripping the frame.

"That fucking conservative cunt! What was she implying? That I'm not qualified because I'm a single mother? Fuck her, I'm a damn good single mother! THIS single mother had a daughter at twenty, worked full time and went to college full time, graduated early suma cum laude with two major degrees. Young, vibrant Brian barely graduated from Catonsville Community College. Is she serious? I'm so sick of people stereotyping young women. Having my daughter at a young age and raising her on my own has never stopped me from doing anything. It's made me stronger and more determined to succeed." Tears start to stream down my face. "I've worked so hard for everything I've ever done and she's trying to discredit me? She thinks she can attack my integrity by saying someone else is doing my work—and get away with it? Her ass is MINE."

"Bryn, you're going to get fired." Imani pleads with me to stop.

"Bryn," interrupts Alex. "What she didn't realize was she offended me!" He points his finger forcefully at his chest. "My son, with my high school sweetheart, I didn't marry his mother!"

"I see red, my fist connecting with her face, and blood spilling everywhere." My eyes cut to Imani. "Please let me out. Talk about me? That's one thing. Talk about my child? Get ready to die."

Imani opens the door.

I'm on the hunt like a wild hyena, stalking the hall to the copier room, eyeing every head perched over the cubicles and peeking from offices. I'm *going* to assault her. Then Bailey pops to my mind. I'm *going* to get legal counsel.

I return to my desk and kick my chair out of the way and forcefully open all my drawers and cabinets, causing the contents to spill out. Section by section, I clear the desk of anything personal. The boxes fill quickly. *I'm going to need help carrying these. Perhaps the man doing all my work can help.*

I slam my desk drawers shut and call Michael.

"Michael speaking."

"I need you to help me carry something to my car."

"Sure, on my way."

"Great." I resist the urge to slam down the phone. I hear Brian poking around his desk.

"Bryn, what's going on?" He peeks around the wall, frightened.

"Brian, it's best I don't talk about it because I may get locked up. But thanks for checking on me. Honestly, I'm just trying to get out of here as soon as possible."

"Do you need help with anything? I can—"

"No thanks. I've got it. Michael's on his way up here. I really don't want you involved. It's only a matter of time before she sinks her teeth into you." I hear Michael talking in the hall. "See, there's Michael right now."

"Hey Brian. Do me a favor, when you see your boss, tell him I need those rate reports." Michael walks into my area. "Bryn, you moving?" He laughs.

"Here, take this." I hand him the box, grab the other one. "Follow me." I walk towards the elevators with all my belongings.

"Bryn, what are you . . ." he whispers, cutting himself off when he sees Susanne ahead. She's smiling and laughing with other managers.

I roll my eyes as we pass her.

"Where is she going?" Susanne says, loudly enough for me to hear.

"To see a lawyer!" I feel unstoppable as I press the down button. I imagine her standing, confused, trying to explain why her analyst is walking out with her desk packed.

The elevator doors open and we walk in. Before the doors can shut, Michael starts with the questions. "What happened? What are you doing? Are you quitting?"

"Michael, relax. I'm leaving for the day before I get an assault charge."

"Against who? Susanne?"

"Do you have to ask?" The elevator opens to the main floor. "I've basically been accused of being a fraud. According to Susanne, you've been doing all of my work."

"What?"

"She's a crazy, miserable bitch. Look, I'm tired of talking about this. I'll call you later."

"Alright, don't hurt nobody."

"Michael, not today."

"I know, I'm sorry. Give me a hug. *You* know I'm not doing your work. I'm just trying to help a sista out. I implemented the system, so I know how it works."

"We don't need to explain ourselves to the psycho. Anyhow, I appreciate your help." I shut my trunk, jump into Betsy, and blast out of the garage.

All I can think about is hitting Susanne. It's such bullshit. It's typical corporate America and their good ol' boy mentality. Throughout the years, I watched my mother come home from work, light up her cigarette, and call her girlfriend, complaining about her day at the office. They would talk well into the night and the same thing would happen at five the next evening. Eventually, she walked away from her corporate job and the phone calls ended. I couldn't understand then, but I sure as hell understand right now.

Fuming, I race home, driving like Danica Patrick. I call my mom for a sanity check. I need to talk quickly because all I've got is two minutes before she takes over the conversation. "Hey Mom."

"What's the problem?"

"How do you know there's a problem?"

"You only call me when there is."

"That's not true."

"What's going on?"

"Susanne," I sigh.

"Bryn, you've got to get a handle on her," she scolds.

"I'm going to put a handle alright. My fist in her face."

"Put her in her place, but keep it professional."

"I plan to visit HR on Monday. I had to get the heck out of there."

"Alright now. Make sure you document everything."

"She's a bully. She harasses everyone because she can. Nobody will touch her because the executives hold her in such high regard. Says she 'bleeds Merchant Bank blue'. It's sickening. She needs to be stopped. And I want to stop her with my foot in her ass."

"Remember what I told you back when you were in grade school . . ."

Here we go. I remain silent and let her give me the 'always be a lady' spiel. I get it. It's irrational to think I can solve my problems with violence, but the anger is still fresh. I'm not the first person to have a strained working relationship with her, she's been picking on people for years, but this time, she's not getting away with it. I hear an incoming call and peek at my screen. It's Shane.

"Mom, Mom . . . hey." I try to get a word in. "Let me call you right back, I've got an important call coming in and I've got to take it."

"Alright Bryn. Call me back."

I click over. "Hello."

"Good afternoon, sweetie, how is your day going?"

"You wouldn't believe it if I told you."

"Would you like to go to dinner tonight? All of us. You can bring Bailey baby."

"Nooooo, I'm not in the mood for a sit-down dinner tonight. I need to get drunk and dance."

"We can do that. TGS and some family are coming into town today, so that's cool. We'll get a party bus."

"Sounds like exactly what I need."

"Bye, sweetie."

I disconnect with Shane and call Jen. "Look, I need to get drunk and give my brain a rest for a few hours. I don't want to go to jail for beating down this bitch."

"Susanne again?"

"Girl, I was ready to swing. But Shane just called, so I'm feeling slightly better. Be ready by eight."

"Don't make me cuss you out."

"Be on time. Bye, I'll call you later." I put the car in park, put on my 'everything is fine' face, and walk inside the school. As far as Bailey knows, all is well. She's trying to hula hoop as I sign her out. She signals me to give her extra time. I arrived early, so I don't mind. I take a seat at the lunch table and wait for her to finish. That way I can secure a sitter for later.

"Hey Mom, can Sidney come over tonight?"

"Oh honey, I'm going out tonight. How about next time?"

"With who?" she whines, handing me her book bag.

"Aunty Jen, Shane, and crew."

"Where am I going? Can I go to Aunty's?"

"I already asked Nana if you can go to her place. She said you two were supposed to finish sewing something anyway."

"Perfect. Can we play Monopoly before you leave?"

I hesitate before responding and force myself to say yes. She brightens up as we walk to the car.

I prepare dinner and set up the Monopoly board while Bailey packs. As we wrap up dinner and roll the dice to see who goes first, my mother rings my doorbell. *Whew . . . just in time.* I give Bailey a big hug and kiss and send her off. As much as I love my child, I can really use a few hours alone without having to be responsible for anything or anyone or having to think about anything other than what I'm going to wear tonight.

I take my time getting ready, choosing a sexy little gold, slightly translucent, bandage dress accompanied by gold strappy heels. My black trench coat is just long enough to conceal the dress. Jen's in her normal party attire, a little black dress.

The party bus arrives to pick us up and it's full.

"She's a brick . . . houseeeeee," sings DeShaun as Jen walks on and takes her seat. I chuckle and give a quick wave to the crew and a few unknown faces. Jen, clearly embarrassed, covers her legs with her pashmina.

"Bryn! Jen!" barks Shane.

I wave to him and take a seat. Terry comes over and sits next to me.

"Who are all these people?" Jen looks up and down the aisle.

Terry points to a man who resembles Shane, wearing a basketball jersey and lots of bling, "Romello." Romello hears his name, looks over, nods, and throws up a peace sign. Terry points to a white man with dark hair and dark eyes who's fashionably dressed (in monogramed smoking slippers). "That's white boy Scott," says Terry. "And those girls?" He points to an Asian girl rubbing another girl's leg, who in turn is sticking her fingers in another girl's mouth. Terry shakes his head in disgust. "I don't know them. I don't want to know them. If you do, ask DeShaun."

The bus takes off.

Seconds later, my phone vibrates in my pocket. It's a text from Shane.

You look beautiful tonight

I smile, return a text, and turn my attention back to Terry who's rambling on about a new coaching opportunity.

We arrive at LOVE nightclub in D.C. "I think Luda is scheduled to perform," says Zander, as we all stare out at the line of half-dressed women wrapped around the building. They must be freezing, because the line isn't moving.

"Let's go!" Shane yells as our four-hundred-pound Samoan-looking bodyguard knocks on the bus doors. He waits for all of us to exit, but stays close to Shane, who takes the lead to the main doors. Thank goodness we're able to walk directly inside. It's packed in here, too.

Shane looks back at me a few times as we maneuver our way through the crowd. Then his security guard leaves him to take my hand. "Shane told me to walk with you. Too many dudes are checking you out," he huffs, out of breath.

I don't mind. This is perfect, his body so large it creates a personal walkway for me.

A hostess waiting in our VIP area has our table set with multiple bottles of Ciroc, Nuvo, and Moet Rose. She pours the first round, but the boys leave their glasses and each of them grabs a bottle and runs to the dance floor.

"Another round," Shane says to the hostess.

Qmar returns with a bottle of vodka for Shane. I make him a cocktail.

"Thank you." He smiles and then takes a sip. "Wow, this is perfect."

I know. I know him so well. "I'll be right back," I say.

"Where are you going?"

"I need to find the ladies' room."

"Wait, hold up," he says, leaning over to his security. "Take her to the bathroom."

The security guard drops me off at the bathroom and waits outside. It's a long line, mainly women primping in the mirror and causing a bottleneck to the sinks. When I finally resurface, I find Shane waiting next to the security guard. "What took you so long?"

"There was a long line in the ladies' room."

"Oh, I thought you were talking to some guy." He stares down at me.

"Seriously? In the bathroom?" I look up at him and smile. "Never mind. You want to dance?"

"I don't know how to dance to Jamaican music."

"Come on." I grab his hand and lead him to the dance floor. "You just need to wine ya waist," I say in my best Trini accent. "I know you can do it. I've seen you dance before." I smile, turning my back to him and pressing my ass against him. His hands fall to my sides as I wine my waist down low to the floor and back up. He lightly taps the side of my thigh and we sway back and forth. "See, you can do it," I say, smiling and looking over my shoulder.

We dance for three reggae mixes before he calls it quits and spins me around to face him.

"Girl, I'm about to tell everyone. I'm about to make you mine." Caressing my cheek, he lifts my chin up to look at him.

"What about Terry? He's going to be mad at you for stealing his girl," I tease.

"I think he'll have to get over it. Come on. Let's go back to the table with everyone. After you." He extends his arm for me to lead the way.

We step over a slew of new people to find an open space for the two of us. TGS, Romello, and the girls have gathered a group of girls from the general area to dance with. Terry finally seems to have given up on the idea of me. Even he's found a tall, fair-skinned, big-boned girl to woo.

Shane excuses himself and walks over to Romello, so I sit down next to Jen, who looks like she's had a few drinks.

"Did something happen? Why did Shane leave?" Jen sways offbeat to the music.

"He came looking for me. He was waiting outside the ladies."

"I saw him bolting out of here." She throws her hands in the air.

"He thought I was talking to a guy . . ." I say, shaking my head.

"That's insane, you're not like that."

"Have you been drinking?"

"Romello made me hold my mouth open and he poured Moet down my throat. But I saw y'all dancing."

"Yeah, it was fun—he really knows how to move his hips." I fall back laughing at the arousing thought that just crept into my mind. "Umm yeah, I need a drink."

I fill a champagne flute with Nuvo and sip it while I watch everyone having a good time. Out the corner of my eye, I see a girl with a heinous tattoo sleeve wearing a tight, black strapless jumpsuit, surveying Shane and slyly making her way over to him. He doesn't see her, but I can tell DeShaun does, because he quickly jumps out of the way to give her a clear path. She tilts her head and slides her hand down Shane's arm. Shane gives her a 'hey, long time no see' look.

I feel slightly jealous of the attention he's giving her. *Do I have the right to feel this way?* We're not *technically* an item, yet.

"Fix your face. It comes with the territory," says Jen, falling against me, then catching her balance. If you're going to date a high-profile individual, work on ignoring stuff like this. You came with him. Remember that."

"You're right. I get up and walk towards DeShaun, since he's staring me down.

"Hey!" Shane mouths 'where are you going?'

I point in the direction of the ladies' room. He excuses himself and reaches for me. "You just went."

"I need to powder my nose."

"You're already beautiful. Come on. Dance with me." He pulls me by the arm and I'm all smiles again.

We dance, drink, talk, drink, and dance again until my feet go numb and I can no longer feel my toes. I take a break. I lean on Shane, pressing my whole body against him, and rest my chin on his chest. He glances down and then clutches my waist. "You know they're looking at us," he says.

"I don't care, let them look." I pull him closer. "You smell delicious."

He blushes. "You having fun? Enjoying yourself?"

"Yessssssssss," I nuzzle my face to his chest. "Thank you, I really needed this, it's been a tough week."

"What about Jen? She's been sitting down all night." He points in her direction.

"She's fine, we don't have to babysit. Romello got her a little tipsy."

"That's my cousin for you."

"You two look alike."

"Yeah, we're really close. We're like you and Jen." He looks directly into my eyes. "Why are you staring at me like this?" He tries not to blush. "Your eyes are so big, sincere. Fuck it. They'll just have to know." He leans down and kisses me on the lips. His lips are full and so soft.

I reach my arms around his neck. We stare into each other's eyes and laugh. He doesn't have to say a word, we have an unspoken connection. He kisses me again. We're lost in our own little world until the DJ plays *Get Me Bodied*, the girls' club anthem by Beyoncé.

The guys immediately line up and stare at all the girls in our area going crazy doing their best rendition of Beyoncé's booty bounce. They're dropping their asses to the floor and have everyone's attention, including Shane's. I'm old school and refuse to mimic them. At least I do until I look over at Jen who's looking back at me as if to say 'whatcha gonna do about it?' At that exact moment, when it's time to drop down low, I conform. Shane covers his mouth.

"Bryn must be drunk!" screams Terry, running over to us with a glass of Moet in his hands. He trips over the edge of the center table and spills his glass on top of my head. "Oops, I'm sorry, B."

I want to punch him. Excusing myself, I walk over to grab bar napkins to soak up the champagne dripping from my bangs, onto my chest and down my dress. I dab and dab, tossing the sticky napkins away and grabbing more. There's a huge wet spot in the front of my dress. I reach behind Jen to grab my trench coat when I feel a hand creeping up my backside. *Shane's so naughty.* Then I hear a girl's voice say, "Shane needs to share that."

"What the FUCK was that?" I snap to a standing position and clench my entire body. The Asian girl from the bus winks at me and walks over to Shane. I hit Jen. "Why didn't you warn me that *girl* was behind me? She touched me. What the fuck, Jen, I thought she was Shane."

"What? I didn't see her touch you." Jen can't see for shit at night, let alone in a dark nightclub. "She was over here asking me if you were with Shane," she slurs.

"Move over so I can sit."

The Asian girl is talking in Shane's ear. She might as well forget it, whatever she's thinking.

"Are you having fun?" Jen asks me.

"Yeah, I think I'm really starting to like him. He's so sweet, caring, and very attentive—a little bit possessive but nothing too serious."

"I forgot to tell you when he stopped by a while ago that he said he wants to be serious with you. He says you're not just a plaything. He really wants me to know and accept things. I think he was kind of asking for the best friend approval. Not necessarily the business side of things. He knows I'll cut him if he hurts you."

"Awww, he's just so ador-wa-ble," I say in toddler-speak. "I'm still laughing about him not wanting me to go to the ladies' room alone."

"You know what that means."

I stare at Jen blankly.

"He's either insecure or jealous. And his behavior, past and present, suggests both."

"Honestly, it doesn't matter. I'm feeling great. I want to dance and enjoy this feeling for as long as it lasts. I'm tired of always analyzing and thinking and trying to figure things out. What is he thinking or why is he thinking it. I want my hair to dry and I want to keep having fun. I don't want this night to end."

Jen looks at her watch.

"What time is it?" hollers Shane.

"Three-thirty," she says.

Shane looks at his Chopard. "Let's go. Never close out the club." He grabs my waist and walks me out.

We fight through the crowd of drunken people to the bus. I walk on first and head straight to the back sofa and wait for Shane. He's staying at the front taking headcount. Once everyone's accounted for, Shane gives the driver the 'okay' and the doors shut.

The strobe lights on the party bus flicker to the beat of the music and hip-hop music plays loudly. Shane works his way to the back and plops down next to me, resting his hand on my trembling thigh. "You cold?" His lips touch my ear.

"Slightly."

He takes off his suit jacket and lays it over my legs. "Better?"

"Yes, much better," I whisper, nipping the tip of his earlobe and laying my head on his shoulder.

"Look at them," Shane whispers in my ear, sending a tingling sensation down my spine. His lips graze my ear; his voice, soft and warm, gives me chills. I smile at his smile. I can't help but laugh at Romello who's now in the center aisle rapping to Jay Z's *Big Pimpin'*. He's drunk out of his mind, using the railings and poles on the bus as monkey bars.

White boy Scott is trying to feel up Jen who's swatting his hand after each attempt (even though he's her type). DeShaun is passed out with a bottle of liquor in each hand and the Asian girl grinding on his lap. Zander is giving a speech to anyone who'll listen about the difference between a visa to travel with and a Visa credit card. Roman is loudly singing a slow song. Qmar is on the phone and Terry is in the far corner sulking.

I giggle, nuzzling my body against Shane's arm. Pulling his hands from under his jacket, I rub my hands with his for extra warmth. His fingers are long and thick. I make a tighter circle around each one of his fingers, changing the intensity at different sections. Without taking his eyes off the guys, he palms my leg like a football. I guide his hand between my thighs. He knows exactly what I want at this point. As his fingertips finally reach my panties, he slips them to the side.

I want to explode like fireworks, but I have to keep my composure.

The bus stops at my house first. Everyone's oblivious to us, so I manage to adjust my dress and hand Shane his jacket unnoticed. Shane follows me off the bus and walks me to the door. He reaches out to embrace me and I give him a tight squeeze. His body is rock hard and my mind recalls him shirtless. He grips my waist, squeezing tightly, the pressure intoxicating. "I need to see you tonight. Can I come back?"

I give him a few pats on the back as reassurance to any onlookers and leave him standing there unanswered.

He pleads again. "Let me make you feel good, Bryn."

I shake my head no, but tell him yes.

Shane breaks for the bus at top speed. The doors shut and the bus peels away from the curb making a terrible screeching sound. I can only imagine what he said to the driver.

22

<u>BLAME IT</u>

"What am I doing?" I whisper to myself loudly, letting out an intoxicated chuckle. I leave the door slightly ajar. Feeling sexy and guilty at the same time, I kick off my heels, drop my purse at the door, and twirl around in my living room. On a natural high, I feel like I can fly. I haven't felt this way in years.

I stare at myself in the mirror above my fireplace and tousle my hair to create a sultry look. A flicker of light shines through the window and I hurry upstairs. The front door creaks and then I hear his heavy footsteps and the door locking. My heart beats in my ears as I scurry to the edge of my bed and position myself in an inviting pose.

Once again, Shane stands confident, *American Gladiators*-like, except now it's at the entrance to my bedroom. Unlike our first meeting, he's not the least bit clumsy. He approaches me with intense bedroom eyes and hovers over me, licking his lips, giving me a boyish grin. He leans in, ever so slowly, and kisses my lips.

He brushes my shoulder strap. His touch is so tender I could cry. My dress practically melts off from his touch. He draws back, appreciating my shape, then slips my bra strap so it falls off my shoulder. He's all smiles as he releases the other strap. Looking deep into my eyes, he kisses me passionately again and again. I close my eyes and exhale.

"You sure you ready for this?"

I'm unsure, but I nod yes anyway.

"You sure? I don't want you to regret this."

"I'm sure."

"I'm going to make you fall in love," he whispers tenderly into my ear.

My body is literally aching for his touch.

I wake up tangled in my sheets with Shane's large arm tightly wrapped around my waist. I can't believe this. Shane's a complete lover. He leaves no stone unturned, I couldn't ask for anything more. I give his shoulder a kiss. He stretches his muscular body and rolls onto his back. "Last night was wonderful. Come here," he says, licking his full lips. "Sit here," he requests, tapping his chest.

I stall. *Is he crazy?* It's daylight and I'm naked. *Fuck, I should've gotten up earlier.* I need my bra. Impatient, he pulls me on top of

Bianca Williams

his chest with ease. I instinctively grab the top sheet to cover my chest, then giggle, trying to seem girlishly shy, when I'm actually horrified because my breasts are real and a size DD. I drop my head and peek through my hair at him. Licking his lips, he yanks the sheet off and grabs my arms which are cupping my girls.

"I want to see. I like to look." He replaces my hands with his. "I love your breasts."

"Really? I think I could use a slight lift."

"They are beautiful. Everything about you is beautiful." He slowly glides his hands down the shape of my body, resting them on my thighs, then squeezes. "Come on," he begs, gently guiding my legs over his shoulder one at a time. "I want you to sit on my face."

Mercy!

I gyrate my hips to the soulful sounds of Lloyd *Certified*, letting the full weight of my head fall back, while holding onto the headboard for support. The sensation of it all makes my legs weak and in my mind, I see myself going limp and falling on top of him. I let out a small chuckle.

"What's funny?" He lifts my hips for a moment.

"Nothing." It's never appropriate to laugh during sex, especially oral, but I think I've got some emotional wires crossed.

"Did you come?"

"Yes, plenty of times."

"Good, my turn." He slowly sits me on top of him and by the first thrust, I'm in ecstasy.

I'm straddling a sleeping Shane who's passed out with his mouth wide open. The sound of his cell alarm wakes him.

"Hey babe." He grabs his cell phone. "I'm late. I've got meetings!" He jumps up, panicked, and quickly searches my room for his things. "Give me a kiss. I'll get fined $10,000 if I'm late." He crawls over the bed with one arm still out of his T-shirt. "I will see you later." He kisses me.

"Wait, I'll walk you to the door." I grab my white plushy robe. He leans down as I reach up on tippy toes to give him a big kiss goodbye. I close the door and lock it. He bolts to his truck.

Frantically, I look for my phone to call my mom and check on Bailey. "Hey Mom. What are y'all doing?"

"Nothing much, Bailey and I are in here making pancakes. Did you have a good time last night?"

"Yeah, in fact I'm still tired. Can I lie back down for a nap and get her after twelve or so?"

"Sure. We're fine, get some sleep."

"Thanks. I'll call you when I get up."

I hang up the phone and walk into my room. My bed is a mess. The blanket and pillows are thrown all over the floor. I put everything into the washing machine, change the sheets, and jump into the shower. The scalding hot water ripples down my body. I close my eyes and I see him, feel him, and get chills reminiscing about his touch.

I get out of the shower, put on the white T-shirt he left behind, and jump into the freshly made bed. Five minutes of snuggling into my pillows and my phone bleeps.

Bianca Williams

Hey baby, I wanna come see you after
work

What time?

50 minutes

Can't wait

Shit, I just lay down. My body is stiff and my girl is sore. *How is this going to work? His ass just left. Uggggghhh.* I jump up and find a sexy panty and bra set to put on. I text Jen and tell her we need to delay our trip to Home Depot because Shane's coming back over. Running into my bathroom in pure panic, I try to do something with my hair which is flat and stringy. I toss it around a bit and apply fresh make-up with lots of lip gloss. I run around for thirty minutes and then like clockwork, he's here.

I open the door and watch him jump out of his Range Rover, skipping up to the door like a five-year-old at a playground. He makes me laugh. He's all smiles as he reaches my doorstep. He removes his gray pullover sweatshirt. I can hear En Vogue's song *What a Man* on repeat in my head, as I get a sneak peek at his chocolate abs.

"How's my baby?"

"I'm good," I reply shyly, heading to the kitchen to grab a drink.

He studies me like a lion studies its prey, ravenous, as if he's going to pounce any second now. I slowly back up towards the refrigerator. "Want something to drink?"

"Just you." He moves in for the kill, lifting me straight up. I wrap my legs around him and he carries me through the house to my bedroom. My legs begin to tremble. I barely have any strength left.

I lie awake feeling completely satisfied. He's sleeping soundly while his playlist is on repeat. I blissfully hum along with Alicia Keys' *Butterflies,* marveling at the contrast of his dark skin against my white sheets. I turn to face him and admire the breadth of his back, and the deep concave of his spine that seems to run endlessly. My goodness, he's so sexy, untamed, and dangerous. I pull myself closer to him, placing my face right in the middle of his back and inhaling his delicious fragrance. He smells expensive. He awakens from my touch and turns to face me.

"I see somebody is awake," I tease, staring at him at full attention.

Smiling, he rolls over and pulls me into his chest. "That was amazing. Your love-making is very flattering." He caresses my cheek.

"How so?" I ask, smiling.

"It's how you respond to me."

"Well, you're pretty fucking amazing." I gently trace the outlines of his tattoos.

He exhales. "Your touch feels so good. Come to daddy." He pulls me in, biting his bottom lip.

For a moment, I feel like I'm going to die. I swear we just went three hours non-stop. He's out cold and although I would LOVE to roll over and go to sleep, I take this opportunity to run into my bathroom. I slide off the bed, slowly pull my top sheet from under his leg, wrap it around me, and dart into the bathroom. I let the hot water run for a while to get it really hot. I look up into the mirror and laugh at the way I look. My hair is tossed all about. My mascara and eyeliner have created huge bags under my eyes. I splash water over my face. When I look back into the mirror, Shane is standing behind me. The top of my head barely reaches his armpits.

"You *are* really short," he says, rubbing his chest and admiring himself in my mirror. "It's funny, because we're the same size in bed."

"You're stupid." I laugh.

He smacks my ass, making it sting. "What are you doing for the rest of the day?"

"Ouch! That hurt." I rub the sore spot. "Terry invited me to his basketball game, so we're going for support."

"Are we going to tell him?"

"No!" I spin around, facing him. "We're not telling anybody."

"Good, I was hoping you'd say that, because I don't want to hurt him. He *really* likes you a lot."

I give him a sarcastic look. As if I haven't heard that a thousand times.

"Alrighty then, I've got to leave, gotta get the kiddies." He touches his scar. "The babysitter is going to kill me, she had to stay extra-long last night." *Babysitter? Really? I'm not buying it.* I follow him into my room and watch him pick up his clothing scattered across the floor. Leaning on the doorframe, I watch him dress.

"I want you to know that we don't have to do this."

He stops in his tracks.

"We can look at it like a one-night thing and keep it moving. Like friends hooking up one time and realizing it was a mistake?"

He turns to me, eyes full of sincerity. "No. That's not what I want. Shit, we ain't stopping now." He caresses my cheek, lifts my chin, and looks directly in my eyes. "Yeah . . . this is mines now." Shane smacks me on the ass again.

I walk him to the door, locking it behind him. I peek out the window and watch him skip to his truck. *He's such a big kid. What have I done?*

A million thoughts rush into my mind, but before I even try to process what just happened, I must get some rest. I plop down on my sofa, snuggle in my chenille throw, and close my eyes.

I jump when I hear Jen open my front door. "Are you decent?" she yells.

"Ha, ha, ha."

She opens the door wide then slams it shut. "So, how did this happen? I knew this was going to happen as soon as you sent Bailey over to your mother's house," she scolds.

I cover my face with a pillow. "Jen, I *must* sleep. You don't understand. I've been up for over twenty-four hours and I'm so weak, I feel like I'm holding onto life by an inch."

"You text me NOT to come over and now you won't tell me anything?"

"Jen, it was amazing. The *best* sex I've ever had in my life. I'll fill you in on the details later. I need at least thirty minutes. Please?"

"Are you still planning on going to the basketball game?"

"Yes, but only if I'm able to rest. I promise on our friendship, I'll fill you in."

"You make me sick!"

"*I* only need fifteen minutes to get ready." I laugh and pull the cover over me.

She slams the door shut.

My phone wakes me, but I need five minutes. I lie awake on my back. I imagine him, hovering over me with a sly grin on his face. I smile, wishing it wasn't a fantasy. *Oh, how I wish I could cancel. I promised. Bryn, get up.* I promised Terry I would be there for his big debut as head coach of his boys' new basketball team. At the very thought of Shane, I feel his tongue tickling my side. *Shit, if I don't get up now, I'll be here all night.* I roll off the sofa and get dressed. Five minutes to game time, it's too late to pick up Bailey.

As Jen and I enter the gym, we see Terry at the home team bench with a look of pride on his face. I laugh and shake my head, *Lord help him.* We both wave at him and he waves back, summoning us over. "Hey y'all. Thanks for coming," giving us hugs. "You tired, B?"

"Exhausted," I say.

"All that dancing you were doing last night, I saw you. You were so drunk."

"Yeah, I know."

"Look, sit on the top bench in the back and wait for Shane, he said he was coming."

"Really? Doesn't he have to check in to the hotel?" Jen glances at me.

"Umm yeah, but he has until six. I know he was moving earlier, but he said he would be here." Terry waves over the referee. "Sorry y'all, we about to start."

"We'll sit back there," I say. "Moving. Really?" I mutter under my breath. *Maybe that was the excuse he gave Terry for being missing most of the morning.* We manage to get seated seconds before the opening buzzer sounds. I take my time climbing to the top of the bleachers, assisting each thigh by swinging my leg over each level.

"Alright, Mildred—pick it up." Jen loudly claps her hands.

"Girl, you have no idea." I turn, hearing a commotion building behind us. What was he thinking? Shane enters and everyone notices.

I sit, saving seats for Shane and crew. Roman runs to me. I stand and greet him with a hug. "You have fun last night, babe?"

"I had fun. How about you?"

"Yeah, it was alright." He adjusts his cap. "You look worn out. That's what happens when you stay up late playing cards."

"Huh?"

"I went to McDonalds and saw Shane's truck outside your house. He said y'all were playing cards."

"Oh right! This is why I shouldn't drink." I give Shane the death stare (moving? cards? He couldn't think of better excuses?) as he takes huge steps up the bleachers, passing over multiple levels. He reaches the top and stands in front of us.

"You not going to speak?" he blurts.

"Shane!" Jen throws her arms around him. He smiles and returns the hug. After he lets her go he turns in my direction, towering over me like a tree, raising his eyebrows.

"Hey." I give him a hug and feel him cupping my ass with both hands, giving it a squeeze. *OMG, I hope NO ONE just saw what he did.*

He releases me, forces a wedge between Jen and me, and takes a seat. He looks over Jen's shoulder as she's texting and throws his body weight into her. She screams at him and he throws his body weight into me and palms my thigh.

"AGH!" I grab his hand.

Startled, he jumps back. "What?"

"I'm sore," I whimper and rub my upper thighs.

"What were you doing last night?" He leans in to whisper in my ear. "Who was you fucking?" He pinches my butt again.

"Shane!" Jen sits upright and folds her hands in her lap and primly asks, "Would you like anything from concession?"

"Yes." Reaching out to give her a high-five, he grabs her hand. "What they got?"

"The normal. Hotdogs, chips and soda."

"They got honey buns?"

"I can check."

"Get me two hotdogs and some BBQ chips, oh and a Fanta. Make sure it's orange! Oh, and a honeybun if they have any. If they don't have Fanta, get a Gatorade. Here, get whatever you want." He pulls a few $20 bills from his gym shorts and gives them to Jen.

Jen stands and asks everyone else if they want anything. Everyone puts in an order.

"I'll go with you," I say, standing up.

"Where are you going?" Shane pulls me back by my back pocket.

"I'm going with Jen to help her carry this stuff," I say, looking back at him.

"Nah, you sit down." He points to the bench. "I'll send one of them. I don't want anyone looking at your butt."

23

EFF THAT

"Mom, Mom, Mom!" calls Bailey, waking me up way too early on a Sunday. She jumps onto my bed. "I got a text from Shane. He asks what we have planned for today. I told him nothing. So, he asked if we can come see him play tonight?" she finishes, out of breath.

"I think it's an eight o'clock game tonight. That's a bit—"

"I'm off from school tomorrow. It's Elementary Conference Day."

"Well, tell him I said yes."

Bailey runs out of my room. I hear her on the phone.

"He says he's coming to pick us up!" she shouts. "He says Jen can come too."

"Sure. Let her know." I pull the covers over my head to get some much-needed rest.

I lie in bed all day. I can still smell his cologne. My sheets are saturated with his scent. I inhale, close my eyes, and let my mind wander until I fall asleep again.

Bailey makes sure to drag me out of bed an hour before Shane is scheduled to arrive. I'm functioning, but at a very slow rate. I toss on a pair of skinny jeans with his jersey.

The doorbell rings incessantly along with rapid pounding on the door. Bailey rushes to open it. Shane's running back to his truck and he leaps into the driver's seat. "Come on. I'm late," he yells from the truck, honking his horn.

"Where's Jen?" he fusses. The back door swings open and Roman helps Bailey inside.

"She's walking out her door right now." He snaps his neck towards her door.

Jen walks to the truck while talking on the phone. "Hold on. Shane, we can't fit back here. I'll drive."

"Roman, come sit on Terry's lap. Jen! Get in!"

"Shane, it's fine. I can drive."

"Jen, get in the truck," he says calmly.

"Look, I gotta go," Jen says to whoever she's talking to, and hops in the back with Bailey, Roman, and me. "Aww. Look. Three peas in a pod."

Shane hits the gas like he's auditioning to be in the next installment of *The Fast and the Furious* series.

"SHANE!!! My equilibrium. Please, please slow downnnn." Jen grips the armrest. Shane turns his music louder than Jen's cries and continues to accelerate. "If I make it out of this truck alive, I swear I will NEVER ride with you again!" Jen covers her face. I believe she's praying.

Roman and Bailey laugh at her while Shane swerves on the beltway and speeds to the stadium.

Ten minutes later, Shane takes a sharp left turn, tossing us around in the back seat. "Hold on!" he belts, coming to an abrupt stop at a security booth. He flashes a badge and takes off again down a winding dark road, pulling into a lot filled with Bentleys, Hummers, Range Rovers, and Mercedes Benzes.

Shane hops out and opens the door for me. "I miss you," he whispers, then runs to catch up with Terry. We follow Shane through a tunnel of fans shouting his name. They're leaning against the metal security gates. Mr. Creeper McCreeper is holding the players' entrance main door. He keeps his eyes to himself as we pass through and into the elevators.

My phone vibrates in my pocket.

Wish me luck

Shane has his back to me.

You are the greatest (kissy face)

Can we celebrate tonight?

Yes, my Champion

"Yes!" Shane shouts and jumps.

"What's up, yo?" Terry hits Shane for startling him.

"*Up* comes out in May."

Shane is failing at cover-ups. He's coming up with the lamest excuses.

"You and Bryn need serious help with the Disney obsession," says Jen.

"Bailey, it's a date," says Shane.

"Yes," she whispers and steps out of the elevator.

"Hey Shane, what's your count?" Ms. Mable, the team mom, reaches for wristbands.

"Terry, take care of that." Shane swings his Louis Vuitton backpack onto his shoulder and hustles away.

"Shane, where's Carice?" she shouts and looks at me.

I shrug my shoulders.

"Taking care of her kids!" he yells back before disappearing into the players' locker room.

"Hey babies, good to see you again. Jason told me the news." She smiles, hands Terry four bands, and motions for us to pass.

We enter what I would consider a small room, small for a fifty-three-man roster and their families. It's filled with round blue plastic tables, white chairs, and a few leather lounge sofas off to the side. In the bar area is a small buffet and what seems like an unlimited number of drinks. I scope out five seats for us at a table with a loud older woman who's wearing a full-length fur coat. By the way she's screaming at the small television, she's a football mom.

Jen immediately makes friends and we find out she's Jason's mother.

"I told Jason if you're as good as everyone is saying, I'll hire you girls to plan my sixtieth. I want to keep it grown and sexy." She's already taken a liking to Jen.

Roman finds us and plops down next to Bailey. "What up, little cookie?"

"Roman, will you walk her over to the food and see what's in there, please?" I ask.

"It's chicken fingers, you want some chicken fingers?"

Bailey nods her head yes. As Roman jumps up, I nudge Bailey to follow him. "Grab me a Sprite while you're up."

"Me too," Jen chimes in, breaking away from pitching an event to Jason's mother.

I tune everyone out and follow Shane's every move on the television.

After the game, Shane's jumping, shouting, running, and high-fiving fans as we leave the stadium.

"Man, that game was nice," says Terry.

"Did you see the way I put Manning on his back?" shouts Shane as we squeeze back into his truck.

"Yeah!" Roman yells from the back seat.

Shane blasts his music and speeds out of the lot and into the city, driving the scenic route home, taking Charles Street to get on 83. We pass Red Maple nightclub, the official after-party of the Nighthawks games, and the line is long. "What time is it?" Shane slams on his brakes.

"Twelve-thirty," says Terry.

"Fuck, we won't make it back in time."

"Shane!" Jen grabs Bailey's head.

"Sorry Bailey, earmuffs. Here." He reaches into his pocket. "A twenty for the swear jar."

"You can say it again if you want," says Bailey.

We all laugh.

I feel a pang of guilt because they want to celebrate this win, and I can't, because I have Bailey with us.

"Shane," says Jen. "How about y'all go to the club and Bryn can take us home and come back to pick y'all up?"

Shane hits the brakes a second time, looking back at me. "Would you do that for me?"

"Of course."

He makes the block and pulls his truck directly in front of the nightclub. They all jump out and I take my place in the driver's seat. Jen gladly takes the front passenger seat. My small body is lost in his seat.

The ride is terrifying and fun at the same time. The truck accelerates at the slightest touch of the foot, unlike Betsy, which feels like pedaling with the Flintstones. The ride is so smooth it seems the tires aren't touching the road. Home in record time. Ninety miles per hour felt like forty.

"What are you going to wear?"

"Are you seriously asking me that? I'm wearing what I have on." I put the truck in park.

"Are you crazy? The Nighthawks just won. Shane was the man. Every hoochie momma in Baltimore will be there tonight trying to 'celebrate'." She winks as if I don't catch her drift. "You need to be on point. You can't afford to get lazy." She pulls up a picture of a video vixen on her cell phone. "This, my dear, is your competition and *she* isn't wearing jeans."

"Help me pick out something," I say as I jump out of his truck.

"I thought so."

Jen sends me back downtown dressed in a sexy, but classy, little black dress with very high heels. I find an empty park directly in front of the club and slither out of the front seat so no one driving by gets a peek.

"Sorry, the door is closed," says the bouncer as I approach him.

"I'm just picking up Shane Smith."

"Oh, that was you who dropped him off?"

"Yes."

He opens the door for me.

Everyone in the club is dancing and I see all kinds of women bent over, touching their toes, for a couple of Nighthawks. The sad part is they have no idea it will most likely end up as a one-night stand. Unfortunately, I hear the way they talk about these types of girls, referring to them as 'club scum'.

I spot Terry, Roman, and Jason and join them people-watching. I notice a disrespectful little girl run over to Shane and start shaking her booty for him. Shane has noticed I'm here and he covers his mouth and shakes his head. She continues to pine desperately for his undivided attention, bending over and lifting her skirt to reveal to everyone that she's going commando.

"She's in for a rude awakening," says Terry, nudging me in my shoulder.

"Why do you say that?" I ask.

"Because Shane doesn't spend his money on women and it's obvious that's what she's about."

"Yeah, well, they both need to do better!" I shout over the music, unable to ignore that Shane now seems to be enjoying the show she's putting on for him.

All of a sudden, I feel someone palm my ass cheek and squeeze it. I quickly turn around and see Roman, who is still standing next to me. "What the fuck, Roman, did you just grab my ass?" I yell, leaning into his ear.

"No, I would never do that," he says, shaking his head. "I swear, I didn't grab your ass," he pleads.

"What the fuck y'all arguing about?" says Shane, butting in and leaning his ear towards me.

"Someone just grabbed my ass and I asked Roman if it was him."

Shane eyes Jason but then jumps back, scowling at Roman. "You grab her ass?"

"I swear Shane, I didn't grab her ass," he bawls.

"I did it," brags Ezra, shoving through the crowd of partygoers.

I give him a perplexed look.

"Nah, not this one brah," says Shane, pulling me into him. "Nah, touch this again and you'll see me on the field." He signals a cutting of his throat.

"My bad. I didn't realize," says Ezra.

Shane looks angry so I move closer to him, hoping to relax him. He leans down and kisses me on the lips.

"Nah, I don't want you around my teammates. I don't want you doing Jason's party."

"Jen just booked another event with Jason's mother."

"Nah. He's going to try and fuck you. Eff that."

24

DING DONG, THE WITCH IS DEAD

Monday morning, as I'm shimmying down the hall, I run into Imani standing at Alex's office door. "Good morning, you two."

"Excuse me, black suit, make-up, and jewelry?" Imani winks at me. Are we interviewing today?" she whispers.

"Let's just say I feel like a million bucks . . . so I might as well look it." I stop and strike a runway pose.

Imani jokingly gives three snaps in the air. "Alright girl. We're in here talking about Alex's best buddy, Susanne."

"Girl, she can kiss my ass."

"Look." She points to Susanne's office at the end of the hall. "It's nine o'clock and it's still dark," says Imani.

"Yeah, Bryn, what did you do with the body?" shouts Alex.

I poke my head into his office. "I had such a wonderful weekend, I forgot all about Susanne."

"Do tell," laughs Imani.

"No." Alex points to Imani. "I need her to share whatever drugs she's on." Alex holds out his hand. "Come on. Don't be selfish! Sharing is caring."

"No drugs. It's a secret. A big, dark secret." I smile and continue down the hall to my cubicle.

"Bryn!" shouts Alex. "Come back. I'm not done with you." He walks over to meet me. "You've been subpoenaed to visit the HR department by Mrs. Gretchen Capparino herself."

"Is that right?"

"Yes."

"Do I need my lawyer present?"

"You don't have a lawyer. But you can thank me later." He hits me on the arm and turns away.

"So there's no need to worry?"

"Not one bit." He looks back, gives me a wink, and then walks into his office.

I sign in at the reception desk and take a seat. "They're expecting you," says a young lady. "Please follow me." She takes me to Gretchen's office where she and the CEO, Hugh Rogers, are seated at a small round table.

"Welcome and please take a seat," says Gretchen, a tall, sickly-thin brunette with a plastic face and extremely arched eyebrows. "I'm sure you know Hugh, the CEO of Merchant Bank? I hope you don't mind. He asked to sit in on our meeting today."

He stands and firmly shakes my hand. "Good to see you again, Bryn."

Should I remind him the last time I saw him, he verbally gave my entire department pink slips? "Same here," I say, taking a seat.

"First and foremost, we must tell you that we value you as an employee. Your hard work and dedication to Merchant Bank are undeniable. Over the years, you have contributed to the many successes of this company. We'd never want you to believe for one moment that you aren't appreciated." She slides a piece of paper in front of me. "We've received your performance evaluation from Alex, along with input from Chris, and based on their recommendations your promotion has been approved, personally by Hugh."

"Congratulations," says Hugh.

I look at the paper and almost let out a gasp. They've given me a fifty percent increase. "Thank you."

"You'll see that we've included a bonus for your commitment to stay with us during our transition to USABankersTrust. We know that you've been looking to leave; however, it's very important to us that our core teams take the lead in the data transfer. I hope we can count on you."

"I will seriously consider it."

"Secondly, on behalf of Merchant Bank, we'd like to apologize for Susanne Kart's behavior. We take our conduct policy very seriously and we have zero tolerance towards behaviors that don't align with the future vision of USABankersTrust. A full investigation was launched after you left the office on Friday, and as of this morning, we've come to an agreement with Susanne for her tenure to end, effective immediately." She takes a sip of water. "As a company, we are embarrassed and we take full responsibility for her actions. We are sincerely apologetic for the grievance she has caused and we'd like to extend personal leave *with* pay for the remainder of the holiday season." She hands me a box that reads 'Smith Island Cakes'. "For you and your family. One less thing you have to prepare."

"Thank you."

"We'll see you after the new year?" She looks at Hugh and it finally dawns on me that her face doesn't move. Just her lips. "Hugh, anything else?"

"Bryn, you exemplify the values of a true Merchant Bank officer." He stands and violently shakes my hand.

"Thank you, Ms. Charles. Enjoy your vacation," Gretchen says.

I take my letter and my cake and sashay out the door.

25

<u>CHRISTMAS EVE</u>

I spent my week off shopping for Bailey and planning Shane's Christmas surprise, so I fell far behind on cooking for my annual Christmas brunch. I'm still wrapping gifts and putting cookies in the oven when I get a text from him.

Where's Bailey?

Out with Jen

I'm out front

Surprised, I rinse my hands, grab a hand towel, and run to open the door. Shane walks in carrying multiple large bags, Best Buy, Apple, Game Stop, Limited Too, Nordstrom, Foot Locker, Toys R Us, and places them all under the tree. "Don't tell Bailey they're from me. Tell her Santa brought them."

"Santa's certifiably crazy. You're spoiling her."

"She's an awesome kid."

"Does this mean you want your gifts now?"

"No, I'll be here in the morning. I didn't want her to see me bring them in tomorrow." He kisses me. "It smells good in here."

"I'm baking cookies."

"You're such a mom."

"Want me to save you some?"

"Nah." He gives me a full-bodied embrace. "Me want your cookies . . . tonight," he says, squeezing my ass.

"Okay, Cookie Monster."

"Yes." He rubs his hands together. "Gotta go. I've got more shopping to do. I guess I'll see you later."

"I'll be anxiously waiting." I close the door and text Jen.

I need you to keep Bailey tonight

Why, what's going on?

Shane brought gifts

I'm taking her and Taylor to the movies anyway

He got everything on the list

That's insane

I know. See you in the morning?

The morning? Have fun

Ha ha ha ha ha ha

You need professional help

Maybe I do, because I can't stop smiling. Shane and I have continued being inseparable. He doesn't care about his schedule or mine. No matter what, he makes it a priority to see me. If I'm busy and can't go out, he'll stop by and sit or cuddle or listen to music. I can't lie, I'm enjoying the attention. The sex is phenomenal, and when we're in sync, the earth shakes.

I'm drinking hot chocolate and listening to *A Charlie Brown Christmas,* sitting on the floor in front of the tree wearing a naughty pair of pajamas and wrapping the last gift, a PSP 3, when Shane rings my doorbell. I leap to my feet and run to the mirror. Hair, check. Lip gloss, check. Cleavage, lots of it!

I pose at the door, arching my back, tossing my hair to one side, as Shane walks in. He's pulling a Louis Vuitton roller bag with a big red satin bow tied around it, which coincidentally matches the bows on the sides of my panties.

Back to the bag, it has my initials monogramed on it in pink and white. I want to scream, but I hold it in. Lately, I'm easily excited about everything when it comes to Shane. I make a silly face as I close the door behind him.

He plops down on the sofa, stretching out his large legs, and assesses my progress under the tree. "You weren't playing, were you?"

"I love wrapping gifts." I try not to ogle the stunning Pégase 55 suitcase, but it's hard. I've been stalking this beauty on the Louis Vuitton website for months.

"Don't just stare at it. Open it."

"For me?" I ask innocently. "Thank you. You shouldn't have." I act shocked and surprised. If I weren't worried about appearances, I'd be running laps around this place. "I don't want to remove the lovely bow. I want to leave it on until I use it. I love it. Thank you." I lean over to kiss him.

"Open it, Bryn," he says in his commanding voice.

"Okay . . ." I'm not sure why he's being so persistent, but I'll go along with it. I lay it down, admiring the signature canvas. It's so strong, durable, and sexy. I can't wait to put it to use. Slowly, I maneuver the bow off without untying it. I have every intention of slipping it back on to put next to the tree. Lying inside is a thick white envelope. My heart starts to pound in my chest. I peek over at Shane. He's smiling down at me. I unfold three pieces of paper: a reservation confirmation at the Jefferson Hotel in Washington D.C., courtside seats to the Wizards game, and tickets at the Warner Theater for Jay Z.

"You see the date?"

"January 16th to 21st. This is the freaking inauguration weekend."

"You said you wanted an experience."

"Shane! All hotels were sold out. How did you do this?"

"I had a little help." He smirks. "Finish opening it."

I feel tears beginning to well in my eyes and open the flaps to the suitcase. It's already packed. "Shane . . ." I don't know what to open first. I touch a winter-white garment. It feels like cashmere. I unfold it, laying it flat. It's a dress, long-sleeved and form-fitting with a deep V-neck. Next to it is a Prada dust bag. I reach inside and pull out classic black leather pointed-toe pumps. They are ultra-sexy. I check the size to make sure he got it right. He did. My heart continues to race as I reach for the next bag. This time, it's a Louis Vuitton dust bag. I peek inside and find a black leather clutch with the gold LV emblem on the front latch. I want to faint. "Shane . . ." I'm speechless.

"Look inside the bag."

"I can't. I feel like I'm going to pass out."

He laughs, staring at me as if he wants to eat me alive. He adjusts himself in his shorts. I realize I'm on all fours at his knees and my pajama bottoms are riding a bit high.

I sit down and tuck my hair behind my ear. The leather smell is invigorating. I pop open the latch and reach inside the clutch and pull out another dust bag. *David Yurman.* I'm sick with nerves. Inside is a linked choker, silver with gold accent, and matching earrings inside a smaller pouch.

"Shane . . ."

He holds his finger to his lips to silence me. He motions me to him and I walk over and stand between his legs. "Now. I'm ready to unwrap my gift." Pulling me towards him, he kisses my thigh then unties my panties with his teeth.

26

THE AMAZING RACE

Bailey's impatience causes me to stub my toe on the nightstand while trying to grab my keys. "Mom?" she cries incessantly. I get it. She's excited and has been for the last week. But I don't need her stressing me out more than I already am. It was stressful enough trying to figure out what to get him. *How do you shop for a man who has everything?* During my week home from work, I figured it out and planned a personalized amazing race similar to my favorite television show. When Bailey handed him his first clue on Christmas morning, he shouted, "A treasure hunt!" I needed an entire day to properly execute the surprise, so since Tuesdays are his only day off, we waited until today.

"I'm coming. I'm coming," I say joyfully through the pain. I'm trying my hardest not to raise my voice at her. I pick up my keys, toss my overnight bag into the closet, and walk downstairs.

"MOM. He's going to get there before us." Grabbing her purse from the railing, she knocks over Taylor's water bottle.

Taylor left her boyfriend to come help us with Shane's surprise. The least Bailey can do is be polite.

"Bailey." I stop in my tracks and give her the 'I'm not playing with you' look. She thinks she's hot stuff with her Juicy Couture cross body bag Santa got her.

"I'm sorry." She picks up the water bottle and hands it to Taylor.

"Can I put my shoes on please? He's always late. Haven't you figured that out by now? Gosh, I was looking for something, something I needed for today." *Technically, for later tonight.*

"Did you find it?"

"Yes smarty-pants, let's go," I say, checking my cell phone as we run out the door to the first pit stop.

Toys R Us is eight minutes away from my house, but I trim the commute down to five. "That's him, right there. That's his Range." Bailey points to Shane's truck, which is illegally parked in the fire lane. *The one time I need him to be late, he shows up on time.* "Who's that with him?"

"It looks like Qmar," I say, surveying the tall, dark-brown-skinned guy with a low Caesar haircut.

"I wanted to see Roman," she cries.

I ignore Bailey and drive to the rear of the shopping center. "Get out here and take the side entrance so he doesn't see you. Taylor, do you have the camera?"

"Yes, Ma'am."

"Listen, this is the first pit stop, he has a total of eight for the day. You two will be at the first and second stops. Jen is already waiting at the third. I'll be at the fourth and so on. It's very important that we keep him to the time schedule." Bailey sighs. "Bailey, Taylor is in charge. She has the clues and you have the prizes. Keep it that way. Remember, he must complete the tasks to win the prize. Most importantly, you two will split for the second challenge. Bailey, you sit with Qmar and wait for Taylor and Shane to finish the second challenge."

"Why can't I be there?"

"Because I said so. Girls, have fun and I will see you later. Oh, and make sure he drops you back to the house after the second challenge. Taylor, check for the keys."

"I've got them," says Taylor.

"Kisses, kisses." I give Bailey a kiss then watch them walk inside before pulling away.

The speed limit is forty and I'm doing about sixty and slamming on the gas at every yellow light. I've got to arrive downtown before he does.

My phone rings. "Yes, Taylor."

"We're on our way to the second challenge."

"Already?"

"Yes, it was hilarious. You're a genius to think of this. Wait until you see the video. You're going to die laughing. Shane was Darth Vader."

Shane's a huge *Star Wars* fan, so his first challenge was to dress as Darth Vader and reenact the famous scene from the movie where he tells Luke Skywalker that he's his father. I provided him a script, which includes battle scenes with light sabers, and instructed him to use the mega *Star Wars* display at the front of the store as his stage.

"He took it very seriously and made a mess of the *Star Wars* game board display. He struck Qmar with the light saber, like really hard. Everyone in the store surrounded us and couldn't stop laughing."

"I'm happy. Did he like his gift?"

"Yes, I can't take him seriously while he's in the front seat playing with a young Anakin figurine."

"He likes toys."

"It's kinda weird if you ask me. Anyway, we're pulling up at the second pit stop. I'll call if I need you."

Shane's going to love his next challenge. I'm sending him to a BMW dealer where he must ride a Segway up and down Reisterstown Road until he lures three people into participating in a BMW test drive with him driving. Since Shane has a heavy foot and drives like a maniac, his challenge is to drive through the back roads of Greenspring Valley Road without causing his passengers to scream. If he passes it, he wins a Lamborghini test drive at a real racetrack. If he fails, he'll be washing three cars. I can't wait to hear what happens.

I feel relieved as I pull onto a cobblestone driveway leading to a beautiful flower-filled courtyard at the Harbor International. I circle the fountain to the valet sign. "Hello, are you checking in with us?" says the valet attendant.

"Yes, I will be checking in but I'm leaving immediately, can you keep my car up front?"

"Yes, Ma'am," he says.

"Perfect." I grab my overnight bag from the back seat and enter the lobby.

"Good morning. Checking in with us today?"

"Yes, I have a reservation for Bryn Charles."

"I can assist you. I will need a valid license and credit card please."

I hand my credentials over and look around the lobby. Large pieces of dark-wood furniture, beautiful oriental rugs, and two huge floral arrangements flanking a grand red-carpeted spiral staircase. *This should be nice.*

Taylor calls again.

"That didn't take long."

"Shane is smarter than you think. He took three people on one ride and purposely drove twenty miles per hour. They didn't care about being smashed in the back. They only wanted pictures and his autograph." Taylor laughs. "So he's on his way to Jen."

"Thanks, dear." I disconnect the call. I've got to get moving. I become anxious waiting for my room key. I'm short on time. I drum my fingers on the marble counter and finally, the receptionist hands over the key.

I hurry to the room and when I push open the door, I see it's decorated old-money style. Antiques everywhere. An oil painting of a general on a white horse hanging above the cedar desk, two double beds with quilted yellow duvets and gold tasseled tossed pillows, antique gold lamps with mustard lampshades. Yikes, nothing about this room screams sex. But, they are known for their amazing harbor views. I set my belongings down and pull back the heavy gold floral embossed drapes. *Is that what I think it is? Oh—no.*

"Hi, this is Ms. Charles in room 215, I just checked in. I need a new room, with a harbor view. My current view is of a gigantic marble crucifix, so yes, I'll pay extra." I've got to get this straightened out before I go anywhere. We're NOT coming back to this room.

They get me into another room with a king bed in the center facing the harbor. It's beautiful. Hopefully, the view will be enough of a distraction from the blush brocade wallpaper, oil paintings, and brass candle sconces. I drop everything and leave, because I'm thirty minutes behind schedule, so I'm glad the valet attendant kept my car at the front.

I check my phone and see I have three missed calls from Jen. "Sorry, I missed your call." She lets out a wail and starts talking to others around her. "Jen, I'm hanging up, Jen!" I yell into the phone.

"Just give me a second . . . Shane's reading his next clue and is about to walk out."

"Did he do the Single Ladies routine?"

"No, I thought it was funny when you first planned it, but I couldn't let him do it with all these women, and men who want to be women, in the boutique. I had to come up with something else. I thought I helped him get off easy by asking him to sing the *Twelve Days of Christmas*, but he didn't know it. So I just gave him the gift."

I'm slightly annoyed Jen changed his task at the last minute *and* let him get away without any penalties. But then again, I'm not surprised, because Shane has a way of disarming people and managing to get exactly what he wants.

"You mean to tell me I sent him to you for nothing? Did you at least feed him?"

"He didn't eat the curry chicken salad I got him."

"Really, Jen? You know he doesn't eat stuff like that."

"Whole Foods Chicken Salad is amazing," she says, sounding offended. "Where are you now?"

"Walking over to the aquarium to get the tickets."

"I still can't believe he's never been to the aquarium. He's got small kids. Anyway, he's on his way."

Irritated, I hang up on Jen and run to the ticket counter to purchase our passes. Taped to the window is a large hand-written sign.

Dolphin Show Canceled

Limited time only: Polar Express 4D experience

They've ruined my plan to embarrass Shane at the dolphin show, but this is even better. Shane's going to love it. I purchase the tickets and walk to the middle of the square, making sure he can easily find me.

Within five minutes, I see Shane making his way towards me with a big grin on his face. "I finally get to see you." He gives me a tight hug.

"Are you having fun?"

"Yes. Definitely. You thought of all this?"

"Yes. You're not done yet. Jen told me you didn't get to eat, so let's detour for a moment and get some food so you can finish the race." He gets cranky when he hasn't eaten.

As we walk into the Cheesecake Factory, the employees and guests alike are happy to see us. I mention we have limited time, so our server expedites everything.

Shane tries to tip our waiter, but I make him put his wallet away and hand him his next clue.

"Are you really sending me to your job?"

"Yes." I hand him a black Sharpie. "Just in case." I wink. "Don't forget to ask for Brian at the security desk. He'll lead you to my cubicle."

Shane's headed to my office to sit at my desk and scribe a letter to me. I added this extra stop for Brian. It's my Christmas gift to him for being a nice office mate and for helping me out with the race. Once Shane's done writing the letter, Brian will hand him his next clue, sending him to the world-renowned Baltimore Aquarium.

Shane returns rather quickly and we hurry to get inside. We walk hand in hand towards the first exhibit and Shane is astonished, even more than the kindergarten group walking ahead of us. He's so excited that he jumps in front of children and stands with his face to the glass to view the fish.

"Look! It's Nemo!" he screams, tapping the small tank with two clown fish. "And there's Dory! Look, it's Dory!" he screams again, ignoring the signs asking to NOT touch the glass. He's the biggest four-year-old in the building. His behavior is rather ridiculous, but as the parents recognize Shane, they become just as childish and giddy as he is.

I jog up to him and place my arm around him, taking a few steps back so the kids can see as well. I'm red with embarrassment. They don't care one bit, only because he's Shane Smith.

He manages to tone down his excitement once we get to the shark exhibit. He pretends he's going to jump off the escalators into the open tank below, to gain attention from his adoring crowd.

"Would you have jumped in to save me?"

"Hell no." I grab his hand and guide him to the theater to stand in line.

Shane and I are the first in line for the Polar Express 4D Experience and he can't stand still. He's doing toe touches, lunges, and jumping jacks. I try and hide behind him, only peeking out when I hear someone call his name. *Jason?*

"Hey, my brother." They do a handshake. "Bryn. What are y'all doing down here with this nut?"

"What are you doing here?" Shane's voice is high-pitched.

"I'm down here with Star." He points to a little girl with her face pressed against the glass. *Please don't say anything about planning. Please don't ask about the event.*

"Sorry J, we gotta go!" shouts Shane as the doors open. He grabs my hand and drags me in to the center row. He plops into his chair and straps his belt before reaching over to strap mine. He puts his glasses on and tightly squeezes the arms of his chair. Once the last person takes their seat, the red curtain opens to an IMAX size movie screen. Shane lets out an unexpected yelp as the hydraulics in our chairs build momentum for the opening scene.

We experience a runaway train ride, snowfall, Santa, and the emotional reminder of the magic of Christmas. If you don't believe in Santa, by the end of the ride you want to.

I exit teary-eyed, wiping my face and handing Shane his next clue.

"You're sending me home?"

"Just for a change of clothes and a quick visit with your kids. I know how much they mean to you."

He kisses my forehead and jogs to the exit.

I'm exhausted. I need a break at the hotel to catch up on sleep so I can make it through the night.

Back in the room, I turn on the television and soak in the tub. Nothing to watch, so I grab my phone to text Jen and see a text from Shane.

What time do I need to pick you up again?

Pick me up at 7:45. Dinner is at 8

When I walk into the courtyard, Shane's Range Rover enters the driveway. *Perfect timing.* The valet attendant opens the car door. Shane reaches over to pull me in.

"Yum, you smell splendid," I say, reaching over for a kiss.

"Thank you, it's the Gucci cologne you got me."

"It smells magnificent on you."

He blushes. "Where are we off to?"

"Ciao Bella's."

I love dinners with Shane.

We dine by candlelight. Tony prepares Shane's favorite meal, penne vodka, which he devours in minutes. "It was perfect," he says with a smile as he rehashes today's adventure. "By the way, I told Qmar."

"I thought we weren't going to tell anyone?"

"Your best friend knows, so . . ."

"What if he tells the boys?"

"He won't. But now for the important part." He reaches into his pocket and pulls out a folded piece of paper with a sketching of a heart with my initials inside it.

"Oh, I almost forgot, the letter you wrote me at my desk."

"Yeah," he clears his throat. "Wow, okay. As we knock down the days and they become weeks, and the weeks become months, I still can't believe this fairy tale we are living. It has been my honor and my EXTREME pleasure to be your lover, but most importantly your friend. Can't wait to create more amazing memories with you." He smiles and hands me the paper.

I can't believe Shane wrote this letter and spelled everything correctly. He's not as uneducated as he acts.

"Aww, that's so sweet."

He has passed his challenge. I hand him his next clue.

"The movies?" he says, his eyes bright, before reading the clue.

"No, read the clue."

Shane refuses to allow me to take care of the meal. He peels off a few hundreds and leaves an extra hundred for the tip. I give him a look as he walks over to me. "You've done enough," he says, pulling my chair out. "Do you know what the most beautiful thing about you is?"

I immediately blush.

"How thoughtful and caring you are. I know this took a lot of time to plan."

He's so charming.

We jump in his truck, off to our next destination, the Christmas Tree Park at the National Mall. "There it is, on the right." I point to an open area where people are walking around. Shane whips the truck around, making a huge U-turn in the middle of the street to take the last free parking space. He maneuvers the truck and puts it in park.

"Perfect," he says, smiling. I reach for the handle to open the door. "No, no. I'll get that for you." He jumps out and runs to my side to let me out. He opens the door with his other hand outstretched. "Madame."

I laugh and go with it, giving him my right hand. He holds my hand tightly as we cross the street at a run. Never letting me go, he walks with me through a Christmas tree park. It's like a scene from a romantic comedy. Truly adorable. We make our way through the twinkling path to the tallest tree.

"Wait here, I want a picture." I back up as far as I can, but he and the tree won't fit in the frame. "It won't fit." A gust of wind blasts us. "I'll have to cut the top off," I say through chattering teeth.

I feel a tap on my shoulder. "Would you like me to take a picture of the two of you?" An older lady reaches for my phone.

"Yes, thank you." I hand her my phone and run over to Shane. He wraps his arm tightly around me.

"You two make a lovely couple." She shows me the picture she took.

"Thanks again." I say. She walks away, hand in hand with an older gentleman. "Look!" I point to where they are heading. "A huge bonfire. Let's go and get some heat."

"How about some hot chocolate first?"

"Great idea."

Shane grabs two hot chocolates and a honeybun from a food truck parked along the street. We sip as we stroll down the Christmas-tree-lit pathway and join other cuddling couples standing in front of the fire. Shane pulls me close and we lose ourselves in each other's eyes. *He's so warm and cuddly.*

"Today was wonderful. I've never done any of these things. You ARE different. You're not like anyone I've ever met. You are simply amazing."

It feels so good to hear these words from him. Up until now, I wasn't sure how I truly felt.

"Sweetie, this . . . right here . . . is perfect."

I close my eyes and imagine a future with him. Is this really it? Is this the real deal Holyfield? Is Shane the man I'm supposed to be with? I've heard stories from married couples about how they didn't like each other at first. Yet they had an amazing friendship that eventually turned into a beautiful love affair. I never thought in a million years this could be my story. One thing is for sure. Right now, I could stay in his arms forever. I feel his love and I feel safe.

A gust of wind tossing soot from the fire chokes me out of dreamland. Shane pulls me in close.

Finally, my knight in shining armor.

27

<u>WHO IS SHE?</u>

I'm headed to Terry's to take him to the airport. He's going to Indiana to meet Shane. Late last night, while Shane and I were in the middle of our cuddle session (as he likes to call it) watching Aladdin, his phone rang. He explained that in past years, once the football season ended, he returned home to Indiana. However, this year, since we've been seeing each other, he's been delaying it as long as possible. When he was summoned back home to attend to a family emergency, it upset me that it came the night before we were due to leave for our weekend in D.C.

I arrive at Terry's condo a little early and have to knock on his door several times before he answers. When the door opens, he's standing shirtless in a pair of superman boxer shorts and long basketball socks. He's all ribs and knobby knees. I burst into shrieks of laughter. "Agh! I'm blind!" I cover my eyes. "Terry please, please put some clothes on!" I peek at him through my fingers and begin to choke.

He rolls his eyes and walks away. He probably hoped for a different reaction, but he lets me inside. The place is spotless, not the average bachelor pad. The décor lacks a woman's touch, but everything has its place. I'm impressed. Most days, Bailey's belongings trail from the front door all the way upstairs to her room.

I take a seat at his dining room table next to a tall glass cabinet filled with sports paraphernalia. I move closer to get a better look. Trinkets, photos, tickets, and access badges creatively displayed on various shelves. It feels slightly creepy, almost like a Shane Smith shrine.

I nose around in the cabinet until Terry emerges from his bathroom, shirtless, wet, and with a towel wrapped around his waist. I try to contain my laughter but fail once again.

"What are you laughing at?" Terry closes his towel.

I silently pray that it doesn't drop. "These pictures," I lie.

"Yeah? I've got more if you want to see them." He struts over to a cabinet next to his television, pulls out a small photo album, and takes a seat at the dining room table.

"So . . . how long have you known Shane?" Terry has more hair in the photos.

"About five years now."

"How did you meet?"

"It was funny how we met, actually. I was a personal shopper at Nordstrom's in Towson Town Center. He came in with his girl at the time. She liked my suit and told Shane that he should get one like it. A month later, he came back and asked me to help him. We've been boys ever since." He opens the album. Every picture is some combination of Terry, Shane, Romello, and TGS. Terry and Zander at dinner, Terry and Shane at a nightclub, Shane, Terry, and Romello poolside at a Vegas Hotel. Terry and DeShaun shirtless on a beach.

"Y'all look so young."

"That was for Shane's wedding weekend."

"Wedding?" I take a sip of water and my heartbeat accelerates.

"Yeah, and this was Shane's bachelor party."

"He's married?"

"No, no. Just engaged." He quickly flips to the back of the album. "That was his fiancée."

"Again, that's not Carice. That whole thing has been very confusing to me."

"How should I put this?" He looks away, thinking. "Technically, I would say that Carice is his girl. *Maybe* you can call her that. Their relationship has always been really strange. What I do know for sure is that she *is* crazy. She's so crazy; Shane makes it a point *not* to upset her in any way. He does whatever it takes to keep her quiet. He even bought a bigger house to shut her up. No one likes her. As you've probably already noticed, Shane never wants y'all around her. I don't blame him because we hate when she's around."

"Hmmm." I flip through the album trying not to react the way I'd like, crazed. "Wow. Look at him." He's wearing a white suit and pink satin vest. To his right is a girl with long dark hair, olive skin, and round, bright eyes. "She's prettier than Carice."

"I know and they're nothing alike. Carice is wild. One time, we were in L.A. at dinner and she didn't like the way a girl was looking at Shane. She took her shoe off and threw it across the dining room, hitting the girl on the head. Next thing we know, the girl's man comes to the table and swings on Romello. A brawl almost broke out in the middle of the restaurant, but security broke it up."

"She was calm when we saw her at the game. She just stared at us like a deer caught in headlights."

"She's not stupid. She knows what Shane's like. She was watching you, looking for any signs. Trust me." He closes the album.

"So what happened to the fiancée?"

"Shane got drunk and got busy with Carice at his bachelor party. Someone made sure his fiancée had pictures in the morning and she left him at the altar."

"Wow, I wasn't expecting you to say that. I didn't know stuff like that really happened."

"What happens in Vegas stays in Vegas."

"On that note, I'm done. I'm afraid about what you may say next. Ready to leave?"

"Yeah, let me finish getting dressed. I came out here because I wanted you to help me choose an outfit. Come into my room." He waves. "I won't bite."

Gross.

Terry's bed is neatly made with luxury linens you'd find in a Neiman's bedding catalogue. "Terry, these linens . . ." I rub my hand across the textured cotton duvet.

"You can have a seat. In fact, it's a sleep number bed. You should try it out. Find out your number. It's excellent support for your back." He enters his walk-in closet and pulls out a mocha brown smoking jacket with black pants and a double-breasted blue suit with a mint green and pink paisley tie.

"Terry, I'm terrible with style. Jen dresses me. You would know more than I do."

He lays them on the bed next to me, then stands back examining them.

"Don't you want to get married?"

"Yes, but only to a man I'm in love with. I'm not going to settle." I'm not sure why he's asking, but my response should remove all hope.

"I'd like to get married too." He rubs his chin. "But Shane doesn't, not after what he's been through." Terry starts to dress in front of me. "I'm going to go with the blue."

"I'm going to go heat the car."

My mind races during our commute to the airport. Terry talks, but nothing registers.

"Uh, huh," I say every now and again. The only thing on my mind is Shane. I don't want to create unnecessary dramas where there are none, but I can't shake this feeling looming in the back of my mind. I need certainty that his ties to Carice are purely for his kids.

I pull over in the departures lane at BWI Airport and let Terry out. "Thanks B. I appreciate it. See you in D.C."

"Have a safe flight."

I dial Jen's number before pulling away. "Hey girl, how's D.C.?" Jen left yesterday to attend the official programs and concerts.

"It's been wonderful! Very inspiring. But you sound funny, what's going on?"

"Well, Terry showed me pictures of Shane's bachelor party."

"What?" she screams into my ear. "Shane is married to that girl?" She pauses. "I repent, Lord. I promised not to judge."

"Wait . . . wait, no. Apparently, Shane was engaged to this really pretty girl. From the rehearsal dinner photos, looked like she came from a nice family."

"I'm confused."

"Well, if you let me finish . . . the thing is, apparently, Carice and Shane hooked up and his soon-to-be wife found out and left him at the altar."

"That sounds like something off reality TV. Ugh, I have nothing else to say. I'm trying to live right."

"Girl, I don't know what to think about those two. He's stressed the fact that he's single, moreover."

"He's with you and Bailey almost every day, so I think it's safe to say, they are not together."

"True."

"Look, no one is perfect. Don't trip and ruin your weekend. I suggest you wait until the weekend is over before even bringing it up. Besides, it's all hearsay and you have to remember that Terry likes you. He might suspect something. I mean, you and Shane aren't the most discreet, so I'm shocked he doesn't already know."

"You're right, I'll stop worrying. Enjoy your day. I guess I'll see you tomorrow night."

"I'll see you when you get here."

"I'm having dinner with Myra. She's flying in from California."

"I completely forgot. Please tell her that I said hello."

"I will. Have fun at the ball tonight, and if you see The Rock, tell him I love him."

D.C. is a parking lot. My driver did the best he could to get me here on time, but I'm late for dinner at the hotel restaurant, Lemaire, with my good friend and mentor, Myra. She flew all the way from Napa Valley for the inauguration. Thankfully, the hotel service is impeccable and I have a seamless check-in. I leave my bags with the bellhop and walk over to the maître d who appears to be expecting me.

"Ms. Charles? Right this way, please." He escorts me to the table where Myra is engrossed in the wine menu. He pulls out the chair for me.

"Thank you."

"My pleasure," he says before walking away.

"Girl, you better get up and give me a hug," says Myra, tossing the menu to the side and giving me a tight bear hug.

"I love the sweater. It's so soft," I say to her.

"I had to come prepared for this freezing weather. I got it when I was in Holland. Speaking of which . . ." She reaches into her purse and pulls out a little white wrapper. "For you."

"Awww, chica. You didn't have to." I unwrap the small paper packaging and pull out a tiny magnet with a pair of hand-painted wooden clogs.

"It's for your collection."

"Only you would remember I collect refrigerator magnets," I say, laughing.

"I have something for my girl Bailey too. It's packed in my suitcase. I'll give it to you on Tuesday before you head back. I'm so glad we get to have dinner tonight before all the festivities begin. And the rooms are gorgeous. How did you find this place?"

"Jen found it. I originally thought Shane did, but it slipped out that she was dropping hints."

"Jen's a mess. You two are always into something. What is she up to these days?"

"Wheeling and dealing as always. Looking for that next big contract."

Our server comes over with a bottle of wine.

"Oh yeah, I ordered the wine. Living out in wine country, I drink a bottle a day."

I laugh and shake my head as he pours the wine for her to taste test. She gives him an approving nod and he proceeds to fill our glasses.

"Next big contract, huh," she continues. "So back to Shane. Thought I was going to miss that, didn't you?" She lets out a loud laugh. "So, you two are seeing each other now? I thought you told me he was married."

"No. Funny you should ask that. He's not married and I just found out he was never married."

"What was that look about?"

"Nothing. Just recalling some hearsay. It's not worth repeating. But the most important part is that he's single—at least that's what he says."

"You sure about that? Because you don't sound too confident," she says with a raised eyebrow. "Now you know I'm about to give you my two cents."

"I know. I expected it."

"You young 'uns trip me out."

Our waiter comes back to take our order and when he leaves, I know she's going to read me my rights. Myra is going to voice her opinion whether I want to hear it or not.

"Bryn, you are getting older. Bailey needs a father figure in her life. You don't want to waste your time with these—for lack of a better word—dogs."

"He's not a dog."

"I recall you telling me just a few months ago all those crazy stories about the strippers and bisexual girls and pimps and orgies."

"Oh yeah. I forgot."

"Uh huh, selective memory I see. Listen, I want you to be happy. But I don't want you to be walking around with blinders on. You're going to have to ask those hard questions and find out if he's really serious about being the man in your life. You don't have time for games."

"I most definitely don't."

"And you don't want to be dating in your thirties either. Trust me. It gets a lot harder then. You glow when you mention his name, so I know how you feel. I was that way about Edwin. We had chemistry that was out of this world. It's been twenty years and he called me last night. He must have sensed I'd be on this side of the country. He keeps saying that he can't forgive himself for marrying that other woman knowing that he still loved me. And I can't sit here and still love him after that. These men Bryn, they don't know what they've got until it's gone."

"What I don't understand is why Edwin married another woman while he was still in love with you?"

"I wish I could tell you darling."

"I think about Shane's past behavior and I try not to dwell on it. I can't hold his past against him, because we all have one. I have to judge him on the way he treats me. I can say I think I love him and I want to tell Bailey.

"I understand completely. Just don't let someone bite your neck, piss on your leg, and tell you it's raining."

"Oh my goodness, that's something my mother would say."

"How is Judge Judy these days?"

Myra and I laugh until we cry. Even though I don't see her often, we are as close as ever. I make my way to my room, slightly tipsy, dive head first into the bed, close my eyes, and fall asleep.

I'm sitting in a parking lot full of cars in a townhome community. The end unit is pulsating. I'm drawn to its front door. Shane's cousin Romello appears to my right. "Don't go in," his deep voice warns, radiating through my body then fading into the distance. I ring the doorbell instead.

"Come in Bryn, how are you honey? Would you like some breakfast?" asks Shane's Aunt Darshelle, an older, thin woman with blonde micro braids in her hair.

"No thanks." I sit at the barstool watching her cook. I hear a commotion brewing upstairs. Bang. Bang. Bang. I look towards the ceiling.

"Don't pay that any mind, dearie." She shakes her head as she continues to stir the eggs in the frying pan.

"Is Shane here?"

"No, baby." Her smile becomes wider than her face. Her front teeth become the size of small saucers.

Eeriness fills the kitchen as children's laughter grows louder and louder, like at a mega Chuck E. Cheese. "What's going on up there?"

"Nothing for you to worry about, baby."

The front door slams and I hear the click-clack of heels smacking against hardwood floors. A strange girl wearing a white tank top, jeans, and a long black weave in her hair points to me. "Who are you?"

"Hi, I'm Br—"

"Where's Carice? Why are you here? Carice lives here. Those are my godchildren. Who are you? Why are you here? Does Carice know you're here?"

A piercing scream shatters the house and it starts to crumble. I duck and run for cover.

Then I'm sitting in my car gripping my steering wheel. A white minivan gets my attention. The driver—it's Shane. His face appears and it is solemn. "I'm sorry," he says. His voice cracks.

"Why didn't you tell me? You could have told me. We didn't have to do this."

"I'm sorry. Bryn, I'm sorry."

The minivan jerks and spirals out of control, lifting from the ground and hovering above my car.

Romello appears in my passenger seat. "GET OUT!" he yells. His eyes are silver daggers.

CRASH!

I fight my way out of the covers, falling onto the floor in a full body sweat. I check my pulse and it's a record one hundred twenty beats per minute. Taking a huge breath, I hold it for two seconds and extend it for the full eight counts down to one, then repeat. My heartbeat begins to slow, but the panic remains on high alert. I take my time going to the bathroom, retrieve my toiletries bag, and dump the contents out into the sink. I take two sedatives and sit on the bench at the foot of the bed, grabbing the remote control to turn the loud action film off.

What the heck was that about? I grab my cell phone. It's 1:30 in the morning. Shane should have been here by now. I call his cell and there's no answer, so I send him a text.

`Hey babe, where are you?`

He replies immediately.

`Hey sweetie, I'll be there first thing in the morning`

`Miss you`

Miss you too babe. Goodnight

I don't reply. I know he's with his family, so I give him space. The last thing I want to be viewed as is needy. He will be here tomorrow morning and we can talk then.

28

OBAMA, BEYONCÉ, JAY Z, OH MY!

I'm snuggled in the armchair with a blanket, perusing the latest edition of *Capitol File* magazine, when my room door opens. It's Shane. He's hiding his face behind a dozen lavender roses. Without thinking, I jump up, dropping everything, and run to him, grabbing the water-filled vase from his hands. "They're magnificent." I bury my nose into one that's fully bloomed. "Mmm, and smell delightful. Thank you, my dearest. They are indeed beautiful." I pucker my lips.

"Anything for my princess." He kisses my neck.

"Yum . . ." I walk my fingers along the closure of his shirt collar and give it a tug.

He takes my hand and places it at my side. "Whoa there, you don't want to wake the Hulk."

"But I've missed him so . . ." I bite my lip and flash him a sultry look.

"Let me get some rest, babe, I've been traveling three days straight." He removes his jewelry, empties his pockets on the nightstand, and climbs into the bed. I set the roses down on the coffee table and climb in bed beside him.

"Is everybody okay?" I ask, caressing his shoulder.

"Yeah, everybody's cool. Romello and the squad came back with me."

My heart skips a beat at Romello's name and the dream comes rushing back to my mind. "Nice. Should be fun."

"Yeah. They'll be hanging out with us tonight and tomorrow. Oh, and I have to leave Monday night."

"You're going to miss the most important part," I whine.

"I know . . . I know." He rubs his face. "But I've got to." He closes his eyes, trying to fall asleep.

"I understand. By the way, speaking of Romello, he was in my dream last night. It was a really weird dream. You were in it as well. You kept saying, 'I'm sorry' over and over again."

"What?" His eyes open wide. "You want Romello or something?" He gives me an accusing look.

"No, silly," I say, pinching him and then pulling him in for a kiss. "I only want my teddy bear." I climb on top of him and give him sweet kisses all over his face until we both fall asleep.

My sleep is constantly disrupted by the ringing of Shane's cell phones. I want to flush them down the toilet but instead, I push them under his pillow hoping to muffle the sound. He shifts, slightly opening his eyes and slowly closing them again. Poor baby, he can hardly catch a break. I lie staring at his sleeping face then kiss him on the forehead. I care for him so deeply and the best part about it is that it feels so natural. When he opens his eyes, he holds me tight.

Even though I'm looking forward to celebrating Senator Barack Obama's presidency win with the entire country, I would be happier staying here wrapped in Shane's arms until morning.

Tonight, in the District of Columbia, the sidewalks are overflowing with foot traffic, passersby, and the homeless alike. Horns honk incessantly in the bumper-to-bumper traffic as we inch past roadblocks and follow new traffic patterns in place for the upcoming ceremony. I check my phone and we're already an hour late for the Wizards game. We left early, but not nearly early enough.

It's halftime when we arrive at the Verizon Center and as soon as we take our seats, Shane's pulled away for an impromptu business meeting. The rest of us, except for Terry (Shane's shadow this evening), sit courtside for the second half.

He doesn't return until the final seconds of the game. "What did I miss?" Shane kisses my cheek. "Sorry, babe, I'm hungry. Let's go."

"Where's Terry?"

"He's outside with the bus. Come on, it's time to eat." He grabs my hand and leads me through the crowd.

"Handsome Bob!" Shane shouts, as we arrive at the bus. He's pointing at Terry who's waiting at the exit doors with the driver, striking a pose with his hands in his pockets.

"I meant to tell you earlier that I like your scarf," I say to Terry.

"Thanks, B. I got it from the Gucci store at Fashion Mall." Terry smiles, follows me onto the bus, and takes a seat next to me. "We stopped there before flying here."

Poor Terry's going to be an innocent casualty of love. I'm starting to feel guilty by simply looking at him. I'm glad the restaurant is only around the corner, because the longer I sit next to him the worse I feel.

When we arrive at Oceanaire, I awkwardly leave his side and join Shane in the restaurant. Shane pulls out my chair next to him. Terry pulls a chair out for Jen at my side. Everyone else sits where they can.

"M, give me updates." Shane stares at Jen and grabs the breadbasket.

"Are you talking to me?" Jen looks left, then right, then back at him.

"Aren't you running shit around here?" he barks. "M, from James Bond!"

"Oh, M. I get it!"

"You think you can top yourself this time? I'm just saying, last party you did might have been a stroke of luck."

"If you feel that way, hire someone else," replies Jen.

"Houston, we have a problem!" bellows Romello, hitting Shane on the shoulder.

They're in a playful mood tonight and the jesting begins. It feels a bit nostalgic, reminding me of Shane's crazy event-planning nights. I can't believe we're gearing up to do it again.

After dinner, the driver drops Jen, Terry, Shane, and me back to the hotel. The boys stay on the bus. I overhear them ask the driver to take them to a 'good' strip club. I don't want to know what 'good' means.

"Let's watch a movie," Shane whispers in my ear as he walks me and Jen to the elevators. "I'll see you soon." He pats his pockets. "I have my key." He jogs over to Terry at a beverage table with real china and silver to prepare hot chocolate like a high tea.

"Goodnight, Shane, goodnight, Terry." I wave to them and Jen and I take the elevator to our floor. "I'm hoping Terry can see the writing on the wall and figure things out on his own. I don't want to play pretenses for the rest of my special weekend," I say to Jen.

"I think Terry is going to be devastated that Shane has been keeping this from him. Shane knows that Terry likes you still. This is going to end ugly."

"I know. I want to tell him."

"Make sure I'm not around when y'all do. I don't want to see the aftermath." The elevator doors open. We walk in different directions. "By the way, I hate to hassle you this weekend, but Jason needs the updated floor plan. And now that

Shane's asking me for updates, I need your results for the venue options."

"Got it. I have my laptop. I'll update the Google doc in the morning."

"Thanks. See you in the morning?"

"Afternoon. I'm hoping I don't sleep until morning.

"Have fun for the two of us."

We laugh all the way to our rooms.

By the time Shane arrives, I'm half asleep.

"You asleep?" he barks.

I stare at him.

"I'll see you in the morning then."

"What? I'm awake."

"No, you're not. You're going to fall asleep as soon as the movie starts. Your eyes are barely open."

"Fine. Come cuddle then."

"I don't want to hurt him," he says in what has to be the most pathetic voice I've ever heard.

"Hurt who? Am I missing something?"

"Terry, he's still awake. I was able to get out because I told him I had to drop off the credit card to Jen." *Is he doing what I think he's doing?* "I'll make it up to you tomorrow. I promise," he says, leaning over and giving me a kiss goodnight.

I sit motionless and let the door close behind him before grabbing a pillow and holding it over my face to scream. *This is not okay. We need to break it to Terry.*

The next morning, I check my phone. No missed calls. I get up and grab my laptop. I don't bother to call Shane. I think it's safe to assume he's still busy with his family or Terry. I connect to Wi-Fi, log into Pandora, and open Jason's layout in my space planner. Jason's template pops up on my screen and simultaneously I hear my room door click.

"Hey, baby," says Shane, walking into the room with Starbucks.

He knows I love Starbucks. "Good morning." I set my laptop down and examine my drink. He even remembered the whip and caramel drizzle. The spice from the chai latte fully awakens my senses as I take the first sip. "Ahh. Perfection."

Shane strips as I sip. Naked, he crawls between the sheets.

I hurriedly finish my tea, tossing the empty cup at the trashcan (and missing it) as Shane impatiently pulls me under the sheets.

Morning sex is always the best sex.

For the first time ever, Shane turns his ringers off and we stay in bed all day. The only time either of us moves is to take a trip to the bathroom or sign the receipt for room service.

My alarm wakes us up to get ready for the Jay Z concert and the first thing I notice is that my laptop has been tampered with. My heart palpitates at the thought of him seeing Jason's floor plan. *Shit.* I hear him moving around the room, so I act like everything is okay and jump into the shower.

I get dressed in the outfit Shane bought for me, pull and clip my hair to hang down on one side, and keep my make-up to a minimum with a red lip. I'm putting my earrings on when he walks up behind me with the necklace.

"You're gorgeous." He places the necklace on and clasps it. "And Terry gets to show you off tonight."

"I'm sorry?" Before I jump to conclusions, I decide to calmly ask him what the hell he's talking about.

"I'm giving him my ticket. I was online while you were asleep and found box seats for the crew. So we don't get a bunch of questions, I figure I'll sit with them." He must be reading the disappointing look on my face because he won't look me in the eyes. "Y'all will have the better seats," he tries to explain.

I scratch my head trying to process and accept this arrangement. At this very moment, I want to cry. I start to think about Carice, this alleged new house, the dream, and convince myself he doesn't want to be seen with me. But I push those thoughts aside, put on my best fake smile and act like I've got a little mascara in my eye.

Terry's all smiles as we enter the Warner Theater. He gladly takes the two tickets and my arm, and leads the way to our seats. I immediately sit and cross my arms while everyone is on their feet.

"Smile, B. It's Jay." He motions for me to stand with him. I shake my head no. "He's about to come out!"

I look away and see Jen bolting down the aisle to her seat in the front row. "Look at Jen." I laugh. "I'm not a huge Jay fan like y'all," I say, continuing to sulk as Jeezy opens the show.

When Jay comes out, I stay seated, bored by it all, until suddenly I hear a familiar melody and Beyoncé's silhouette appears on stage. I jump to my feet. "She's here?" The screen lifts and it's her, looking absolutely gorgeous in her signature black bodysuit. "Oh my God, it's Beyoncé." The beat drops and my separation anxiety from Shane is instantly cured.

Terry wraps his arm around me. We're laughing, singing, dancing, and having a good ol' time. But Shane soon comes down and stands next to me.

"Y'all down here having too much fun," he growls, descending on us like a black cloud. He's jealous and I love it. The only person he needs to be mad at is himself. It was his idea. "Sit down," he says into my ear.

"Why? It's Beyoncé!" I'm doing the booty dance looking up at him with a smile so bright it could cause flowers to bloom.

"I don't want these dudes looking at your ass."

I bounce my hips side to side and flip my left hand. "Oh, oh, oh . . ."

"You better be sure the bark is worth the bite!" he roars to someone behind me.

I peek over my shoulder to see who was on the receiving end of that reprimand, and then back at Shane. I flash him my left hand, point to my ring finger, and resume singing along with Beyoncé.

He gives me a smile, rests his hand on my lower back, and doesn't leave my side.

29

SOMETHING SPECIAL

It's night and Shane should have landed back in Indiana already.
I send him a text.

Hey babe, I miss you.

Why don't you let me come over then?

My heart drops to the pit of my stomach as I type.

Where are you? I thought you were gone.

We missed our flight. Leaving in the
morning

I call Jen, who answers the phone half asleep, and I beg her
to wake and sit with Bailey. I must see Shane before he leaves. "I
hate you," she slurs. "I can't believe you're calling and waking
me up."

Jen, Myra, and I left the hotel at dawn and walked to the mall on Washington to watch the inauguration ceremony. The closest we got to President Obama was the Lincoln Memorial, because there were already millions of people, of all nationalities, standing shoulder to shoulder as far as we could see. We spent the entire day on our feet and just got home an hour ago.

"I owe you one."

"Send her over."

"She's asleep."

"You're going to have Jason's budget file to me tomorrow."

"Thanks, Jen."

"Whatever!" she shouts and hangs up the phone.

I text Shane.

`Let's do dinner? I'm hungry`

`I'm on my way`

I rush to dress and go out to his car, a Black BMW 7 series, where he's been waiting.

"Hello gorgeous." He leans over to give me a kiss.

"New car?"

"I test drove this one on my scavenger hunt."

"Amazing Race!"

"Yes, my Amazing Race."

"I like it." I don't know why, but I'm extremely nervous. My stomach clenches the entire way to Ruth's Chris Steak House. *Bella's Lullaby* from Twilight plays through the speakers.

"You have fun this weekend?"

"I had a wonderful time. Thanks again."

"You're welcome, sweetie."

He valets the car. They seat us in a booth and we order.

"How are things with the family?"

"They will be fine," he says, sticking his finger in a candle flame.

"Good."

"How's Bailey? We haven't been to the movies lately. I need to call and check on her."

"She's well." I take a sip of water. "Preparing for auditions."

"She's going to be a star. I know raw talent when I see it."

I smile, but I'm trying to drum up the courage to say what I really want to say. "Can I ask you something?" I ask with trepidation.

"Don't ask me anything you can't handle the answer to, because I'm not going to lie to you." He yanks his hand from the candle flame and squeezes his finger. "But first, I have a question for you."

"Shoot. But go ahead and stick it in your glass of water first."

"Ha, ha. You saw that, didn't you?"

"Why, Shane? Why?"

"I don't know. I'm drawn to things I know I shouldn't touch." He laughs.

"Anyway, what's up?"

"I don't ever want you to be angry with me. I don't know how I would be able to handle that. But when I was booking the extra Jay tickets for the squad, I saw that you were working on something for Jason."

"I—"

He cuts me off. "Are you still working for Jason after I asked you not to?"

"I am. It's my job. I've been assisting Jen." I didn't want to tell the truth, but I don't want to lie to his face.

Shane takes out his phone and makes a call. "Jennifer. Hire someone else to help you with the business." He pauses. "Bill me for it." He disconnects the call. "It's taken care of."

"Shane, we built Platinum Events together. Ummm, that's my other job. And it could be my only job if I don't find another soon."

"You don't need a job. You've got me. Whatever you need, whatever Bailey needs, it's already done."

I sit silently, not knowing if I should take him seriously. Jen is sending text messages back to back to my phone.

"Anyway, what did you want to ask me?"

"I want to know about the true nature of your relationship with Carice." I reach to touch his hand. "Please be honest."

"She's the mother of my children. That's it."

I look at him, wanting more than he's probably willing to offer.

"That's all she's ever going to be. I'm single and I date who I want."

"So, you're saying she's okay with you and me."

"She doesn't have to be okay with us. I mean . . . she might not like it, because she still wants me, but I want you. So, it really doesn't matter. I mean y'all will probably never meet 'cause I don't want drama."

"Drama?"

"B, she ain't nothing to worry about."

The waiter brings our food.

"Umm, is that right?" I place the cloth napkin in my lap.

"We not together. We ain't been together. Her job is to raise my kids and that is it. That's all she's ever going to do," he says adamantly and then starts to eat his sizzling steak.

"Well, I heard you just bought her a house."

"I bought my kids a house. You're listening to hearsay now? Everybody's got something to say about Shane Smith."

"I just want it to be very clear that I'm no one's side chick."

"Do I treat you like a side chick? Do you even know how side chicks get treated? They don't get time. They don't go out on dates. They know their place. They just get fucked!" Shane abruptly gets up from the table and walks to the men's room.

On his way back, he shields his face and plops down onto the seat with a look of defeat. "I'm not sure what it is, but we've got something between us. Something I've never felt before."

"I feel it too."

"Exactly, that's my point." He pushes his plate away. "Babe, listen . . . I only want you, and you have to trust that. You and me? We've got something special. Don't ruin it."

30

<u>VEGAS</u>

The sunlight shines through my bedroom window. Out of habit, I reach for my phone to check for messages from Shane. Tears of disappointment fill my eyes. It's official. For the first time, Shane's stood me up.

Trampling footsteps sound in the distance and grow faster and louder as they reach my bedroom door. I yank the covers over my head.

"Mom," whispers Bailey. "Are you awake?"

"Morning, babe," I say sleepily.

"Shane's picking me up to see a matinee."

"Oh yeah?" I peek from under the duvet. "What time is he coming?"

"He said in an hour."

"Okay, babe, you can go. Have fun." I check my cell phone. Nothing. *It's so unlike him.* When we spoke last night, he was leaving the club with Terry and DeShaun. He called again when he was ten minutes away. Then nothing. When I called him back, his phone went straight to voicemail. And now . . . hours later . . . he calls Bailey to make plans for a movie date?

I make sure to seem busy when he stops by to pick her up. He doesn't knock on the door, he simply pulls up and Bailey goes running out.

"Bailey, I'm going out so text me when you're done!" I shout out the door behind her. She waves her arms wildly and reaches for the front door handle. "Back seat," I remind her and then shut the front door. Loneliness engulfs me.

I call Jen even though I know she's busy. "Let's go get lunch, I need to talk. Put the laptop down and meet me in the car."

"Fine!" she barks.

Jen walks out of the house with her laptop bag and collapses into Betsy. She looks into the back seat. "Where's Bailey?"

"She's with Shane."

"So, when did Bailey make plans with Shane?"

"I have no idea." I back out of the driveway and drive to a local restaurant. "He got back in town on Monday and he was supposed to come over last night and that never happened. The next thing I know, Bailey's getting dressed and telling me Shane's on his way to take her to a movie."

Jen goes silent.

"I mean, hello?"

"Give me a minute. I'm thinking." Jen thinks the remaining way to the restaurant.

I take a deep breath and let out a melodramatic sigh as I schlep towards the hostess. "Two please, a booth if possible." The hostess grabs two menus and takes us to our table.

"Your server will be right with you."

"Thanks," I say, kicking my feet up on the opposite seat.

"Your daughter is hanging out on a Saturday afternoon with a professional football player who adores her." She stares at me. "And you're upset?" I know she's looking for a substantial comeback.

"Did you just completely miss the fact that I said he stood me up?"

"Maybe he fell asleep."

"We've been playing phone tag since Monday. All week he's been busy with business meetings for TGS."

"And on Saturday, he's with your daughter. I'm sorry, your point? Haven't you been busy with work?"

"Yes, the transition to USABankersTrust has been draining, so we planned to make time last night. Honestly, I think it's because I asked him about Carice."

"I doubt it. I think y'all are coming off that three-month honeymoon period. Most relationships are lucky to get that far."

The waitress comes to the table and takes our order. Jen pulls out her laptop. "Star's event is around the corner."

"I sent you everything I promised to send."

"That's not the point. We are partners in this."

"Yes, but it's also causing problems with my relationship with Shane. He said to hire someone else."

"I can bring my assistant, Sasha, on full time, I guess."

"I'll do anything that doesn't involve his teammates."

"All of our contracts involve him and his teammates. This is ridiculous, I can't believe we are having this conversation. He needs to get over himself."

As we're finishing our meals, my cell phone beeps with a new message. "Bailey's on her way." I've lost my appetite. The thought of seeing him makes me feel crazy. "Am I PMSing?"

Jen ignores me.

Bailey walks into the restaurant smiling from ear to ear and with a bounce in her step, making her long ponytail swing like a pendulum. Screeching in the restaurant lets me know Shane isn't far behind. I see him lower his cap as he hurries to our table and scoots into the booth next to Jen.

"What up?" he sings. He starts fiddling with the salt and pepper shakers. He avoids eye contact with me. I give the top of his cap the death stare and wait for him to raise his head.

"What's wrong, Mom?"

I perk right up. "Oh nothing, honey. My stomach hurts." I pat my middle. "I don't think my tummy agreed with it." I point to my half-eaten plate.

"What, you pregnant?" Shane barks, finally looking up at me.

I don't respond to his ignorance. Instead, I roll my eyes and give him the fakest smile I can muster. "No, I waited too long to eat," I lie. I want to say, 'you turned my stomach, you JERK'.

"Umph." He looks me up and down. "What y'all doing this weekend?"

"Nothing, I was supposed to do something last night, but it never happened," I say.

"Oh, is that right? Y'all wanna go to Vegas? It's Terry's birthday," he says, slapping the table before standing up.

"Sure," Jen and I say in unison.

Jen, Terry, Shane, and I board our flight to Vegas. When we land, a limo awaits and takes us straight to the Bellagio. The Bellagio water fountain spectacular, synchronized to Frank Sinatra, is playing as we pull up. "I can never see this show too many times, it's simply amazing," says Jen.

"Simply amazing," says Shane in a snooty voice, mocking her.

Jen rolls her eyes and grabs her purse. We enter the huge lobby and as Shane heads to registration, I stop and admire the extravagant $10 million chandelier made up of two thousand multi-colored hand-blown flowers.

"We've got to go," says Shane, startling me. "I booked an area at Foundation Room."

I've heard of this place. It's located at the top of the Mandalay Bay Hotel known for its sprawling view of the Las Vegas strip.

The private room is large with a gigantic hundred-foot projector screen, a pool table, and lots of plush seating.

"Shane. This room is too big for four people," Jen says.

"Jen, what did we discuss we'd work on?"

"I'm sorry, Shane, my protective nature just kicks in."

"Right, I get it, but it takes the fun out of things. Relax and enjoy it."

"Forgive me." She takes a seat and kicks her feet up. I sit on the plush suede seating next to Shane who's already engrossed in the elaborate menu.

"You still mad at me?" he pouts. "I fell asleep."

"You couldn't tell me?"

"Terry drove me home. I couldn't have him drop me off to your house. I was so tired I didn't charge my phone. I fell asleep on the couch. I even let Terry take my truck." He steals a kiss. "Baby, don't be like that. What would you like to eat?"

"I'm not sure yet. Let me check out the menu for a second."

"When you're ready, just tell her what you want." Shane points to the waitress. "Come on y'all, order, 'cause I'm hungry!" he yells to Jen and Terry. His phone lights up and vibrates on the footstool. He answers the call in a kind voice. "Yes, sweetie, we are here. Tell them I said to bring you up." He waves Terry over to him and whispers in his ear. Terry nods and leaves. Shane turns back to me, smiling, and plants another kiss on my lips. "Smile, it's Terry's birthday."

Fuck Terry! Who was that on the phone? I force out a 'yeah' and wave my hands.

"That's right," he says, leaning close into my ear and whispering, "you are so sexy. I can't wait to eat that pussy tonight." He bites my earlobe and sends a rush through my body. I'm instantly reminded of how much I miss his touch.

Terry returns with three very young, scantily clad girls. Two of the blondes look like trailer trash, but the one in the middle just walked off the strip. She's short like me, but has a head full of platinum-blonde clip-on extensions, and she's wearing a tight, black, revealing dress exposing her quadruple Ds.

Shane's all smiles and he jumps to his feet, bouncing around like a jackrabbit to walk his acquaintances over to the sitting area. "Bryn, this is Lexi and her friends Brandy and Tara. Ladies . . . this is Bryn and Jen, my event planners."

"Hi, nice to meet you." I stand and shake their hands with a frozen smile. Jen is distracted, on her phone. "That's Jen over there, working. She never stops. Yup, that is what we event planners do." I tilt my head with a scary grin on my face. "Here, have a seat. I'll go check on Jen and see how work is coming along." The girls take a seat and Shane swoops in with menus like he's on some damn magic carpet. I hear him tell them to order anything they want as I approach Jen.

"What are you doing over here? Do you see this shit?"

"Yes. Shane has me looking for rooms for them, but all hotels are sold out. They have very poor reception in here."

"Excuse me? Rooms?"

"Yes, Terry just came over here and told me Shane said to find them a room to stay overnight."

"Overnight? This is bullshit. This isn't going to work." I wave my finger.

"Stop! You look crazy." She stares at her phone. "Excuse me, excuse me," she says, waving to the waitress. "Do you have a computer in an office I can use? I'm trying to book a hotel reservation and my phone Internet connection isn't working."

"I'll check with the manager," the waitress replies.

"Thank you." Jen sets her phone down and looks at me with an exhausted expression. "Look, it's been a long day." She rubs her face. "He just flew us out here for Terry's birthday. We are in this sick area to watch the fight. Forget about him and enjoy yourself." She makes herself comfortable with extra pillows from the next seat.

I look over my shoulder and see Shane running his mouth to the Girls Next Door. Terry, leaning on the pool table, is engrossed in a basketball game on one of the smaller TVs. In my sexiest Beyoncé walk, I grab two pool sticks, handing one to Terry. "Wanna play? Birthday boy?"

His face lights up. "Sure."

"You break," I say.

Terry breaks and gets solids. "I didn't know you played." He's excited and takes a few more shots until he misses.

"My turn." I bend over, eye level to the table, to inspect *nothing*, but it gets Shane's attention. I line up my cue stick, hoping to hit this striped ball into the left pocket. But first, I picture Shane's face on the front of the cue ball then strike it with all my anger. It goes in. "Yes!" I scream, like it is my twenty-first birthday, taking a short dance around the table with my tongue sticking out.

"That was luck!" roars Shane from across the room.

"Mind your business. This isn't your game," I shout, seductively walking towards him and then leaving him wanting. I bend low to the table again. Shane is definitely staring at my ass. Another ball goes in the pocket. Luck is on my side again. I dance with the stick this time, acting very mischievously and certainly not ladylike. But I know what he likes and it's working, because he leaves the Dixie Chicks and yanks a pool stick out of the wall cabinet, practically breaking it.

"Let's start a new game," he barks at me. "Terry, go check on Jen. She's been gone too long." He angrily collects the balls and resets the table. I shimmy over to him, looking up at him with my finger in my mouth. "Let's put a wager on it," he growls.

"What did you have in mind?" I lick my lips.

He suggestively looks at his dick, grabs his drink, and swallows it in one gulp. He slams the glass on the table edge. "You gotta swallow. Tonight!"

I let out a hearty laugh. "Is that right?"

"Yeah, that's right." He undresses me with his eyes.

"BET!" I feel a raging tornado inside me. I'm so fired up I could lift the table off the floor with my pinky finger.

"Let the game begin." He breaks, proceeds to knock all the solid balls in the pockets, and wins. "That was too easy. Best two out of three?"

I nod yes. Thankfully, I'm still in the game.

The second game ends faster than the first. I'm not sure how that was possible. I didn't get a chance to move.

"I tell you what. Next game, winner takes all." He holds his dick and laughs uncontrollably. He breaks and three of his balls go into various pockets. He laughs again, starts imitating me swallowing, and wipes his mouth before taking another shot. Shane's knocking in balls left and right. He continues to taunt me and I feel defeated. Then somehow, he misses. "Your turn."

All my balls are still on the table and he's down to one. *This sucks.* I take my turn and miss.

"Ohhhhhhh!" screams Shane. "She swallowed it!"

"Shut up," I say to him, pouting.

Shane looks me in the eye as he sets up his last shot. "You suck," he says with a grin. "Literally." He lets out cries of laughter and takes his last shot. The cue ball is perfectly lined up to send his last ball into the side pocket. Then, magically, the ball curves slightly right and hits the eight ball instead, sending it to the corner pocket.

I win.

I smile from ear to ear, vindicated. Shane throws his stick on the table, almost breaking it, and silently walks back over to his guests. I want to chuck a ball at his head and send him to the nearest emergency room. *I wonder if Lexi and friends will nurse his wounds.*

"Terry, where exactly is Jen?"

"She's in the management office."

I hand him my stick and storm out of the room into a packed bar. I find our waitress and she leads me to Jen. "Why are you still in here?"

"Everywhere is sold out. I don't know what he wants me to do. The only rooms available are suites at the Bellagio."

"Oh, hell naw." I'm wild-eyed and leaning over the desk.

"Bryn, I don't have time for this. I didn't fly across the country for this." She holds her head. "Yes, I'm still holding," she says into the phone.

"Well he—"

"GO DO SOMETHING ABOUT IT!" Jen cuts me off.

I storm back to the room and Lexi is dropping it like it's hot in front of Shane. I daydream of crashing a bottle of liquor against his head. Snapping back to reality, I walk back into the bar area before I kill everyone in this room. I close my eyes and try to calm down, feeling my throat constricting. *Breathe, Bryn, breathe. Don't freak out. Don't freak out. Don't freak out.*

"What's wrong with you? Why are you out here?" I hear Shane bark.

"I figure you needed space."

"Where is Jen?"

"She's still looking for a room for your bunnies." I cross my arms at my chest.

"It's not like that. They're my friends."

I look him directly in the eyes. "I shouldn't have to put up with this."

"Put up with what? Bryn, you have to understand that I know a lot of people. You've got to learn to accept that. I can't be rude to them, just because you're jealous."

"Jealous? And you're not being rude? I'd say you're being rather accommodating. You introduced me as your event planner!"

"You are!"

"Oh, I'm your event planner when it's convenient for YOU! But you've pretty much banned me from event planning."

He stops and stares at me. I can tell he wants to say something, but he won't. "What's happened to you? I thought you were different. Don't act like these other girls act. Don't be like that."

"Really? I'm acting like everyone else? I'm acting like any self-respecting woman would act if their man is openly flirting with other women. If they stay, I'm staying with Jen tonight and I'm flying HOME first thing in the morning. The Jonas sisters can keep you warm tonight."

"Fuck that!" Shane storms off and returns with Jen seconds later before going back over to his guests.

Jen joins me at the bar. "What just happened? Shane burst into the office, grabbed the phone out of my hand, slammed it down, and yelled at me to stop looking. I mean he was crazed, manic."

"Jen." I turn to face her. "I just calmly told him that if those girls stayed, he would be sleeping alone tonight and every night after that."

"What happened? Your eyes are bloodshot."

"I . . . I feel like I'm about to lose it."

"Hold it together. I'm not sitting in an emergency room tonight. Y'all are ridiculous. Let's move."

With a look of venom, I walk into the room and witness Shane telling The Girls Next Door he can't get them a room.

Hours later, Goldilocks and the two sluts follow us back to our hotel and ask for a tour of Shane's suite. "Y'all can tour Jen's," he says, walking away towards our room.

"Where is your room?" Goldilocks starts eyeing me.

I raise an eyebrow and before a word can form on my lips, Jen whips out her room key. As they enter Jen's room, I kick my heels off and beeline after Shane. The door is shut by the time I reach the end of the hall. I tap on the door three times.

"Who is it?"

"Open the door, it's me."

The door flies open and he grabs my arm and yanks me into the dark room. "Shane, I can't . . . see."

"Come here." He kisses me wildly and forcefully spreads my thighs. "You're wet," he whispers. "Let me put it in." He spins me around, pushes me against a doorframe, and frantically unbuckles his belt. Yanking my dress, he splits the seam as he pulls it above my waist.

"Shane, my goodness. What's gotten into you?"

He smacks my ass and then rips my thong clean off my body. "Bend over," he huffs. Pulling me over to the window, he yanks the curtains back. With my face pressed against the glass, Shane drops to his knees and takes me whole, into his mouth. My legs, my waist, my entire body start to convulse. He lifts me on his shoulders and leans my back against the wall. Slowly, he guides me onto him and fulfills his need.

I'm on the floor, out of breath, when he stands and puts his pants back up. He reaches in his pocket and hands me a ticket.

"Here, get the bags." He kisses me on the forehead and walks away.

"Where are you going?"

"To the casino." He tosses me a bottled water from the mini bar.

I lie naked on the floor in disbelief with the damn ticket in my hand. "To be clear, you're leaving me in this room?"

"I just need you to wait for the bags. I've got to get down there, because Lexi has to go back to California soon."

"Are you serious?"

"Now you know what jealousy feels like."

"I'm confused."

"I know you've still been working with Jason . . . after I asked you not to, after I told Jen to hire someone else." I feel a pang of guilt. I open my mouth, but nothing comes out. He takes my silence as an 'okay' and shuts the door behind him.

Shit! I knew working with Jason would come back to bite me in the ass. I've tried to disengage myself with the planning as much as possible, but Jen constantly needs my help. I call her. "Jen, Shane just flipped out because he knows I'm still working for Jason."

"Don't fall for it. He's positioning himself and deflecting."

"For?"

"He knows he was wrong. Inviting those girls was downright inappropriate. Don't fall for it. I say you hold out and don't give him any tonight."

"It's too late."

"You, my dear, are dick-ma-tized."

"Don't say that."

"I'm sorry, but you are. I don't have any sound advice for you tonight. You two have worn me out."

"He just left to go cater to Lexi."

"And you gave him some?" she shouts. "You're on your own tonight. Goodnight. I'm going to rest for tomorrow."

The doorbell rings. The bags arrive just in time.

I shower and change into a red dress and a pair of nude heels. My hair is bone straight and my make-up is minimal. I look gorgeous and give myself a pep talk in the mirror. "You're the baddest bitch!" I say, adding an extra layer of gloss.

The casino is at least a mile's walk from the room. *Where is this asshole?* I say under my breath, canvasing the floor as if I'm on the hunt for my enemy. Middle-aged men at the poker tables are practically falling out of their chairs staring at me as I walk by. I hear a few whistles and catcalls which I ignore. With Shane nowhere to be found, I head towards the crap tables.

"Babe." He leans against a crap table, reaching for me and pulling me against his body. "Aww baby, why do you look so mean? Daddy didn't make it better?" He kisses my neck.

"Where are your girlfriends?" I catch the man across the table staring at my cleavage and wink at him. Embarrassed he got caught, he lowers his head and flips through his chips. Shane places his hand on my shoulder and presses his hard dick against my back.

"You're turning me on," he says into my ear. "I want to take you on this table."

"About the Jason thing."

"Not now. We're next, you want to roll? Maybe bring Daddy some luck?" He places the dice in my hand. "Make sure you hit the back wall."

Talk about pressure. I close my eyes and realize it's not appropriate to say a prayer. I'm gambling. All bets are placed and it's time for me to throw the dice. With a flick of my wrist the dice soar and bounce off the red velvet wall and onto the table.

"Seven," the dealer says.

"Oh no," I pout. "I crapped out on the first roll." I feel like a loser. Everyone is cheering and getting chips, including us.

"No babe, it's okay this time," he says, grabbing his chips and placing more bets. "Roll me a five."

I blow on the dice and let them loose.

"Five!" shouts the dealer.

"You're fucking kidding me." Shane rubs my back, sending shivers down my spine.

Next, I throw a five. Then a nine. Then a six. Our table gets crowded and all eyes are on me. I'm having a great time. I take the dice, do a little shimmy and shake before releasing them. It feels like they're settling in slow motion.

"Seven!"

Fuck. I crapped out.

Shane smiles, pulls me towards him, and places a handful of black, purple, and yellow chips in my hand. "You've earned them."

31

VEGAS: THE MORNING
AFTER

Shane's cell phone rings at dawn, waking me up. He's still snoring. We had marathon sex until we both tapped out. I debate whether to wake him, but then he starts to stir. The ringing stops, only to be replaced by a different ringtone from another caller. I rub my feet against him so he'll wake up and make it stop. He rolls over and cups my breasts instead. The ringing continues.

"Babe, your phone. Please, maybe it's important." I watch him as he pulls back the white sheets, revealing his naked body. I'm obsessed with his build. I get excited watching him sit on the edge of the bed. His back is broad and his muscles are so defined it makes his body look fake. He stands, stretching, and his dick dangles like a vine. *That anaconda, woo wee.* What a rush, an enjoyable aching sensation that awakens my desire to feel that monster inside me again. I touch myself and I'm wet.

He takes the call in the seating area and quickly returns to the bedroom. "Getting started without me?" Shane tosses the phone on the floor. He pulls the sheets back and motions for me to slide over to the middle of the king-size bed. "Don't stop. I like to watch." He kneels on all fours. "Yeah, get my pussy wet." He watches, licking his lips like an impatient animal waiting to be fed. He quickly joins in.

Ring, Ring . . . Ring, Ring . . . This hotel phone is loud as shit. I pull the covers over my head. Then I hear a *ding, dong. Bang! Bang! Bang!* Finally, Shane jumps out of bed. *What is it now?*

I hear the room door open and shut and Shane walk back into the bedroom. "It's afternoon, babe. Get up and go shopping. I'm going to hang out with Terry."

I leap out of bed, shower, and toss on a pair of cigarette pants, a white top, and my Prada pumps. For a pop of color, I dig in my suitcase for my red clutch and head down to the casino to cash in my chips. Jen is already waiting for me in the lobby, so we take the shortcut towards Caesars Forum shops. But first stop, Chanel in the Bellagio shops. I spend a good half of my winnings purchasing a quilted black Chanel flap bag. It's timeless. Jen is drooling over a gigantic tote.

Next stop, Dior. Jen stops to chat with the fashionably dressed sales rep while I pick out an amazing pair of large tortoise-framed shades and a bottle of Ms. Dior Cherie perfume. All this excitement is making me hungry.

We stop for lunch at The Cheesecake Factory. Seated in the fake outdoor area, the painted cloud ceilings make me forget we're in a mall. "I need you to help me pick out something for him." I place my shopping bags in the extra chair.

Jen shakes her head. "Yesterday you were all crazy and today you can't stop smiling."

"He makes me smile."

"Give me eight grand to shop with and I'll be smiling as well."

"What should I get him?"

"A tie. Wear it tonight."

"That's so cliché. They did that in *Pretty Woman*."

"Who cares, it works. If it ain't broke, why fix it?"

"Good point. I'll find him one from Hermès."

When I return to the room later that evening, Shane texts me directions to where he's sitting in the casino. I put everything away and go back down. When I find him, Zander is sitting at the poker table too. "What are you doing here?" I ask Zander, giving him a hug.

"I flew in for my cousin's big day."

"Where is he?"

"He doesn't gamble, so I called Jen to take him shopping." Shane winks. "So tonight, it's just us." He pulls over an extra chair from behind us, kisses me on the lips, and then turns his focus back to the table. I watch and let him try to explain the game of poker to me, but I can't catch on. An older Asian woman with a shit load of chips sitting across from us keeps staring at us. Finally, she asks him, "Is she your lady?"

"Yeah." Shane smiles and pinches my butt.

"She very pretty," she says. "You treat her good."

"I do." He pulls my chair closer to him. "She's got me under her spell." I give him a wink and blow him a kiss. Shane's so adorable when he blushes.

As the game ends, everyone throws in their cards except Zander, who's shouting with excitement. Shane has a dead hand, but he still pushes all his chips into the center. The remaining players throw their cards in. The dealer reveals his cards, Zander's hand wins and he takes the pot, jumping and screaming.

"Come on, baby, let's go. Congrats yo," Shane says, exchanging a brotherly embrace with Zander. Then he grabs me by the waist and guides me through the tables.

"If you had a dead hand, why did you put all your chips in?"

"I wanted him to have them," he says sincerely.

"Wow," I say and continue to walk with him towards the restaurant.

"When I was in college, I was dating this girl. She came from money and I didn't have money then, well, not like I do now. I went out to dinner with her family to a five-star restaurant. Everything on the menu was market price. I didn't want to order anything and it made me feel some kinda way. When it was time to take care of the check, I pulled out my money to contribute and her father grabbed the check and told me to put my money away. He said that when he was my age, he lived paycheck to paycheck and now that he was a successful businessman, his money lasted longer. He told me to remember that and made me promise if I was ever in that position, I'd do the same thing. So I vowed I'd always do that."

The more I learn about Shane, the deeper I fall. I wipe a tear from my eye.

"You alright?"

I rub and squeeze his hand as tightly as I can. "As long as we're together."

Shane and I dine by candlelight on prime rib and whale-size lobster accompanied by a bottle of Egon Muller Scharzhofberger Riesling Auslese. We feed each other dessert, and for the very first time, it feels like we are an official couple. I know things won't always be perfect and that like every relationship, we'll have our struggles. But at this moment, I know that he's mine and I am his.

32

DR. SEKYLL

The next morning, Shane's dark mood from Saturday has returned. His ability to turn off the crazy and turn on the charm keeps me on my toes. We take ten steps forward then five steps back. The suite is pretty much silent as we pack. Right as we're ready to head out, he says he needs to stay behind to 'call his mother'.

"Go ahead and get Jen. I'll meet you downstairs. Leave your shopping bags. I'll bring them. Yeah, that way Terry won't catch us." It must sound like a good excuse to him. I give him a disbelieving look. "Bryn, Terry told me after D.C. that he wants to marry you. He's not ready to find out. Not right now. It will crush him." I'm still not convinced, but leave him in the room to make his call.

Jen's in the hallway waiting for me.

Terry, all packed and ready to go with a new Gucci murse strapped across his chest, is in the main lobby with Zander. "Where's Shane?"

"I guess he's in his room."

"The limo is waiting. He needs to come on." Terry takes out his cell phone and starts to dial. "Man, he's not answering."

Seconds later, Shane is walking up to us. "Yo, I called you," says Terry.

"No, you didn't."

"Yes, I did. Check your phone."

Shane reaches in his pocket and pulls out a phone. He pats his other pockets frantically. "Fuck," he yells. "I left my other phone." Shane turns to me. "You still got my key?"

Without saying a word, I reach into my back pocket and give him the key. Shane hands me the shopping bags and heads back upstairs. Zander looks away intentionally, and then directs his attention to Terry, who's staring at me. Jen grabs her bag and walks to the limo.

I don't know if I should say anything, so I just follow Jen. When I catch up to her, she shakes her head. "Feeling better, dearie? You look like you've just had sex."

"It hurt so good."

"Yuck. Terry's got to be stupid if he doesn't know now. Zander asked him if you and Shane were fucking. Apparently, you two were very obvious at the poker table."

"I'm tired of hiding things from Terry. It's turning into a crutch. Initially, I got it. No one wanted to create any animosity between the two of them, but now it's getting in the way of me and Shane. Especially how I'm being treated in public when he's around."

"You already know I don't believe in secrets. It's betrayal. Shane knew that Terry liked you in the first place. He should have manned up a long time ago." She signals that they're walking up behind us. We all get in the limo and head straight to the airport.

With all this talk of Terry, I didn't have the guts to tell her I need to quit.

I stand by the gate looking out at the service crew turn over our plane. There's a lot on my mind. I'm happy, but sad, disgusted, yet charmed. I love him and I hate him at the same time. *Look at him, over there practically licking his King magazine, not paying me one bit of attention while I stand here alone.*

Once again, because of Terry, we're acting like strangers waiting to board our plane.

33

THE CALM BEFORE THE STORM

"Mom. Shane's here." I hear the door open and shut.

I grab my coat and scarf and lock the door, following her to his truck.

"You're hanging out with us?" Shane asks me, lifting Bailey into the back seat.

"Yeah, Bailey begged me to come with y'all today."

"I'm so glad you could join us. I thought you were still treating me funny because of Vegas."

"Stop it. Don't try it. That was two weeks ago."

"I'm just kidding. I'm ecstatic. Now I have two of y'all to beat." He turns on the soundtrack to *High School Musical* and he and Bailey start singing on our way to Dave & Busters.

Shane's bombarded as we walk inside. He's such a professional, humbly thanking his fans for the love and politely requesting privacy. Bailey, on the other hand, stands huffing and puffing with her arms crossed over her chest, red with anger. "They're so rude. I wish they'd leave us alone."

"Bailey, relax . . ." I say, rubbing her back. I stare at Shane at the counter getting the game cards and attract his attention with my eyes widened. Without Bailey noticing, I point to her and frown, exaggeratedly poking my bottom lip out. He lets out a chuckle.

"Here, sweetie," he says, handing her the card. "I put $500 on there so let's get it in." Shane grabs her hand and they run towards the racecars.

Bailey perks right up. I find a seat in a booth and get comfortable, wanting to give them time together. This is their last outing before Shane leaves tonight and he'll be gone for three months for his off-season training.

She's just as saddened as I am about him leaving. They have established their own fun relationship. She texts him and tells him about her day, her report card, or any random thing. It's so cute. She's able to relate to him in a way that she hasn't related to any other male, including her father. Shane happily assumes the role of the male figure in her life and encourages it. He makes a point of making her feel special and I love that about him. It makes me love him more.

They run around until Bailey passes out, unable to keep up. Shane carries her to the car. The ride home in the rain is quiet until Shane breaks the silence. "I would say dinner and a movie later, but I've got to pack tonight, so how about just dinner?"

"Sure, babe, that's fine," I say, squeezing his hand. "Thank you for today."

"Anything for my beautiful girls," he says, blowing me a kiss. "I'll pick you up in an hour. Make a reservation at Ruth's Chris." He jumps out and lifts Bailey out of the truck and gives her a big bear hug. "Take care of your mom while I'm away. Keep her out of trouble."

"What trouble are you talking about, silly?"

"Work trouble." He takes her hand and walks us to the door. "I'm going to miss you, Bailey baby."

Her eyes tear up.

"Don't cry. It will go by really fast, I promise." He gives her another hug and hands her the Dave & Buster's play card. "Keep this safe for when I return."

Her face lights up and she runs into the house.

"See you in a few, babe."

I close the door, walk into the house, and plop down on the couch to check my email.

Dear Bryn Charles,

On behalf of The Lawson Company, I'm pleased to offer you the position of Accounting Manager . . .

I landed the job I wanted.

Today is truly bittersweet.

It's too cold outside for a sexy dress, so I throw on a pair of jeans with a sexy top. As I finish my smoky eye, Bailey pokes her head into my bathroom. "Yes, my dear," I say to her in my stuffy old-English-lady accent while applying my eyeliner.

"Where are you going?" She picks up my lip gloss and starts to apply it. "When did you say I could wear make-up?"

"Thirty."

"Thirty?" she screams, looking up at me.

I lean down to give her a kiss. "Just kidding . . . twenty-one," I laugh.

"Mom!"

"Maybe somewhere between sixteen and eighteen. I keep telling you . . . you don't need make-up like Mommy. You don't turn pale yellow in the winter like I do. You've got that natural Trinidadian glow from your grandfather."

"How do I look?" Bailey mocks my voice and shakes her head with a face full of sparkly bronzer.

"Like a beauty queen. Now make sure you wash all that off tonight when you take your shower. You don't want break-outs."

"Um, yeah, you didn't tell me where you're going?"

"Out with Uncle Shane to discuss his next project."

"Ooh, can I go? Is Roman going to be there?"

"I don't think so. Besides, Aunty said she wanted you to watch *Princess Diaries 2* with her."

"Can I make microwave popcorn?"

"Let Aunty Jen make it."

"I think that's her now." She runs downstairs to meet her.

Just as she arrives, so does Shane. I open the door of Shane's truck and his arm is outstretched over the center console. He gently pulls me in. "Hey, baby," he says, kissing me on the lips.

"You know Bailey's looking through the window."

"She can't see through my windows."

"Make sure you wave to her when you turn the bend."

Shane rolls his window down to wave to Bailey who's sitting with her face plastered against the glass. "Babe, hold on, this is my Mom calling. I gotta take it. "Yeah," he says into the phone. "No. I said everyone is responsible for his or her flights. No, my babies fly out with me. I couldn't give a shit. She can walk. I love you too." He hangs up the phone, glancing over his shoulder at me, and then focuses his attention back on the dark windy road in silence. I've gotten really good at reading his body language.

"Planning for Hawaii?" I ask, staring out at the road over the dashboard.

"Yeah, see I was trying to get y'all there, but my family . . ." He stops at the red light, looking both ways before making a right on red, avoiding eye contact. "I haven't been for a couple of years and this is the last year we can go to Hawaii, so Mom wants to go as a family . . . you know?"

"I completely understand." I keep a straight face, listening to his seemingly rehearsed response. Somehow, I believe 'his family' includes Carice.

"Oh, you know this song?" he blurts, turning up the volume on *No One* by Alicia Keys. He sings along for the rest of the way.

They are kind enough to seat us at a candlelit table for two in the wine room for privacy.

"To us," he says, lifting his glass for a toast. "So beautiful," he continues, with a look of admiration and then adds, "congratulations on the new gig."

"Thank you."

"You should be receiving something on Monday."

"Aww, you didn't have to."

"I know. I wanted to," he says, gulping his wine then smacking his lips loudly. "So," he says, leaning back in his chair. "I still can't believe we're doing this. Like, I'm ready to tell Bailey."

"As long as it's forever."

Shane takes my hand. "What do you think she will say?"

"I have no idea what her reaction will be."

"That's my girl. I can't wait to tell her. She can call me step-dad. Would you let me adopt her?"

"That conversation is for another day."

"I feel so honored to be here with you. Like when I first saw you I was like . . . I'm not on her level, she would never date a guy like me. I mean, I never thought I could get you, but here we are."

"Thank you sweetheart, and yes, here we are, who would have thought?" I say, rolling the stem of my wine glass between my fingers, back and forth. He was right. I would have never guessed it either. It wasn't love at first sight, but it was love. I feel like I've fallen in love with the innermost part of him and it feels great.

After dinner, Shane takes the scenic route back to my house. I reminisce about the night he held me close in front of the fire.

I relax and try not to let the fear of him leaving put a damper on our last night together.

"I love you," escapes from my lips.

"WOW," he says, jumping in his seat and turning his body towards me. "You've never said that before." His eyes widen.

I shift my body to face him. "I'm saying it now."

"I'm just—I have a hard time saying those words. I got hurt by the one woman I said that to," he says, fumbling around with his iPod.

"Well, I didn't say it just for you to say it back to me. I said it because that is how I truly feel and I want you to know it and remember it while you're away."

An unusually quiet Shane hits play on his iPod and reaches for my hand, giving it a tight squeeze as Alicia Keys' *Tell You Something* begins to play. I can see him thinking. The remaining five-minute ride home is the longest I've experienced. He holds my hand as I focus on the lyrics.

We pull up in front of my house and Shane jumps out to open my door. His hand is outstretched for mine and I gladly take it and jump out onto the curb. He uses his body as a shield from the rain as we run to my door.

"I'm going to miss you, babe."

"I know. This will be the longest time we've been away from each other. I'm going to miss you more," I say, reaching for a hug.

He plants the sweetest kiss on my lips.

"Goodnight, sweetie. Dream sweet dreams of me."

I give him another kiss before opening my door to leave him, fighting back tears. It only lasts until I shut the door. Still seeing a glimpse of his motionless shadow, I peek through the sheers to find Shane standing in the middle of my lawn with his head lowered. He puts his phone in his pocket and runs to his truck.

My cell phone chimes.

`I love you too!`

34

SIDELINED

I'm quitting Platinum Events, today. I don't know how, but it must be done. A week has passed since I've heard from Shane and I can't stop thinking that it's because of a conversation he could have had with Jason during their flight to Hawaii, or in the locker room, or in the shower after practice. I don't know, but I can't think of any other reason he hasn't contacted me.

Jen will think I'm being irrational for choosing my relationship with Shane over the business. I'm not prepared to give Shane up. I fix myself a drink for some liquid courage. I'm startled when my phone rings.

"Come open the door," says Jen.

I drop the hand towel on the counter and let her in. I'm throwing a Pro Bowl potluck party for a few friends.

"Can you ask Bailey to come help me bring in the chicken?" She struggles through the door with a lemon pound cake and a few liters of ginger ale.

"Bailey, come help Aunty Jen with the food. "Girl, drop those sodas, please, before you drop that cake."

"Mom, where is it?"

"Bailey, it's in my car. Lock the door when you finish." Jen drops her keys.

"Ugh," I say, exasperated.

"Don't start that crazy sigh. What's that for? You talk to your boy?"

"Actually no. Not for seven days. Since he's been in Hawaii, no bueno."

"I'm sure he will call," she says, as she starts to set up the food table. "I only got a pan of fifty wings. Will that be enough?"

"It's plenty. It's only your people, Michael, and Imani."

"Well, you know how my family eats. I'm just saying."

"I don't even have an appetite so there's extras right there."

"Lovesick, I'm assuming." She plops down on a chair to catch her breath.

"Yeah, I just miss him like crazy."

"Aww how tweet," she says, bending over and dry heaving.

"I will not tolerate this type of reaction to my affections."

Jen starts to choke.

"Aunty, are you okay?" Bailey walks into the house with the chicken.

"She's fine, dear, God doesn't like ugly," I say, looking at Jen.

"Oh Aunty, can I help set up the table?"

"Sure honey," says Jen, trying to catch her breath. "Look," she says to me, "you know what my aunty told me, 'if a man lies, he'll cheat. If he cheats, he'll steal. And if he steals, he'll kill.' Remember that."

"He hasn't lied. Well, not technically."

"Withholding the complete truth is lying. Like I said, he needs to tell Terry. But I mean—that's y'all business." She balls the plastic bags and tosses them into the recycling bin. "He should be careful, you know what they say about karma."

"We're going to talk to *everybody*."

"Yeah, well, like I said. I don't want to be around for it." She shakes her head. "Know the plays, or get sidelined."

"What are you talking about now? What are you . . . like a quote machine now?"

"Know the plays, or get sidelined. It's that simple. Terry got played." She coughs. "This time," she says under her breath.

"What are you insinuating? Speak freely, please."

"Ignore Shane's plays and you'll find yourself on the outside looking in. Terry didn't realize what he was up against. I can't, in good conscience, say that I believe you know what you're up against."

"My eyes are wide open. I'm in love."

"Whatever. Keep telling yourself that. I've got my own set of problems to deal with. Jason's mother just added a hundred people to her dinner. You know what that means. I need you on the phone with the caterers first thing Monday morning. No offense, but your time is so consumed with Bailey and Shane you haven't made time for Platinum Events in weeks. I've been carrying things on my own, and frankly, I have a serious issue with it."

I nod and finish my cocktail in one gulp. I don't know how to respond, but I do know that now isn't the time to break the news to her. "Excuse me, I'm going to change before my guests arrive."

When I return, Bailey and Jen have done a wonderful job of the décor. The event planner in me rearranges a few of the dishes on the table and voilà, perfection.

Throughout the AFC vs. NFC game everyone is focused on the screen and enjoying Michael's famous buffalo wing dip and chips, listening to his commentary on every play. I'm walking around completely stressed out trying to be a fun hostess.

"Alright Bryn, where are the drinks? We need more drinks before the game is over!" he shouts.

"I'm on it." I run upstairs and check my supply and I've only got a bottle of tequila left. A thunderous roar fills the basement. I quickly line the glasses together on the tray, open the bottle, do my best rendition of Tom Cruise in *Cocktail*, and steadily take them downstairs. Halfway down, I hear the final minutes of the game. AFC is ahead with a one-point lead.

I make it around the room handing out shots to everyone.

"Alright! Alright! On three, y'all. On three! AFC!" yells Michael.

Everyone raises their shots.

"One!" shouts Michael.

My mind swiftly drifts to Terry. We'll tell him first, soon as Shane returns. No more secrets.

"Two!"

Bailey's next. She'll be so excited.

"Three!" Michael wails.

Fuck! I've got to tell Jen I'm quitting.

"Go AFC!" the entire room roars. The AFC wins with a field goal.

Troubled, I make my way around the room collecting glasses and placing them back on the tray.

"Hey B, look, your boy is on. He's about to do an interview!" shouts Michael.

"Hush. Hush everyone," says Jen, standing up and motioning for silence. She grabs the remote and turns it up to almost maximum volume.

Reporter: Shane Smith, what a game!

Shane: Yes, it was exciting, glad to be a part of it.

Reporter: Congrats on your second nomination to the Pro Bowl, how do you feel about them changing it up for next year, breaking tradition and moving it to Miami?

Shane: Well, you know . . . all great things come to an end sometimes. I'm just glad I was able to make it this year with the entire family.

Reporter: Yes, and congratulations on the new addition.

Shane: Yes, thank you. My son, he's here with me.

Reporter: Oh look, he's headed our way.

The camera zooms in on Shane taking his son from Carice. Her hair is dyed Nighthawks blue and styled in a mohawk. She has a big dumb smile on her face as Shane drapes his arm around her shoulder.

Shane: I'm so privileged to share this win with my children and my fiancée.

Reporter: Congratulat—wonk, wonk, wonnnnnnnnnkkkkkkkkkkk

My legs buckle.

Somehow an anvil smashes my chest.

I gasp for air.

Everything goes dark.

35

<u>INTUITION</u>

I'm standing at the bottom of the Philadelphia Museum of Art looking at the seventy-two stone steps in front of me. There is an unknown urgency luring me to reach the top. Like Rocky Balboa, I start my crossing, fueled by pure desire. I'm manic, panting for air, as I reach for the top. Lifting each foot to take my final step, another seventy-two appear in front of me. I'm running in place. I turn to look back and find myself alone at the bottom of the stairs. No cars, no sign of life anywhere. I run again and again and again and finally after the third time I reach the top platform. Before me is an extravagant white cathedral with pure gold accents.

A gong sounds and the doors of the church swing open with force, revealing a one-hundred-foot red runner down the center aisle. At the very end, a couple and a preacher are standing at an altar.

"Speak now, or forever hold your peace," says the preacher, staring at me with sad eyes. It's Qmar.

No one makes a sound. The pews are occupied by faceless mannequins.

"Noooooooooooooooooo!!!!" I scream and sprint towards Shane in record time, my eyes filled with tears. "Shane, don't do it!" I cry.

His face is like stone. He reaches for her left hand.

My once-forward motion violently stops as I run in place, fighting a huge vacuum-like pull sucking me backward towards the entrance. I can't endure the struggle and rest. The force pulls me outside as I watch the doors slam shut in front of me. A drawbridge is lifted and closes with a bang, leaving me on the outside staring up at the stone castle walls.

I find a ledge. I'm confident I can make this jump and scale my way to the top. I can't let him do this. I take a running start and leap with every fiber of my being, arms outstretched. Mid-flight, the stone ledge disappears and I fall into dark swampy waters, murky and foul smelling. I offer no resistance and sink to the bottom where my legs finally find freedom. As excitement fills my body, I continue to fall and land in a soft cushiony chair. I see Shane sitting in the chair to my left. He reaches for my arm and cuddles into me, looking at a huge movie screen at Cadillac Records.

It's Beyoncé with platinum-blond hair and a blue patterned dress in a studio, singing I'd Rather Go Blind.

I remember this night vividly, Christmas 2008.

"Baby, why are you crying?"

"I don't know . . . I just really feel this song," I whisper in his ear.

"Bryn, don't worry, I'll never leave you. Bryn! Bryn! Bryn! Bryn! Bryn!" he says, wiping my forehead with a cold wet washcloth.

I hear Bailey scream. "Mommy!" I open my eyes. There are twelve sets of eyes hovering above me as I lie on a plush fuzzy throw draped across my leather chaise. A wet washcloth falls into my lap as I try to shift to a seated position. My head is heavy, so I slide back down. "Bailey, can you get Mommy some water?"

"I've got it," says Jen, and then quickly sends everyone home and Bailey next door with Taylor, reassuring her that I'm okay.

I sit, struggling to shift through my thoughts to figure out what's real and what's a dream. *Who am I kidding?* This is very real. *What the fuck?*

"I'm an idiot," I say aloud to Jen who is sitting across from me silently staring for what seems like hours. I can see her trying to choose her words.

"Well, Bryn . . . I think that is rather harsh. You had no idea. Well, you had a feeling, but he led you to believe that she was out of the picture."

A tear escapes and slowly makes its way down my cheek. "I . . ." My voice cracks. "I don't know what to say."

Jen walks over, handing me a tissue. "Bryn, you are my best friend and you didn't do anything to deserve this. It's his loss. I'm surprised he chose to do it this way, considering y'all friendship, but there's no excuse. He should have been honest. The only honest thing he's ever said was that you were too good for him. He *never* deserved you."

"What do I say? How do I even bring it up?" I say, wishing this heavy weight could be lifted.

"It's not for you to bring it up. He should come to you."

I catch myself staring off into the distance. "You're right," I say, getting up from the leather chaise. I look down at the broken glass on the floor before turning back to Jen seated on the edge of the ottoman. "I need a minute . . . alone." She obliges and slowly walks upstairs. I bend over with the tray and begin to carefully pick up the pieces of broken glass.

I'll never ignore my intuition again.

36

<u>WHAT NOW?</u>

My heart skips a beat when my phone rings, the same as it has for the last two weeks. Holding my breath, I check the caller ID and to my dismay, it's Jen.

"Hey," I say, rolling over and adjusting my pillow under my neck.

"How are you making out?"

"I'm holding on. I'm just really tired that's all."

"Bryn, I've been calling you every day and Bailey tells me you're asleep by 6:30. That's not holding on."

"I'm just tired, like really tired." I yawn in her ear.

"Let's go out tomorrow. Maybe I'll call Michael and we can get some drinks and make you laugh."

"Eehh, we'll see."

"I don't like the way you sound. I'm coming over after my meeting with Jason's mom."

"No, I'm in bed and I really just want to be alone. Seriously, I was half asleep when you called. Goodnight. Call me in the morning," I say and quickly disconnect the call.

I lie in the dark. No television, no iPod or any background noise, just me and my relentless thoughts. *What could I have done differently? I thought I did everything right. I don't deserve this.*

I turn my ringer off. I don't want any contact with the outside world. The one I love most is right here with me. She's the only one who truly loves me and cares about me. Good thing I didn't tell her anything. That would be horrific. I'm already embarrassed. I'm even too ashamed to pray. Maybe it sounds crazy, but how do I ask God to help me through this when I clearly ignored the warning signs? Regardless of what Shane said and how he made me feel, deep down I *knew*. I've rehashed everything countless times in my mind trying to figure out where things went wrong. I simply can't put my finger on it and I no longer have the energy to try. *Lord, help me.*

I close my eyes, hoping to fall asleep.

My morning alarm sounds and on my phone, there are a few new alerts.

I miss you. How is my baby?

3 Missed Calls: Shane

Daddy will be home before you wake up

He must be joking, right? No freaking way. My eyes must be playing tricks on me or someone at the phone company has stolen Shane's identity and I'm being punked. He couldn't have the audacity to call me three times and send me two text messages two weeks too late. Although I'm irritated, I feel a shift in the balance of power emerging.

There's absolutely no way I'm waiting until 9 to call Jen, even though she'll curse me out for waking her up early. She'll have to forgive me. She answers after the seventh ring on the third try. I don't even give her a chance to speak before I start ranting.

"You're not going to believe this shit!" I yell into the phone.

"Brynnnnnnn . . ." she says in a groggy voice. "What is it?"

"This mother FUCKER texted me and called me three times last night."

"Saying what?" she slurs.

"Ummm, saying he'll be home before I wake up. What the heck? Saying 'Hey babe' like everything is fine. Has he lost his mind?"

"That's strange. I'm thinking he believes you didn't see it."

"Two weeks, Jen. He let two weeks pass," I say, pacing my room, anger rising in me.

"Listen, don't respond right away. Go to your new job, focus, and try to ignore him today. Let me think of a response."

"Come up with a good one, because right now I only want to rip his face off."

"Relax child, and get Bailey to school."

I don't normally do a two-step in the mirror while getting dressed, but I've got a surge of energy, even if it's fueled by anger. Bailey notices too, laughing at me on the way to school when I surprise her by belting out a few Weezy lyrics she had no idea I knew.

"Have a wonderful day, babe," I say, giving her a huge hug and kiss. She shuts the door and runs through the double doors, disappearing into the school. There are a million things I could say to Shane and none of them are Christian-like. Before pulling out into traffic, I check my center console for my old faithful break-up soundtrack, Kelly Clarkson's *My December*.

Yes. I wipe off the dust and try to scrape sweet and sour sauce from the bottom of the case, then put it in the CD player and crank up the volume on track one, *Never Again*! I sing with passion along with Kelly. Hitting the highway to work, I set it on repeat. I wail with Kelly as the tears fall again.

As I pull into the parking lot at work, I notice the lights to my office shining through the blinds. I grab my purse and put my game face on and head into the building.

Mandy, the office manager of The Lawson Company, is not at her desk (no surprise) so I hang my jacket on the back of the door and take my seat. I boot up my computer.

"You're early," she says, walking into the room with a bagel and a cup of coffee.

"I get here at this time every morning," I say with a chuckle, trying not to sound rude.

"Really?" Mandy acts surprised.

"Yup . . . really," I say, returning my attention to my desktop. *She can't be serious . . . but somehow, I know she is.*

"It's country day." Mandy runs over to the radio.

"Yes, it is," I say, shaking my head. This woman is too funny. My first week here she was breaking it down to Two Live Crew and doing the running man, and the next day she was doing the Honky Tonk down the hall. We agreed we'd switch up from R&B and country every other day. I don't care since I like all kinds of music. What I didn't expect this morning was Keith Urban's *Only You Can Love Me This Way* followed by Lady Antebellum's *Need You Now.* It's like pouring salt into the wound.

I offer to check our mailbox near the front desk, choking on my tears. She nods and continues to sway to the music. I wipe my tears as soon as I clear our office, praying I don't run into anyone. I make the final right turn at the end of the hall to find Mandy standing at the copier next to the mailbox.

"I have to scan a contract, so I just grabbed the mail," she says, handing the pile to me.

"Oh, okay." I smile. She must have taken the back way. I can't deal with her today and return to my desk.

Sitting at my desk listening to this music and watching the snow fall is the perfect recipe for an emotional breakdown. I ramble through my purse and pull out my iPod and headphones. I hate to do this to Mandy, but I've got to listen to aggressive music to stay angry.

Before I hit play, I hear Mandy shuffling into our office. "Oh my, Bryn."

What is it now?

"They are beautiful," she says, placing a huge vase with a dozen red roses on my desk. "Come on, you're holding out on me. You said you were single. Who's the lucky man?" She puts her hands on her hips and glares at the card attached. I can tell she wishes for supernatural vision to read right through the card stock.

It becomes harder to swallow as I reach for the card. I'm more surprised than she is as I grip the ivory card with the single letter 'B' printed in italics. "Excuse me," I say, turning around for privacy. I carefully open the envelope and take out the enclosed card.

Daddy's home
Love, SS

Wow, he's really something. I place the card back in the envelope and stick it into my purse for safekeeping.

"Red, let's see . . . it must be a lover," says Mandy, trying to connect the dots. "And it's winter so these had to be shipped. And you know what? They came by courier, so they spent a lot of money to get them here so early."

And she's off. Yeah, they are from a friend all right. Bryn, Bryn, Bryn, what are you going to do about this one?

If I heard he was seeing other people, I could prepare myself for that. If he told me he wasn't ready, I could accept that. I could even handle a break-up since he was leaving for the off-season, but to announce a fiancée? A fiancée? You don't just become a fiancée overnight. I have to stop thinking about this before I pass out again. I must focus and get through the day.

Jen picks Bailey up for me this evening because the traffic is a nightmare. I hope she gets her dinner. I don't have an appetite. I've been snacking on saltines and ginger ale for the last few days trying to settle my stomach. The thought of him touching her in the way he touches me makes me want to vomit.

The spark of spunk I had earlier has left. The roses he sent set me back further. Wondering if he knows is driving me crazy. Trying to figure out if the flowers are from guilt or love pisses me off. Either is inappropriate because he still has to speak to me. My phone rings and my stomach drops as if I just took the plunge in a gigantic rollercoaster. It's Jen.

"Did you talk to Shane?"

"I didn't," I say, pulling into my driveway. My trashcan reminds me that tomorrow morning is trash day and now . . . I have to take it out myself. "Bastard!"

"Yeah," she sighs, "he called me today . . . and he wants to meet up."

"Does the fucker know that we saw him?"

"He didn't mention it. He just said he needed to meet with me to talk business."

"Oh really. The asshole can call you about an event but he can't . . . I can't." *I'm so thankful I never told Jen about my plan to quit Platinum Events.*

"I know, this is awkward and this is why you can't mix—" She stops herself. "Never mind, it doesn't matter. I think you two should talk. I don't think you can salvage the friendship, but maybe you can at least get closure. You definitely deserve that."

"I'm walking through the door." I hang up, walk in the house, and find Jen perched in her favorite spot in my living room with the latest *O* magazine. "I'm getting you a subscription for your birthday this year."

"Whatever, why should I get it when I can just come over here and read yours?" she says, crossing her legs and turning a page.

"Where's Bailey?"

"Homework."

"Ugh, I don't know how she does it," I say, dropping my laptop bag at the door. "I don't even want to think about work."

"She's a great student. You raised her well. She'll do great in college."

"When are you meeting Shane?"

She looks at her cell phone. "About ten minutes."

"Where? Here?" I scream, leaping over the three steps leading to the living room.

"Relax, Mayweather. He asked me to go to his new house."

"His new house? Exactly, HIS new house, the one he bought for his kids. Whatever. Don't give him any updates about me. I better not run into him in the streets."

"Watch out now, mini Joan, you sound just like your mother," she says, laughing and putting the magazine on the ottoman. "I'm going to find out everything . . . promise on our friendship." She stands and walks out through the front door.

Jen's more like a sister than a best friend. We're over-protective of each other and I know she's looking out for me when she says she's going to take care of it. Adding the friendship oath confirms she's serious. We only use that in emergency situations.

I've yet to start the five stages of grief or perhaps I'm stuck in the first stage of denial. I won't even allow myself to think about it yet. I can't, or I'll hate him and I don't want that. I need to pull myself together for Bailey's sake. I lock the house down and head upstairs to see my baby girl.

"Hey, sweetheart. Done your homework?"

"Yup," she says, putting her notebook in her book bag.

"Movie night?"

"*Aladdin*?"

I cringe. "How about *Beauty and the Beast*?"

"Bonjour, Bonjour, Bonjour . . ." she sings as she changes into her pajamas nodding yes. The last movie I want to watch is *Aladdin*, Shane's favorite. Every time it comes on we watch it and if we're not together, I text him and he gets super excited. It's a thing we've got going on . . . hard to explain, one of those things that connects us . . . that's all.

"Awesome, my room in fifteen minutes. I'll get the popcorn."

Bailey falls asleep before Belle's father even reaches the castle to meet Cogsworth and Lumiere. I finish watching the movie alone. I can't help thinking how I've lived my very own version of this movie. When I first met Shane, I was afraid of him and his strong brutish features weren't attractive to me. Each day we spent together, I grew fonder and fonder of him and fell in love with him, the inner person. All the external things that I was once appalled by became beautiful to me, and his rude ways quickly diminished. There was no magic rose to change him, only me.

Apparently, I fell asleep because loud pounding on my front door awakens me. I grab my cell to call 911, peeking through Bailey's bedroom window hoping to get a glimpse of whoever it is, but the bay window in the living room hides my view. I tiptoe down the stairs, relieved I set the alarm earlier. If they try to break in, the police will still come. I dial Jen.

"Are you home?" I whisper.

"No."

"Where are you?"

"I'm out."

"Whatever, someone is banging on my door and I don't know who it is."

"It's probably Shane."

"What? Why would it be Shane? Jennnnnn?" I walk to the bay window to peek. I'll be damned. She's right. My heart is pounding in my chest. I hang up on her, because clearly, she's on a date. For some odd reason, she acts all secretive. No one is going to judge her for meeting someone online. She works like a crazy person, so it's really the only way for her to get a date. She'll forgive me for my abrupt exit.

I open the door and look at Shane standing outside the storm door. I'm silent.

"Can we talk?"

I cross my arms and stare at him blankly, responding coldly, "I'm listening."

"Can I come in?" he pleads.

"No, Bailey is asleep and I may wake her cussing you out," I say through the glass.

"I need to clear something up before I leave town," he says, looking at me with sad eyes.

I can't believe I'm feeling sorry for this jerk. My heartbeat starts to slow. "Let me grab a sweater. We can talk in your truck."

It's so hard to stay mad at him, but this is serious and I hope he realizes. I shouldn't have to spell it out for him. He royally fucked up. I follow him to his truck parked in my driveway and hop into the passenger seat. He reaches out to take my hand and before I realize it, I swing, hitting his arm, and then break down crying.

"Baby no . . . don't cry. It's not what you think," he says, rubbing my back. "Let me explain."

"How could you?" I wail.

"Babe, it's not what it looks like. I'm not with her and she's not my fiancée."

"You just announced to the world that she is."

"Bryn, relax."

"Don't TELL ME TO RELAX!" I scream, outraged.

"I didn't want her there, but she had to be there for me to bring my kids. My mom was supposed to have them, but last minute, Carice threatened to tell the media I kidnapped my children. I don't need this drama right now, especially because I'm in the middle of negotiating my contract. You know this."

"Yes, I know about your contract, but I don't know SHIT about that girl."

"It's all for publicity. I fired Xavier. My new publicist told me to do what she says right now. I mean, how can I be with her when I'm with you every day? Babe, she's got me by the balls right now. I had to give her my HOUSE. This is my chance. This is my time. I'm in the prime of my career and I can't let her destroy it."

"Why would she do something like this? Love doesn't try to publicly humiliate a person."

"She's spiteful!" he yells.

"It's no excuse!" I shout accusingly at him. "You broke my heart."

"Baby, I never meant to hurt you," he says, reaching out for me.

I pull back and hit my head against the passenger window. "Ouch! No, don't touch me. I don't know about this. This is a lot to deal with and maybe you can't be in a relationship until you work this drama out." My lips tremble. "Maybe . . . maybe we just need to be friends." *I can't believe I'm saying this because it's the opposite of how my heart truly feels.* I want to lie in his arms and tell him I forgive him, but I can't.

He reaches for me, but I stop him. "Shane, when it's good, it's *great*, but when it's bad, it's destructive. When I saw you two together on television it felt like I'd been taken out. It blew me out of the water. It's taken weeks for the heaviness in my chest to go away. I don't think I have it in me to handle another blow."

"Bryn, I—"

I cut him off. "I'm not playing this game with you—"

"Who's playing?"

"Let me finish. You had the opportunity to fix this, but you never called. I waited and waited. I'm not waiting on the sideline while you try to work this out. I have to protect what's left of my heart." My heart literally aches. Tears stream down my face. "I love you Shane. I mean I *really* love you. I love you so much it hurts. But you, you managed to break our something special."

By the look on his face, he expected to hear something different.

"Bryn, I never meant to hurt you. This is not what I want," he stutters. "I respect your decision, but I'm not going anywhere until you at least forgive me," he says, holding his head down.

"Shane, look at me." His eyes are bloodshot. "If it were possible, I'd wish it all away. But I can't. I pray that I can forgive you, but it's impossible to forget."

He wipes a fresh tear away. "Baby, stop crying. I will make it up to you. I promise on my children."

I want to remove all hope. "Shane, you've made me feel like I'm not enough. It's time for me to go." I jump out of his truck, leaving him sitting there. I lock my front door and peek out the window to see him still sitting in my driveway. I search for his contact info in my phone and delete it, and then try to convince myself that I'm at peace with my decision.

<u>EPILOGUE</u>

I've been feeling dreadful for the last few weeks now. Thank goodness it's Saturday and I don't have to rush off to work, although Bailey still has dance. I call my mother and beg her to take Bailey to class so I can squeeze in a few extra hours of rest.

I wish I could stay in bed all day. Unfortunately, I promised Jen I would meet her at Starbucks for a late lunch. This is her way of forcing me to get out of the house and interact with society again.

As I try to get up, the urge to throw up is real. I'm a bit lightheaded and my mouth keeps watering. I hope I don't have food poisoning, because emptying my stomach sounds like a good plan. I make it into the bathroom and glance in the mirror. The dark circles under my eyes make me look as bad as I feel. I'm pale as well, so it must be the flu.

Suddenly, a pang hits me in the abdomen. *I think something is coming up.* I cover my mouth and run to the toilet. I start to dry heave, forcefully. I fall to my knees and lay my head against the seat between bouts of projectile vomiting. *Oh, my God . . . this feels terrible.*

I crawl back to my bed to retrieve my cell phone. *Please, answer. Shit!* I got Jen's voicemail. *Ugh!* The feeling of barfing at any moment stays with me every move I make. But I've got to get some Motrin or Pepto.

I sit still on the floor and give myself a pep talk to get into the shower.

Being clean helps. I dry off and throw on a pair of cotton grannie panties before searching around my room for my sports bra, which has apparently shrunk because my girls are spilling out of it. *Wait a minute I think,* when my phone rings.

"Jen, where are you?" I ask.

"I'm at Starbucks waiting for you. Where are you? You were supposed to be here."

"What are you talking about? I called you. I got your voicemail."

"I was on a call with he-who-shall-not-be-named."

"Listen, things are a little weird. I'm dry heaving, pale, and constantly nauseated."

"I'm sure it's stress."

"No Jen, my boobs. They're spilling out of my bra."

"What? Are you still coming? What are you implying? You're pregnant? I'm sure you're fine but if you're worried, go and grab a test on your way here."

And that is what I will do. I hang up with Jen, throw on a tank top and a sweatshirt, and grab my Uggs from my closet. I drag myself down the stairs and into the car and drive to the local Rite Aid pharmacy, slowly. Any sudden turns might get me going again.

This is so embarrassing. I haven't bought one of these in eight years. What does it look like for me, an unmarried woman in her late twenties, walking into a pharmacy to buy a pregnancy test? How could I have been so irresponsible? Thank goodness I don't see anyone I know.

I ask the man to double bag the test. Thankfully, he has a stash of small brown paper bags. *Looks like I'm not the first to ask for the special packaging.* I nod and hurry back to my car.

When I arrive at Starbucks, Jen is seated on the brown leather couch at the front window.

"You do look sick." She sets a folder on the table in front of my seat.

"I'm telling you, I was dry heaving all morning and the last time that happened, I was pregnant with Bailey."

She takes a sip of her tea. "But you told me y'all always had protected sex."

"Yes, we did, except once when we were in Vegas when he attacked me. No, I'm lying . . . that entire weekend."

"Bryn," she says, reaching for my hand, "you are fine. Please, we need to meet and finalize the plans. He signed the contract and scanned it to me last night."

"He agreed to pay double?"

"He said money didn't matter."

"Did you remind him that you are his single point of contact and *not* to call me for anything? May I remind you, the only reason I'm doing this is because of you?"

"I know, and I appreciate it."

A vision of Shane with his family flashes before me. "I'm not sure how I'm going to do this, because he no longer deserves the best of me."

"I've got to give it my best. I've only got four weeks of severance pay left."

"The fucking asshole. I'm sorry. Repressed anger. I'm looking forward to happier days."

"Great, I'm glad to hear. I'll get you a chai tea."

"I'm feeling too sick for that and the smell of this coffee is already making me want to hurl."

"I'm sure it's stress. Look, before we get started, why don't you go take the test in the bathroom? Do you have it with you?"

I tap my purse. "Right in here."

"I'll grab you a water while you're gone."

I grab my purse and make my way past the long coffee line to the bathroom. I secure the lock and take the package out and hang my purse on the back of the door. I take out one test and pull the purple plastic tip off and lean over the toilet. I replace the cap and sit it on the flat surface of the metal toilet paper holder. This has got to be the longest two minutes in history. I'm counting every second . . . waiting for my phone to confirm a minute has passed. I peek at the test and see the urine slowly flowing from the square to the circle to show it is complete. The dark blue negative line is bright as we hit the first minute. I feel relieved as I continue my second count to sixty. I walk away from the test and wash my hands to speed up time. I return to grab the test. I gasp for air. A vertical blue line has appeared. It's positive.

Surprisingly, I don't feel anything besides the horrible sick feeling I had this morning. I pack the contents back into my purse, exit the bathroom, and walk straight-faced to Jen who is typing on her laptop. I take a seat in the soft chair across from her.

"Well?" Jen takes a sip of her drink before looking up at me.

"I'm pregnant."

"Oh shit!" Jen covers her mouth, knocking her latte onto floor.

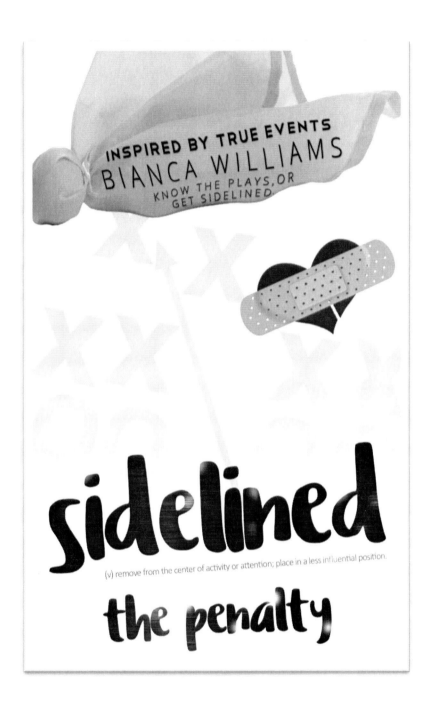

INSPIRED BY TRUE EVENTS

BIANCA WILLIAMS

KNOW THE PLAYS, OR
GET SIDELINED.

sidelined

(v) remove from the center of activity or attention; place in a less influential position.

the penalty

PROLOGUE ACCORDING TO JEN

I'm not afraid of you, you big bully.

Only a small round table at my favorite Starbucks separates our stare-down. I fully expected something like this. Anything less isn't his style.

He stretches his neck and forms a fist.

I dare you, I think, leaning in.

"No deal!" He bangs on the table with his bear-paw-sized hands.

"Have it your way." I'm pissed, but I remain calm while gathering my belongings. "As always, Mr. Smith, it was nice doing business with you. I wish you well." I snatch the contract from in front of him and shove it into my bag.

"What is this? A dick-measuring contest?" Shane pounds on the table again, except this time, his tantrum causes customers in line to turn and look over at us. "Stop trippin' and sit back down and let's finish what we came here to do!"

And this is exactly why I vowed never to work with him again. "Why must you always be so combative?"

"Football. I get hit in the head a lot. Now take a seat!"

I take a deep breath and reluctantly return to my chair. "Shane. Let's try this again. Double payment is what we previously agreed upon." *Keep it up and I'll make it triple.*

"Tell me why, again? I mean y'all have done this already," he argues, putting his hand in my face. "One! It should be less work. Two!" He starts counting on his fingers. "Less time. Am I right?" He turns to ask his 'best friend', whose input is as useless as a pair of rubber scissors.

"True dat!" replies Will, briefly raising his eyes from his cellphone.

"And therefore, less money." Shane returns his attention to me and steadily holds three fingers in my face.

"Shane." I shoo away his hand. "You present a valid argument, however, the fee is non-negotiable. Bryn—"

He cuts me off. "Bryn ain't running shit! Where she at?" He looks around the cafe. "She ain't even here! What's she hiding for? She's gonna have to show up at some point!"

"Yes, but we agreed—"

He cuts me off again. "I agree to disagree." He folds his arms across his chest. "I thought you made the rules."

"Bryn and I are a team."

"She's Team Smith forever, baby!" He laughs but I can see his pride is a little hurt. "Bryn is frontin'. Nah, for real, where she at anyway? You know I'mma get her back." He nods, agreeing with himself. "Yeah. I'm confident of that."

"Really?" I smirk.

His smile disappears. "I know she ain't seeing somebody else!"

I go silent. I know his ego can't handle any competition.

"Bryn is bossin'," interjects Will.

Will irritates me. "By the way, where is Terry?" I ask.

"If you must know, Terry's dumb ass decided to go back to school, so he's useless to me right now. Will's his temporary replacement." He reaches across and smacks Will upside his head and says to him, "Write the stupid check!" He turns back to me, signs the contract, and then pulls out his phone. "I'm calling Bryn. You think she'll answer?"

"I seriously doubt it."

"Yo, why is she still ignoring me? I told her I was sorry. It was a set-up, man."

"You should be thankful all she's doing is ignoring you."

"You know what?" He smiles sinisterly. "She can't ignore me anymore!"

"How so?"

"Shit! I paid. Y'all work for me now!" he says matter-of-factly. "I'm her client. She gotta pick up! I'm the boss now." He smacks his chest.

Here we go. "Don't forget. We also agreed to doing things differently this year."

"We are. I gave y'all more time and money."

"Right, but I also recall us agreeing to keeping things professional. I need to trust that you and Bryn won't be going behind my back, for the second time. We will make it through this event without any back-alley hanky-panky, Mr. Love Me Longtime."

Shane's smile widens. "Tell her I said . . ." He takes the check from Will, signs it, and then flings it at me. "Tell her. She's my forever. Yeah, I like that."

"I can't."

"Why not?"

"She's vulnerable. Besides, I'm not choosing sides. You two aren't doing this to me."

"Does she ask about me?"

I roll my eyes.

"Never mind then." He jumps to his feet and grabs me in for a hug, practically cutting off my circulation. "Y'all family now."

"Love you too, Shane."

"Will!" Shane shoots his water bottle into the trashcan. "I'm the best! Untouchable is what they call me!" he sings as the door swings shut behind them.

Lord knows I don't know how Bryn tolerated him. She claimed that he was a different person with her but I swear I can't imagine this cuddly teddy bear she was always gushing about. Barf. He's a textbook sociopath. If I didn't know any better I'd swear he was dropped on his head as a child.

For the life of me, I don't understand why she still loves his crazy behind. All I can hope for is that she sticks to her guns and doesn't take him back. It's bad enough she'll be around him planning this event. But if she holds out, like I pray she will, we'll come out on top.

I fold the check in half and place it in my wallet for safekeeping. One thing is for sure, Shane knows what he wants and he'll do whatever's necessary to get it. Now that's something I can respect.

It's getting late. Bryn should be here by now. I make sure Shane's out of sight before I call her.

"Jen, where are you?" she groans.

"I'm at Starbucks waiting for you. Where are you? You were supposed to be here." I give her attitude for effect.

"What are you talking about? I called you. I got your voice mail."

"I was on a call with he-who-shall-not-be-named."

"Listen, things are a little weird. I'm dry heaving, pale, and constantly nauseated."

"I'm sure it's stress." I slide Shane's signed contract into my portfolio.

"No Jen, my boobs. They're spilling out of my bra."

I see an empty sofa and collect my things. "What? Are you still coming? What are you implying? You're pregnant? I'm sure you're fine but if you're worried, go and grab a test on your way here." Bryn's in need of tough love right now and I've earned the right to give it to her.

Fifteen minutes later, Bryn arrives looking like the walking dead and plops down in a chair across from me. "You do look sick." I've seen geriatric patients with more pep in their step and her skin is some hue of lavender. I retrieve the signed contract and place it on the table.

"I'm telling you, I was dry heaving all morning and the last time that happened, I was pregnant with Bailey."

My godchild Bailey is exceptional and I love her but if Bryn spits out another, she's on her own. My days as a nanny are behind me. She starts dry heaving in front of me and it makes me want to vomit. She needs to take that show into the bathroom. "But you told me y'all always had protected sex." I cover my mouth and think of happy thoughts so I don't puke.

"Yes, we did, except when we were in Vegas he attacked me. No, I'm lying . . . that entire weekend."

Although she looks pretty banged up, I'm convinced it's the flu. "Bryn." I reach for her hand. "You're fine. Please, we need to meet and finalize the plans. He signed the contract and scanned it to me last night," I lie.

"He agreed to pay double?"

"He said money didn't matter."

"Did you remind him that you are his single point of contact and *not* to call me for anything? May I remind you, the only reason I'm doing this is because of you?" Bryn's eyes are big and wild, borderline manic.

"I know, and I appreciate it."

She sinks back into the chair. "I'm not sure how I'm going to do this because he no longer deserves the best of me."

Personally, I agree but we need to table opinions for now. This is business. "I've got to give it my best. I've only got four weeks of severance pay left."

"The fucking asshole. I'm sorry. Repressed anger. I'm looking forward to happier days."

"Great, I'm glad to hear. I'll get you a chai tea." I point at my drink.

"I'm feeling too sick for that, and the smell of this coffee makes me want to hurl."

"I'm sure it's stress. Look, before we get started, why don't you go take the test in the bathroom? Do you have it with you?"

She taps her purse. "Right in here."

"I'll grab you a water while you're gone."

Thank goodness there isn't a line, so I get her water and myself a breakfast sandwich. Sitting back down, I thumb through a travel guide of Dubai. It'll be my reward for a second round of contracted servitude with an abusive master. Envisioning myself relaxing on a beach, riding a camel, and hopefully at dinner with one of these fine men, yum they are sexy, it all becomes worth it again.

I'm halfway through when Bryn returns and I put the booklet down and look up at her. "Well?" I ask, taking another sip of my drink.

"I'm pregnant," she says with a deadpan expression.

"Oh shit!" I scream, knocking my latte onto the floor.

ABOUT THE AUTHOR

Bianca Williams was born and raised in Baltimore County, MD. She discovered her love for creative writing at college while pursuing a dual Bachelor of Science degree in Finance & Management. After graduating at the top of her class, achieving a 15+-year career in finance, and co-founding an event planning company, Bianca began penning her autofiction series. When she isn't writing, Bianca is an active volunteer in her community. She currently resides in Maryland with her daughter and four-year-old Morkie. Sidelined is her debut novel.